Praise for the Zoe Cham

"I loved *Bridges Burned*. The acti never lets up. Zoe's on the case, an through the mystery's twists and turns strong and bold, but vulnerable and relatable. I adore her, and you will, too."

– Lisa Scottoline,
New York Times Bestselling Author of *Betrayed*

"New York has McBain, Boston has Parker, now Vance Township, PA ("pop. 5000. Please Drive Carefully.") has Annette Dashofy, and her rural world is just as vivid and compelling as their city noir."

– John Lawton,
Author of the Inspector Troy Series

"I've been awestruck by Annette Dashofy's storytelling for years. Look out world, you're going to love Zoe Chambers."

– Donnell Ann Bell,
Bestselling Author of *Deadly Recall*

"An easy, intriguing read, partially because the townfolks' lives are so scandalously intertwined, but also because author Dashofy has taken pains to create a palette of unforgettable characters."

– *Mystery Scene Magazine*

"Dashofy has done it again. *Bridges Burned* opens with a home erupting in flames. The explosion inflames simmering animosities and ignites a smoldering love that has been held in check too long. A thoroughly engaging read that will take you away."

– Deborah Coonts,
Author of *Lucky Catch*

"Dashofy takes small town politics and long simmering feuds, adds colorful characters, and brings it to a boil in a welcome new series."

– Hallie Ephron,
Author of *There Was an Old Woman*

UNDER THE RADAR

**Books in the Zoe Chambers Mystery Series
by Annette Dashofy**

UNDER THE RADAR

A ZOE CHAMBERS MYSTERY

ANNETTE DASHOFY

HENERY PRESS

Copyright

UNDER THE RADAR
A Zoe Chambers Mystery
Part of the Henery Press Mystery Collection

First Edition | February 2020

Henery Press
www.henerypress.com

Trade Paperback ISBN-13: 978-1-63511-575-8
Digital epub ISBN-13: 978-1-63511-576-5
Kindle ISBN-13: 978-1-63511-577-2
Hardcover ISBN-13: 978-1-63511-578-9

Printed in the United States of America

To Ray, my partner in crime and life

ACKNOWLEDGMENTS

My ninth book. Wow. I couldn't have gotten here without a lot of help. If I named everyone, I'd double the size of this volume, but here are just a few of the people I can't function without:

As always, I rely on my team of experts in my attempt to present a believable mystery. Thank you to Chris Herndon for her help with all things autopsy-related; to Charles Van Keuren for keeping me from making too many blunders with the legal process; and to Terry Dawley, a retired cop and a fabulous writer in his own right, who totally shot down an entire scene only to give me "Signal One" and make that entire final confrontation one hundred percent better than my inaccurate first draft. If there are any other mistakes in any of these areas, I take full blame.

I can't imagine a writing world without my fabulous critique buddies, Mary "Liz Milliron" Sutton and Jeff Boarts. I not only trust them with my life, I trust them with my words. Thank you, thank you, thank you!

Thank you to Belinda Turner for allowing me to use her name. A member of my street team (Zoe Chambers Mysteries & Friends on Facebook—check us out!), Belinda entered and won a contest I ran to have a character named after her. I hope you're pleased with the results.

Many eyes see these pages before the final product goes to press. Thank you to my early readers Donnell Bell and Edie Peterson. A huge thank you to my freelance editor Erin George for your insights and eagle eye. Speaking of eagle eyes, thank you to my team of proofreaders: Anne Tiller, Wanda Anglin, and Sheri Bradshaw.

I am most grateful to the team at Henery Press for all they do to bring Zoe and Pete to the world. Kendel, Art, Maria, Christina, and all the rest—THANK YOU.

Pennwriters and Sisters in Crime are directly responsible for my being published at all and continue to provide an amazing amount of support. Along with the previously mentioned street team, you're my feet on the ground, my publicists, and my staunchest reader base.

Ramona Long and her Writing Champions crack the virtual whip at me every morning, holding me accountable for putting words on the page for at least an hour a day. They've kept me going through busy times and rough spells. Without you, I'd never meet my deadlines.

I owe a huge debt of gratitude to my dear friends Gretchen Archer, Julie Mulhern, Wendy Tyson, Cynthia Kuhn, and Meredith Schorr. I love you, ladies.

To my readers—a million thanks. Without you, Zoe and Pete (and I) wouldn't have gotten past the first books. You are the real reason I keep plugging away and battling to put out the best story I possibly can.

Finally, to my own partner in crime, my husband, Ray. Thank you for always having my back.

ONE

"Did it seem odd to you?" Zoe Chambers asked her paramedic partner, Earl Kolter, as the pair stepped out of Walden's Cafe. "The way Tony shooed us out?"

Earl adjusted his grip on the plastic bags holding his half of the ambulance crew's lunch order. "I figured he was hungry."

Zoe wasn't buying the simple explanation. "There was something more."

The cold breeze of early November blew a mist of rain into her face. Hands full with bags containing the rest of the takeout order, she tipped her head so the bill of her ball cap shielded her eyes. The leaden gray sky had been dumping rain on them all morning and most of the previous week. At first, she thought their crew chief, Tony DeLuca, had merely hustled them out on the lunch run due to the lull in the heavier precipitation. But she'd known him too long. He wasn't hungry. He was worried.

Her concerns amped up when she and Earl rounded the corner at the top of the hill. Below them, a crowd gathered on the sidewalk in front of their ambulance garage.

Earl saw it too. "What's going on?"

Zoe scanned the throng. Still too far away to make out expressions, she didn't sense upset or fear radiating from the small mob. She'd worked on Monongahela County's EMS long enough to recognize the emotions surrounding an accident or crime scene and saw none of that. Instead, they appeared curious, jostling for a better view into the large front window.

Earl shifted his takeout bags to one hand, dug out his phone, and thumbed the screen.

"Who are you texting?"

"Tony. I want to know what we're walking into."

Zoe picked up her pace. "We'll find out soon enough."

The industrial-sized garage door in front of the first bay rumbled open as they approached, and a man Zoe had become all too familiar with led a small entourage out onto the sidewalk.

"Charles Davis," she muttered, more to herself than to Earl.

"Oh, goodie. How did we manage to become a campaign stop?"

Dr. Charles Davis, forensic pathologist and candidate for the county coroner's position, popped open a black umbrella against the drizzle. He lifted his face and spotted them. "Ah." His voice carried, rising over the spatter of rain on Zoe's ball cap and jacket. "Ms. Chambers. I was hoping to run into you."

She sensed every eye in the crowd turn in her direction. Even Earl looked at her.

Davis was determined to put the current coroner out of a job, which would subsequently eliminate her part-time gig as deputy coroner. She doubted the candidate was here to offer her a position on his staff. Especially since most of the Reelect Franklin Marshall signs dotting Phillipsburg's and Vance Township's roadsides were her doing.

Battling her desire to veer from her path and go anywhere but the garage, she braced for the confrontation and closed the distance between them. Earl kept with her, moving like one of the Steelers' offensive linemen.

Zoe stopped in front of Davis. "You came here just to see me?" she asked, knowing it wasn't true.

"Of course not." He sniffed. "I've come to talk to the good people of Phillipsburg, including the brave first responders of the county EMS. I'll be working closely with everyone here in the near future. I thought I should get to know them."

She didn't miss his use of "them" rather than "you." Maybe he thought he had the power to fire her from this job too.

Tony, who hadn't returned Earl's text, appeared through the

crowd and took her takeout bags from her. Was he afraid she'd drop the guys' lunch? Or was he hungry and expected this conversation to take a while? She caught and read his pained expression. "You knew he was coming," she said sotto voce.

"His campaign manager called earlier and said he'd be here at noon." Tony matched her low tone. "I hoped he'd be in and out before you guys got back." He and the crew's lunch headed for the safety of the EMS office.

Davis kept his cold eyes and saccharine smile directed at Zoe. "I did want to speak to you too, Ms. Chambers. In case you held out any delusions of continuing to work for my office once I'm elected, I thought it only fair to inform you, your services will not be needed."

She hoped her poker face, honed through many Saturday night card games with her local friends and colleagues, held firm. "Are you using a Magic 8 ball to predict the future these days?"

His smile wavered closer to a snarl, but he recovered. "I don't need a Magic 8 ball, Ms. Chambers. I have polls that place me solidly in the lead. As it should be." He aimed his voice over his shoulder to the voting public behind him. "Monongahela County's residents are tired of living in the dark ages where truth and justice are laid in the hands of butchers and funeral directors. Men..." He raised an eyebrow. "...and women who aren't qualified to dissect a frog but are given the responsibility of determining how crime and accident victims died. How many killers have gone free because these inept amateurs declared a death to be from natural causes when, in fact, murder was involved? How many incompetent medical doctors have avoided legal actions because nothing deemed suspicious was detected during autopsy?" Davis used the hand not gripping the umbrella to make air quotes around "autopsy."

The phone inside the garage rang, but Davis didn't bat an eye.

Had they not been surrounded by a couple dozen townspeople plus a handful of local reporters, Zoe wouldn't have graced the man with a reply. He was well aware of how the coroner's office worked. The public, however, appeared to be buying his lies. "As I'm sure you're aware, Coroner Franklin Marshall contracts with a licensed forensic pathologist to perform all autopsies. And I think even you have to agree that Dr. Abercrombie is more than qualified."

Davis beamed triumphantly. "Thank you for bringing that up. Yes, in its current sad state, the coroner's office must pay to have *qualified* personnel perform autopsies. That's taxpayers' money going toward an unnecessary expense, one that will be eliminated once I'm elected."

Zoe cringed. She'd taken the bait and set Davis up for one of his key campaign promises.

"*Zoe,*" Tony shouted from the office doorway. "*Earl.*" The crew chief flapped a slip of paper. "You're up." He faced the crowd. "Please clear the front of the station so we don't run over anyone."

She and Earl were not the team who was supposed to take the next run. Tony was rearranging the order to get her away from Davis and his followers. She owed her crew chief a big favor, although the swap meant she would miss lunch.

Earl led the way, herding the crowd back as he strode toward Medic Two. Zoe followed in his wake without another glance at the coroner candidate or at the faces of his audience. Earl shoved his takeout bags at Tony and headed for the driver's door. The crew chief handed the paper to Zoe and caught her arm as she passed, pulling her close enough to whisper in her ear, "The caller was Horace Pavelka. He claims he shot and killed a man. Police are en route."

Zoe met Tony's gaze. He'd refrained from mentioning a shooting in front of the media and Davis to save her and Earl from being followed to the scene. But it was the caller's name that explained why Tony told Zoe instead of Earl.

She gave her crew chief a quick nod of appreciation, climbed into the passenger seat, and told Earl, "Langstown."

Earl whooped the siren as a woman with a camera stepped in front of the ambulance to snap a photo. She scuttled backward, tripped, but regained her balance. As the woman lowered her camera, Zoe caught a glimpse of her face. "Is that...?"

The woman turned away before Zoe could be sure.

Earl wheeled Medic Two left onto Main Street and hit the gas.

"You gonna tell me what this call is or are you saving it for a surprise?"

Zoe erased the mental image of a woman she hadn't seen in almost a year...and probably hadn't seen a moment ago either. "Horace Pavelka claims he shot and killed someone."

"Horace...who?"

Zoe repeated the last name. "We were friends in high school."

"Never heard of him."

"I'm not surprised. He was very quiet, reserved. Shy. Still is."

Earl glanced her way. "Still? You've seen him recently?"

"He works at Brunswick Bakery. I've stopped in a couple of times about..." She let the thought trail off. The stress of rushing into an emergency situation involving a shooting couldn't compete with the stress of planning the happiest day of her life.

"About your wedding cake?" Earl asked with a grin.

"Yeah." She picked up the mic. "Control, this is Medic Two. Show us en route."

Earl grew quiet, and the wail of the siren filled the silence. As they approached the turn from Phillipsburg's Main Street onto the road to take them up Langstown Hill, Earl asked, "Your shy wedding cake baker friend shot someone?"

"So he says."

In theory, Vance Township Police Chief Pete Adams had Saturdays off. In reality, neither the calendar nor the weather kept him from responding to a homicide call in his jurisdiction.

Langstown was one of the many former coal mining towns dotting Vance Township and southwestern Pennsylvania. It had fared better than most. When the coal petered out and the mines shut down, a steel production company took over and operated until a few decades ago. While the old mill still limped along, employing a skeleton crew, the once-thriving town's nicer homes suffered the same neglect as the cookie-cutter company houses.

Pete tugged on his ball cap, stepped out into the cold

November drizzle, and took in the scene. A tarp covered a human-shaped mound at the end of a narrow driveway, a baseball bat a few feet away. Pete's weekend officer, Nate Williamson, held a shotgun—not his department issue—and loomed over an older model red Chevy Malibu coupe, its headlights and passenger-side window shattered. The windshield showed evidence of blunt-force trauma, although it remained intact. A man with thinning red hair perched on the edge of the driver's seat, hugging his left elbow close to his body. Sirens keened in the distance.

Pete approached his officer. "What've we got?"

Nate tipped his head at the man in the car. "This is Horace Pavelka. He lives here." Nate glanced over the car's hood at the body. "The deceased is Dennis Culp. Shotgun blast to the center of the chest." Nate hefted the twelve-gauge shotgun, an inexpensive tactical pump with an eighteen-and-a-half-inch barrel. The kind used for protection, not hunting. "Horace admits to discharging the weapon and willingly surrendered it to me."

The man in the car raised his round, tear-streaked face. "I was afraid he was gonna kill me."

Pete knew Culp. Tough guy—or so he fancied himself. Opinionated and convinced that his take on any topic was the only one that mattered. But any time Pete had gone toe-to-toe with the man, Culp had backed down.

A cluster of onlookers huddled on the sidewalk several houses away, some with their phones out, taking photos. Neighbors gathered on the porches of the surrounding homes. Pete noticed a woman watching them from the house next door, an address he used to be well acquainted with. He met her emotionless gaze, expecting she'd turn away or lower her face. She did neither.

A pair of Pennsylvania State Police SUVs made the turn onto the street and cut their sirens, although more filled the air.

Pete looked at Nate. "Did you call for EMS?"

"Yep." He tipped his head toward Pavelka. "He needs his arm looked at." Meeting Pete's gaze, Nate's lips curled with a hint of a grin. "Recoil." The grin vanished. "And I called the coroner."

"Tag and secure the weapon. Then rope off the area and

handle crowd control." Pete gestured toward the amateur paparazzo. "I want any pictures or videos they've shot. And question the neighbors. Anyone who saw what happened." He looked at the neighbor woman, still standing on her porch, watching. "Except her. *I'll* talk to Mrs. Gates."

"On it, Chief."

As Nate strode away, Pete turned to the man in the car. "Mind if I ask you some questions?"

Pavelka glanced after Nate. "I already told him what happened."

"I know you did." Pete gave him a sympathetic smile. "Unfortunately, you'll have to repeat your story a few more times before we wrap this up."

Pavelka cradled his left arm and rocked like a mother soothing her child. "Okay."

Pete opened his notebook. "Tell me what happened."

"I was coming home from work."

"Where's that?"

"Brunswick Bakery. I saw Dennis and his buddies standing on the sidewalk in front of my house, waiting on me."

"How did you know they were waiting on you and not just hanging out."

"Because it's not the first time."

A marked Monongahela County Police cruiser rounded the turn at the end of the block and rolled toward them.

"Not the first time?" Pete echoed.

"They've been...harassing me. For months."

"Who are 'they'?"

"Dennis. Grant and Stanley Jennings. And Reese Perkins."

Pete jotted down the names. Along with Culp, he'd encountered the Jennings brothers all too often. Drunk and disorderlies by the dozens. A handful of simple assaults. But Reese Perkins? Never heard of him.

"All four of them were standing there when I drove up. Blocking my driveway so I couldn't get in. Dennis had the bat. Was swinging it around and leering. Calling me names. Yelling I should get out of my car."

"Did you?"

Pavelka's eyes widened. "No. I was scared. Terrified. For my life. You know?"

A black unmarked sedan with red and blue lights imbedded in the grill turned onto the street. An ambulance followed.

"What did you do?" Pete asked.

"I tried to drive through them. Tried to get into my driveway. I hoped they'd get out of my way. But Dennis wouldn't move. He started bashing on my car. The hood. The headlights. The windshield."

Pete surveyed the interior of the car. Glass pebbles glittered on the passenger seat. "And the window?"

"Yeah."

"Then what?"

Horace stared at his knees. "I shot him. Through the broken window."

"What did the others do?"

"They ran."

Smart move. "You carry a shotgun in your car?"

The soft splat of footsteps approaching on the rain-soaked road drew Pete's attention. Zoe and Earl had parked their rig in the middle of the street and lugged a pair of medical bags and portable defibrillator with them. County detective Wayne Baronick trailed behind.

Pete met Zoe's gorgeous baby blues and answered her unspoken question by nodding toward the tarp-covered mound. To Earl, he said, "This gentleman seems to have injured his arm."

Instead of diverting to the deceased's body as Pete expected, Zoe paused, looking at Pavelka.

"Horace?" she said.

"Zoe?" he replied, his voice quivering, pleading.

She looked to Pete, to the body, and back to the man in the car. "I'll talk to you in a bit," she said. "Okay?"

"Okay."

She crossed in front of the car to deal with the body. Pete didn't have to watch. He knew she'd begin in paramedic mode, even though the man was clearly beyond help. Once she confirmed the fact, she'd note the official time of death and slip into deputy coroner mode, photographing and processing the body.

Earl set his jump kit on the hood of the car and removed a blood pressure cuff and stethoscope.

Baronick, attired in a long dark raincoat and fedora, acknowledged Pete with a nod and followed Zoe.

While Earl took Pavelka's vitals, Pete resumed his questions.

"The shotgun. Why did you have it in your car?"

The man's voice was little more than a whisper. "Protection. From those men. Dennis and his gang."

"You mentioned they'd been harassing you? How?"

He looked up at Pete, his eyes brimming. "Following me around stores in town. Crowding me. Pushing me. Dennis tripped me outside the bargain store in Phillipsburg two weeks ago." Pavelka held open his palms revealing healing abrasions. "I was scraped up real good. They laughed. Said I was a clumsy oaf. Called me all sorts of names." He winced as Earl palpated the elbow he'd been shielding. "I had a dog. I found her—" His voice broke. "Dead. Poisoned. I know it was them. I can't prove it, but I know it was them. Last week, they threw a rock through my kitchen window. Again, I can't prove anything. But I know."

Pete gazed at the surrounding houses. Horace Pavelka's home was plain but neat. Jan Gates no longer watched him. Dead hanging baskets decorated her now vacant front porch. Pete scanned the small crowd behind the yellow tape Nate had strung. She wasn't with them. The state troopers and county officers worked the locals, asking questions. Someone on this street had seen what transpired. If no one else, Jan Gates most assuredly had.

"Chief?" Earl said. "Do you mind if I take him over to the ambulance to immobilize his arm?"

Pete held up a finger. One minute. "Mr. Pavelka, I have to ask. If these men have been intimidating you for months, as you say, why haven't you reported them to me?"

He slouched forward. "It was their word against mine."

Pete opened his mouth to tell him he should've gotten the threats on record.

Pavelka cut him off. "And because they said they'd kill me if I said anything."

TWO

One look at the body beneath the tarp told Zoe that Dennis Culp was dead. The shotgun blast at close range, center mass, left a hole the size of her fist in his chest. His lifeless eyes stared at the sky, a look of surprise frozen on his face. She wiggled her hands into a pair of Nitrile gloves, clipped a blood ox meter to his finger, and checked his pupils for the nonexistent reaction. She spread open his unzipped jacket, slipped her scissors from her pocket, and cut the front of his sweatshirt, allowing her to attach the EKG leads. The flatline on the monitor officially confirmed what she already knew. She looked at her watch and noted TOD: 12:57.

What the hell had happened? Sweet, soft-spoken Horace Pavelka had taken a life?

"Can I give you a hand?"

She shook her head, clearing it of personal assumptions and looked up at Wayne Baronick, who waited patiently for her to shift from life saver to death investigator. "In a minute. I need to get some photos first."

"All right. I'll check on our witnesses and be right back."

By the time she'd put away the defibrillator and taken photos of the body as she'd found it—wider angle shots showing the man's position on the sidewalk and closer shots to catch all the details— Wayne returned.

"What do you need me to do?" he asked.

"Help me roll him."

"You do know it was a shotgun, right? There isn't gonna be an exit wound."

She gave him her best "duh" look. "I still have to roll him and photograph what is or isn't under the body."

Wayne winked at her. "Oh."

"You're not funny."

"Pete tells me the same thing."

Nate Williamson wandered over as Zoe held the victim's head and Wayne knelt next to the body, reached across, and log-rolled the man toward him. Wayne had been right. No exit wound. Nothing under the body either. "Hey," Zoe said to Nate. "Grab my camera and take some pictures for me."

Unlike the county detective with his warped sense of humor, Nate remained stoic as he accomplished the requested task. Once they'd returned the victim to his back and Zoe gingerly settled his head on the pavement, she stood and retrieved the notebook she'd been using to record her findings. "What can you guys tell me about the weapon used?"

"H & R Tactical shotgun," Nate said. "Twelve-gauge."

"Ammo?"

"Buckshot."

Zoe added the information to her notes. She'd been working with the coroner's office long enough to know about Franklin Marshall's zest for detailed reports.

Wayne turned to Nate. "My county guys have been talking with some of the neighbors. No one saw what happened. Only the aftermath. What about you?"

"The neighbor over there—" Nate lifted his chin toward the house to the left of Horace's place. "—said he heard raised voices and got up to look but heard the gunshot before he made it to the window."

"What about the neighbor on the other side?"

"Chief said to leave her to him. Got the impression he knows her."

Pete's voice confirmed Nate's suspicion. "I do."

Zoe spun to find Pete standing behind her. "Is that a good thing or a bad thing?" she asked. "You knowing the neighbor lady, I mean."

He shrugged. "Depends on what she tells me." He fixed his icy gaze on Nate. "Have you knocked on all the other neighbors' doors already?"

He slumped. "Not yet, sir."

Zoe concealed a grin. Nate Williamson towered over all of them and may or may not have been a professional football player depending on whether you believed the rumors, but Pete had the commanding presence to wilt even the big guy. "He was helping me process the body," she said.

Nate shot a grateful glance her way.

"Fine." Pete jabbed a thumb toward the other side of the street. "Get back to work." He eyed Wayne. "You too."

"May I remind you, you aren't my commanding officer."

Pete kept him locked in that cold, hard stare.

Wayne growled in annoyance. "But I guess I should check on my men."

Through the gloves, Zoe fingered the diamond ring on her left hand. If they hadn't been standing over a dead body, she'd have nudged Pete's shoulder with her own, an innocent, crowd-safe gesture of affection they'd developed.

"Do you know this guy?" he asked.

She looked down at the man at her feet and then over at the ambulance's open rear doors where Earl was placing a sling on Horace's arm. "Which guy are you talking about?"

"I already gathered you know the shooter. What about the victim?"

She brought her gaze back to the body in front of her. "I haven't seen him in years, but I know who he is." Dennis Culp was a bully. But she wasn't going to offer her opinion as part of a homicide investigation.

"How well do you know the shooter?"

She pictured Horace's frightened face, his eyes, wide and beseeching. His red hair, tinged with gray, had thinned, and lines creased his still babyish face, but the expression hadn't changed much in two decades. "We graduated high school together."

"That's all?"

"We were friends then. He's a baker now at Brunswick Bakery. A good one too." She paused before continuing. "I've stopped in a couple of times to talk to him recently." She paused again. "About doing our wedding cake."

"Oh." Pete sounded surprised. His opened mouth hinted at a rare moment of speechlessness. The arrival of the county coroner's van rescued him from further comment. And saved her from having to reveal more of what she knew of Horace's past. She'd get Pete alone and share later.

Franklin climbed from the passenger side and strode toward them. He greeted Pete with a nod before squatting next to the body. "Update?" he said to Zoe.

"Shotgun blast to the chest from close range." She handed him the notes she'd jotted. "I've taken photographs and done a preliminary exam. No other obvious injuries."

Franklin looked up at Pete. "Did anyone disturb the body prior to Zoe's arrival?"

"Nope. Nate didn't move him." Pete gestured to a group of neighbors and their cell phones. "Just covered him to protect him from the looky loos."

"Good." Franklin turned to Zoe. "Let's prep him for transport."

Pete knew from the look in her eyes that Zoe had more information about the shooter. He'd get it out of her later. For now, he left her and Marshall with Dennis Culp's body, climbed the next-door neighbor's porch steps.

Jan Gates' late husband, Everett, had been a well-known and much despised alcoholic who'd raise hell at several of the seedier local bars before going home and beating the crap out of his wife. On average, Pete and his officers would respond to a couple of domestic dispute calls a week at this address. Sometimes, she'd let them haul Everett off to jail. Sometimes, she'd tell them to leave her alone to handle the drunken bastard. Pete never understood why she refused to leave him or even file a PFA. At the time, she'd claimed she didn't have any kids to protect and insisted she could take care of herself—in spite of a black eye and bloody lip.

The frequent calls to this address in Langstown ended a couple years ago when Everett drank himself into a stupor at Rodeo's Bar, then failed to negotiate one of the bends on Langstown Hill, crashing through the guardrails and rolling his pickup down a steep embankment. He might've been saved had the wreck not gone unnoticed until mid-morning the next day.

The woman who answered Pete's knock sported an oversized flannel shirt and threadbare sweatpants. Ample gray-peppered hair that hadn't seen a brush for at least a couple of days. And she wore the same dead-eyed expression as the day he'd delivered her husband's death notice.

"Chief Adams," she said flatly.

"Mrs. Gates. Do you mind if I ask you a few questions?"

"As if it matters whether I mind or not." Stepping back, she gestured him in. She did not, however, offer him a seat.

"Did you see what happened out there today?"

"Hard to miss." She wiped her nose on the sleeve of her faded flannel shirt. "That good-for-nothing Dennis Culp got what was comin' to him."

Pete pulled out his notebook. "Tell me what you saw."

"Heard it first. Dennis and his buddies were at it again. Hounding poor Horace out there in the street."

"Again? You've seen them torment Horace before?"

"Lots of times. Almost every day lately. They either yell at him when he's inside his house or, like today, try to block him from getting into his driveway. I've seen them throw rocks at him and at his car."

Pete thought about what Horace had told him. "Did you happen to see them doing anything to his dog?"

The hard, emotionless mask lifted for a moment, revealing either anger or sadness. "No. I didn't see anything. I know Horace believes they poisoned it. Wouldn't put it past them."

"You keep saying 'them.' Besides Dennis Culp, who else was

out there? In the past and today."

"The same. Always the same bunch. Dennis was the ringleader. But the Jennings boys were just as bad."

"Anyone else?"

"One other guy. Don't know his name. He ain't from around here. Tall. Dark hair."

"Does the name Reese Perkins sound familiar?"

She pressed her lips into an inverted "U" and shook her head. "Nope. That his name?"

"According to Horace."

"Well, he'd know."

Pete looked at the woman. She held his gaze. "You've witnessed a history of their harassment toward Horace. What else happened today?"

"I heard the yelling again. I went out on my porch to tell those men to leave Horace alone. But they ignored me. Dennis had a bat and was beating the hell outta Horace's car. Next thing I knew...*bam*! Horace shot him. I don't think Dennis even knew what hit him. Damn shame too. I'd like to have seen him know exactly why he got what he did. Would've served him right to suffer some."

Pete studied Jan Gates, looking for some sign of embarrassment over what she'd said. There was none. "What did the other three do when Horace shot Dennis?"

"They ain't fools. They took off before he could unload on them too."

"Is there anything else you can tell me?"

She shook her head. "Just that the world's a better place without Dennis Culp in it."

Pete thanked her and pocketed his notebook, making a mental note to never get on Jan Gates' bad side.

Back on the street, the coroner's van pulled out with Culp inside. Zoe, Earl, and Horace stood at the rear of the ambulance with Baronick. Horace looked more like a traumatized victim than a criminal, which made the next step all the more difficult.

"The next-door neighbor supports everything you told us," Pete said to Horace. The quartet looked at Pete, but he met only

Baronick's gaze.

The detective gave one nod and turned to Horace. "I'm placing you under arrest for the homicide of Dennis Culp."

Horace appeared resigned to his fate. Zoe, however, stepped between him and Baronick. "It was self-defense."

"That's not up to us," Pete told her.

She looked at Horace. "Do you have an attorney?"

"Yeah. I do."

"You need to let him call his lawyer," she said to Baronick with a glance at Pete.

"I will," the detective replied. He lowered his voice. "I'm not interested in railroading your friend. But we have to go through the process. You know that."

"He needs to have that arm checked out too."

"I'll make sure he gets medical attention."

Zoe caught her lip between her teeth, having run out of arguments.

Horace reached toward her with his free hand but didn't quite touch her. "I'll be okay. I killed a man. I knew what I was doing."

She shushed him. "You have the right to remain silent. Use it."

He shook his head. "I'm not hiding from what I did." To Baronick, he said, "I'm ready to go."

Pete, Zoe, and Earl watched them walk to the unmarked sedan. Once the car had pulled away, Earl placed a hand on Zoe's shoulder. "We need to get back in service."

She exhaled, her shoulders sagging.

"Hey," Pete said to her before she could head to the front of the ambulance. "We need to talk. About Horace."

There had been times in the past when Zoe had been secretive about her friends in misguided efforts to protect them. This time, she met his gaze, her baby blues clear, her jaw set. "Yes, we do. Can you come by the ambulance garage later?"

"You bet."

Nate approached him as the ambulance pulled away. "We've finished talking to everyone we could find who saw anything. No one contradicts the story that Culp and his pals have been tormenting Pavelka for months, and everyone agrees that Pavelka is quiet and keeps to himself."

"Anything else?"

Nate thumbed a couple of pages in his notebook. "Pavelka has a girlfriend. Name's Belinda Turner. She's his only frequent visitor that I can tell."

"Got an address on her?"

"No."

"Track her down. And see what you can find on Reese Perkins."

As Nate strode away, Pete withdrew his phone and keyed in the number for another one of his officers. When the call picked up, he said, "Seth, meet me at the station in ten minutes."

THREE

Zoe was relieved to see Dr. Charles Davis and his merry band of followers had moved on by the time Earl backed Medic Two into its bay. She didn't have the energy to deal with him on a good day, but especially not this afternoon.

Earl cut the engine. "I hope no one ate my lunch."

Lunch. Zoe had forgotten about it. "I'm not hungry."

Earl was halfway out of the ambulance but stopped and looked at her as if she'd sprouted another head. "You? Not hungry? Maybe I need to run you to Brunswick Hospital for a complete checkup."

She made a face. "Ha ha."

He chuckled as he climbed the rest of the way out and slammed the door.

Zoe slid down from the passenger side and followed him into the office.

Tony sat at the desk. "Zoe." He jerked a thumb over his shoulder. "You have a visitor."

A woman beamed at her from the bench next to the large front window. Zoe stared. "Lauren?"

The reporter stood and extended her hand. "I thought you might've spotted me earlier." Other than sporting a shorter, edgier haircut, she hadn't changed much since Zoe'd last seen her.

She grasped Lauren's hand. "I did but wasn't sure it was you. What are you doing here?"

"Reporting." Lauren glanced over Zoe's shoulder at the two men. "I know you're on duty, but is there someplace we can talk?"

Tony's chair creaked as he climbed to his feet. "I can take a hint." He slapped Earl on the back. "Come on. We're missing the Pitt game anyway." They headed toward the door to the crew lounge. Tony paused and called to Zoe. "Your lunch is in the fridge."

Once they were alone, Lauren made a shooing motion. "Go get your food. I'll talk while you eat."

"I'm not really hungry."

Lauren shot her a look. "One thing I know about EMS is you eat when you get the chance. You might be on runs for the next twelve hours."

"You have a point."

Two minutes later, they perched on opposite ends of the vinyl-covered bench with Zoe's BLT from Walden's between them.

"What happened to the newspaper job you'd taken in Detroit?" Zoe asked.

Lauren slung an arm over the back of the bench and made a face. "The press went out of business. Besides, I liked it here. And Marcus was homesick." The troubled teen Lauren was fostering.

"How's he doing?"

"Better. To be honest, I'd have left Detroit even if the job still existed. The city wasn't a good fit. Marcus was getting mixed up with a bad crowd. Moving back..." Lauren picked at a piece of lint on her dark gray slacks. "Well, I thought Pete might be able to adjust his attitude again."

Zoe took a bite of her BLT and chewed, letting her mind wander to last winter and the fights Marcus had gotten into. As well as the contentious beginning to her relationship with Lauren. At one time, Zoe had pegged the reporter as willing to do *anything* for a story. She'd been wrong.

"Speaking of Pete," Lauren said, "I understand congratulations are in order."

"Thanks." Zoe resisted the almost involuntary reflex to flash the ring. She suspected Lauren had a "thing" for Pete at one time and didn't want to flaunt her victory in the competition.

"By the way, I don't suppose you need any help at your barn, do you?" Lauren asked with a hopeful grin.

"As a matter of fact, my cousin left for Florida this week to spend time with my mother. If you want to come out and help, I'm sure Patsy's offer to ride her horse still stands."

"That would be great. Time on the farm is exactly what both Marcus and I need. But we can talk about all of that later." The reporter reached into a leather satchel at her feet and came up with a notebook and pen. "One of the reasons I'm here is all business. What can you tell me about the call you took earlier? I understand there was a shooting?"

Zoe swallowed. "Why weren't you at the scene?"

"I was busy finishing up with Dr. Davis. Would you rather answer questions about him?"

She coughed. "No."

Lauren grinned triumphantly. "Then tell me about the shooting."

"Who did you say you were working for?"

"I didn't."

Zoe took another bite. She wouldn't answer Lauren's questions with her mouth full, but Lauren didn't have any excuse.

"I'm freelancing for the Monongahela Edition of the *Pittsburgh Reporter*."

Zoe waited, sensing there was more to the story.

"I'm hoping if I can prove myself, they'll put me on staff."

Picking up a napkin, Zoe wiped mayo from her fingers and mouth. Lauren was back where she'd been last winter career-wise. "Okay. Yes. There was a shooting in Langstown." She relayed the facts of the case—Horace Pavelka, Dennis Culp, the type of weapon.

Lauren huffed as she lowered her pen. "Come on, Zoe. I got that much from the police radio and your crew chief's report. Help me out here. I know you were the deputy coroner on scene. Give me something I can really use."

"You mean a scoop."

Lauren's lips slanted into a hint of a grin. "A scoop would be good."

Zoe debated how much to share. She wouldn't mind offering

her thoughts about Horace's current situation or his past to a friend. And she intended to tell Pete all about it. But while Lauren might've grown into a friend over time, at the moment, anything Zoe said was destined for print.

Reading Zoe's hesitation, Lauren offered, "I don't have to use your name. I can say 'a source with the county EMS.' Or the coroner's office."

Great. Franklin would love that. "Like either of those would conceal who spoke with you."

"Off the record then?" When Zoe shot Lauren a skeptical look, she added, "Give me a starting point. I'll have to work to get another source for confirmation, but at least I'll have an idea of what direction to go."

Zoe picked up a piece of bacon that had fallen from the sandwich, popped it in her mouth, and used the chance to ponder Lauren's offer. "Off the record. Dennis Culp and his cronies had been bullying Horace for quite a while. Today, Dennis took a baseball bat to Horace's car with Horace inside. So he shot him."

"Self-defense?"

"Yep. But that's not the whole story. I've known Horace since high school. He was always the quiet, sweet kid. Kinda nerdy. He'd never pick a fight or even stand up to anyone else who started one." Zoe hoped Lauren wouldn't pick up on the small lie. Off the record or not, she wasn't prepared to share the rest with anyone. Except Pete.

Lauren studied her. "This wasn't the first instance of bullying he's faced."

"No. Not the second or third or even tenth. He's been picked on and pushed around all his life. I think today, he decided he'd had enough."

"You mentioned Culp's cronies. What are their names?"

Zoe reached the end of her willingness to help. "I'm sure you can find out easily enough. You wanted a place to start. I've given you one." She picked up what was left of the BLT and took a bite.

"Fair enough. The history of bullying makes for a good angle." Lauren eyed her. "I said today's shooting was one of the reasons I'm here. The other is more personal. For you, anyway."

"Oh?" Zoe said around a mouthful of sandwich.

Lauren came forward, her gaze unwavering. "I heard about what happened this spring."

Zoe stopped chewing, a chill settling over her.

"I think I can find your brother."

Grant and Stanley Jennings shared a double-wide on a plot of land surrounded by what used to be their grandparents' farm. The land had been broken up and sold off over the years, leaving the brothers with an acre bordered on one side by a newly remodeled brick house, and on the other side and back by fallow cornfields.

The rain had stopped by the time Pete and Officer Seth Metzger pulled into the driveway occupied by a one-ton dump truck, an empty lowboy trailer, and a battered GMC pickup. Jennings Bros Construction was stenciled in chipped paint on the dump's doors.

"I hope I didn't interrupt anything important on your day off," Pete said to Seth, who normally worked the graveyard shift on weeknights.

Seth hesitated just long enough for Pete to know the next words out of his mouth weren't entirely true. "Nope. Nothing."

Pete eyed him askance. "You could've brought Abby along, you know. The more the merrier." Abby was Vance Township's newest officer, Wayne Baronick's kid sister, and the woman who'd claimed Seth's heart.

A rush of red singed Seth's neck and crawled into his cheeks. "We're supposed to have dinner later."

"You might still make it. Any progress with the task force?" A widespread string of thefts had prompted the Mon County PD to pull together a multi-jurisdictional team in a so far unsuccessful attempt to catch the culprits. Pete had assigned Seth and Abby as Vance Township's representatives.

"That's part of our dinner plans. Going over the files. I keep thinking we're missing something."

Pete knew that feeling well. "It's a working dinner."

"Kinda."

He opened the car door. "Remember what they say about all work and no play."

No sidewalk led to the front entrance of the recently re-sided house, so Pete and Seth slushed through the puddles to the rear stoop. Pete pressed the doorbell. He didn't detect chimes or footsteps inside. After a minute, he pounded on the storm door.

Stanley Jennings yanked the door open fast enough for Pete to believe the man had been lurking inside, his hand on the knob. Stanley's eyes darted from one cop to the other, settling on Pete. "What do you want?"

The glass of the storm door began to fog from the cold outside air. "Is your brother home?" Pete asked.

"Maybe. Why?"

"We'd like to talk to both of you."

"What about?"

Pete fixed him with a hard stare through the hazed glass.

Even with the nearly obscured view, a few seconds of Pete's intense gaze was all it took for Stanley to crumble. "Grant! Get out here."

Grant appeared at his brother's side. Their family bonds were obvious in their shared longish dirty blond hair, gray eyes, and their thin, hard physiques. Stanley stood a few inches shorter than Grant, a deep scar across his left cheek.

Grant opened the storm door but blocked the way in case Pete and Seth intended to enter. He took in the two law enforcement officers as well as their weapons and glared at Pete. "You here about that scum Horse Ass Pavelka gunning down Dennis Culp in cold blood?"

Pete winced, wondering if that was a nickname he'd had to put up with all his life. "I understand you both were witnesses."

"Damned straight. Saw the whole thing."

"Then you won't mind telling us what happened." Pete didn't pose it as a question.

"I told you. Pavelka gunned Dennis down."

"In cold blood. Yes. Where can we talk?"

Grant indicated the room behind him with a nod of his head. "In here."

Stanley turned, but Pete stopped him with a raised hand. "No. Stanley, you stay and talk to Officer Metzger. Grant, you and I will speak inside."

Stanley shot a wide-eyed look at his brother, who glared back at him. Pete could read the unspoken order—*play it cool*—as clearly as if Grant had barked it out loud. Stanley gave a quick nod. "Okay." He grabbed a light jacket from next to the door and brushed past Pete.

Once inside, Pete looked around as Grant shoved the door closed behind him. "I ain't payin' to heat the outside."

Pete knew Seth's body armor and winter coat would keep his officer sufficiently warm. He wasn't so sure about Stanley's jacket.

Grant led the way from a surprisingly neat kitchen to a living room decorated with varying shades of brown and beige. Mismatched frames on a shelf held photos, including one of the brothers, arms draped around each other's shoulders, the dump truck behind them. Another was an older photo of what appeared to be prior generations of the Jennings family. There were a couple of Grant and Stanley standing in front of what Pete guessed were their building projects. One photo showed Stanley cheek-to-cheek with a cute strawberry blonde, who seemed blissfully unaware that she could do much better. And in another, three men—Stanley, Grant, and Dennis Culp—knelt with the trio of antlered bucks they'd bagged.

"What d'ya wanna know?" Grant asked.

Pete picked up the hunting photo and turned it toward Grant. "What were the three of you doing in Langstown?"

"What difference does it make? Last I checked, it's still a free country."

Pete set down the photo. "You're going to make this difficult, are you?"

"No." Grant folded his arms across his broad chest. "Just don't see why it's police business what we was doin'. Now, what we seen? *That's* police business."

"All right. Tell me what you saw?"

"Horse Ass shot Dennis Culp. Killed him in cold blood."

"Where was Horace when this happened?"

"In his car. He tried to run us over."

"Where were you when this happened?"

"On the sidewalk."

"And he drove onto the sidewalk?"

Grant's eyes shifted. "Uh. Yeah."

"Huh. That's odd. There's a stretch of grass between the road and the paved sidewalk on that street. As wet as it's been, there would've been tire tracks. There weren't any. Are you sure you weren't in his driveway when this happened?"

"Uh. Maybe. But he tried to run us over."

"What did you do when he tried to run you over?"

"What d'ya mean?"

"Did you jump out of the way?"

Grant thought that one over. "Yeah. We did."

"And then what?"

"He shot Dennis."

"Through his window?"

"Yeah."

"Did he roll the window down first?"

Another hesitation. "No. He shot right through it. Busted the glass."

"You sure it wasn't Dennis who broke the glass? With a baseball bat?"

"No way."

"Then how did Horace's car get smashed up?"

"I dunno. Maybe he hit a deer on the road or somethin'." Grant's eyes lit up. "Or maybe he really did run into Dennis. I mean, Stanley and me got out of the way, but come to think of it, I bet he hit Dennis."

"Hard enough to shatter the headlight, mash the hood, and

break the windshield?"

Grant's head bobbed in agreement.

"Poor Dennis must've been pretty busted up by the time Horace shot him. Talk about adding insult to injury."

"I know, right?" Grant smiled, pleased that Pete had laid out his story for him.

"I have a few problems though."

Grant's smile vanished.

Pete held up one finger. "First, the deputy coroner at the scene didn't find any injuries on the body other than the gunshot wound." He held up a second finger. "Second, the broken glass from the passenger window was all over the inside of the car. If Horace had shot through the closed window, the glass would've been on the outside." Pete held up three fingers. "And witnesses at the scene reported Dennis had a baseball bat and was smashing the car with it—after all three of you had been taunting Horace and trying to keep him out of his own driveway." Pete closed his fist. "Would you like to try again?"

Grant's face darkened. "If Dennis hit Horse Ass' car, it was to protect himself because he was tryin' to run us down."

"Which brings me back to my first question. What were the three of you doing hanging out in front of Pavelka's house?"

"I don't need to answer that." Grant's jaw jutted like a spoiled child's. "I don't have to answer any of your questions. We didn't do anything wrong, and you can't prove otherwise. There ain't no law against walking down a public sidewalk."

"No, there isn't. However, there is a law against making terroristic threats."

Grant stuttered, "T-terroristic threats? We ain't no terrorists."

"But you did threaten Pavelka with physical harm. Not to mention simple assault, harassment, and stalking. By the time I go over all the witness statements, I might throw in a few other charges as well."

"Stanley and me, we didn't do none of that stuff." Beads of sweat bloomed on Grant's colorless forehead.

"Doesn't matter. Dennis did. You were with him. That makes you accomplices and as such would be charged with the substantive crime."

"*What* crime?" Grant's voice had jumped an octave.

"You and your brother can be charged with the same crimes as Dennis committed, whether you swung the bat or not."

Grant's mouth hung open as he processed this whole new set of circumstances. And the potential of jail time.

He started to speak a couple of times, then dropped onto the sofa. "Look. We was just havin' some fun. Horse—" Grant eyed Pete and wisely decided continued use of the nickname wasn't in his best interest. "Pavelka practically asked to be teased." He looked at Pete as if pleading for validation.

Pete didn't give it to him.

Grant's shoulders slumped. "Dennis maybe pushed too far. *Maybe*. But he didn't deserve to be gunned down in the street. He wasn't gonna hurt no one. None of us was."

"You were just having fun." Pete made no effort to hide the sarcasm in his tone.

"Exactly." Grant appeared relieved that Pete "got" it. "You're gonna arrest Pavelka, aren't you? For murder?"

"He's been taken into custody."

"Good. Hey, you need me to testify at his trial, you say the word. Me and Stanley will be there with bells on."

Pete grunted. Horace Pavelka would likely never stand trial, but Grant could learn that from someone else. "What about the fourth man?"

"What fourth man?"

"Reese Perkins. Another friend of yours?"

What little color had crept back into Grant's cheeks drained. He stuttered again. "N-no. I don't know who you mean. Never heard of him. There was only me, Stanley, and Dennis. No one else."

He'd rattled the statement off without taking a breath. Pete studied him. "Why would Horace say Perkins was there if he wasn't?"

"Don't know. I've told you all I can." Grant glanced toward the door. Seeking an escape? Or wondering what his brother was telling Seth? "And I'm done answering your questions. You wanna ask me anything else, call my lawyer."

FOUR

"My brother?" Zoe folded the remainder of her BLT in the waxed paper it had come in and pushed it aside. "He's dead."

Lauren raised a knowing eyebrow. "That's not what I understand."

Zoe's heart and head had been at odds since last spring when she'd learned of the child her father had sired prior to marrying her mother. The joy of meeting the man who reminded her of her dad, who shared her blonde hair and blue eyes, who stepped up to take care of her and her farm, had soon been quashed by the lies. She'd watched him die that horrific night and continued to grieve in spite of the truth. In her heart, he was still her brother. She'd given up trying to make sense of her feelings and instead simply kept them buried. "He's dead," she repeated.

"I know about Jason." Lauren bent down and came up with an envelope from her satchel. "I know he's dead. And you know he's not the one I'm talking about."

Zoe stared at the envelope on Lauren's lap. "How'd you find out?" Zoe hadn't told anyone about last spring's phone call from her mother. Except Pete. She'd decided she wasn't ready to act on that tidbit of information. Wasn't ready to risk having her heart shattered again.

"I have sources."

Zoe looked at the reporter. "What kind of sources?" Kimberly wouldn't share that kind of information. She'd hung up on Zoe the first time she'd mentioned it. For Kimberly, admitting her husband's high school affair to Zoe had been gargantuan. No way would she talk to a reporter.

"It doesn't matter."

"It kinda does. And to be honest, I don't even know if my missing sibling is a brother or a sister."

"You have a brother." Lauren's eyes gleamed.

"How do you know?"

"Wouldn't you rather hear *what* I know?" Lauren held the envelope out to Zoe.

She looked at it. The thing might as well have been Pandora's box. As long as Zoe remained unaware of the facts, she couldn't be hurt any worse than she'd been last spring. She missed her father so badly she'd turned a blind eye to reality and nearly lost Pete in the process. She wouldn't take that risk again. Pete was all the family she needed.

Lauren heaved an exasperated sigh. She opened the envelope and removed two folded sheets of paper. "A boy child was born in Clarion, Pennsylvania, to Melanie Wilson fifty-one years ago. The father was Gary Chambers. The baby was put up for adoption as soon as he was born."

"Clarion. Where is he now?" The words whispered from her mouth unbidden.

Lauren replaced the papers. "I don't know."

"You don't—" Zoe choked. A gift she hadn't realized she wanted had just been dangled in front of her and then snatched away. "But—the other stuff..."

"Any investigation takes time and effort." Lauren tapped the envelope. "This is all I've come up with so far. I was hoping, if you wanted to dig deeper, we could work on it together."

Zoe stared at Pandora's envelope in Lauren's lap, her mind reeling.

"If you don't want to search for your brother, fine." The reporter stood. "But if you do, you have my number." She left the envelope on the bench and strode out of the office.

The cold drizzle had intensified into a soaking rain by the time Pete and Seth made the trip back to the station in Dillard.

Pete upped the wipers from intermittent to low. "Did Stanley give you anything useful?"

"He was pretty squirrely. I doubt he's used to talking or even thinking without his brother's input."

Pete chuckled. "I had the feeling Grant was worried about what his brother might say." He shot a glance at his officer. "So?"

"He insisted Pavelka gunned Culp down without provocation. Claimed he knew nothing about a baseball bat and swore they were all innocent bystanders."

"Following the party line. What did he say about the fourth man? Reese Perkins."

"Nothing. Said he never heard of him. Maintained there were only the three of them. When I pressed the issue, I thought he was going to barf on my shoes. I don't know who this Perkins guy is, but I can tell you, Stanley Jennings is scared shitless of him."

"Horace didn't make the guy up. Jan Gates mentioned the fourth man as well but didn't have a name." Pete negotiated the hard right at the bottom of the hill. "Call Nate. Tell him to meet us at the station."

Five minutes later, Pete wheeled into the parking lot. Nate's cruiser was already parked in its spot and the "Out on Patrol" sign had been removed from the door. Nate handed them each a cup of coffee as they entered.

"Boot licker," Seth told the weekend officer. "You're making the rest of us look bad."

Pete accepted the mug with a wink at Nate. To Seth, he said, "Well, you have been slacking." He led the way into the conference room and took a seat at the long table. "What'd you find out?"

"Belinda Turner, Horace's girlfriend, lives outside of Brunswick." Nate eased his muscular frame into one of the chairs. "I passed the address on to Detective Baronick. He said he'd question her about Horace's history with the victim and the

Jennings brothers."

"What about Reese Perkins?"

Nate huffed a laugh that sounded more like a growl. "I got nothing on the dude."

"What do you mean, nothing?"

"The only Reese Perkins I found in our database was an older bald guy who's been arrested on multiple DUIs."

Pete shook his head. "Jan Gates said the fourth man was tall and dark-haired."

"There are a bunch of people with that name on the social media sites. Some are girls. The others aren't from around here and don't fit the description. I even ran different spellings."

"Horace was the one who gave me the name. Call Baronick back and tell him to ask our shooter about this fourth guy he and Mrs. Gates claim was at the scene."

"*Claim* was at the scene?" Nate asked. "You think maybe there were only Culp and the Jennings brothers?"

"No," Seth replied before Pete had the chance. "Stanley Jennings was too freaked out when I asked him about Perkins."

"Agreed." Pete drummed his fingers on the table. "Same with Grant. Reese Perkins, whoever the hell he is, has both brothers spooked."

"He's a ghost," Nate mused.

Their radios crackled to life. "Vance Thirty-five, this is Command."

Nate fingered the mic clipped to his shoulder. "Command, this is Vance Thirty-five."

"Resident requests an officer at 1507 Ridge Road."

"Ten-four, Command." Nate pushed his chair from the table and stood. "Duty calls."

As Nate left the room, Pete checked his watch and eyed Seth. "Looks like you can still make your date."

"You sure you don't need me for anything else?"

Pete flapped a hand in a shooing motion. "Go. Have fun. I'm outta here too. I promised Zoe I'd stop by the EMS garage."

"Thanks." Seth climbed to his feet.

"Hey. Ask Abby if she's heard anything about our ghost." The younger Baronick had, until recently, worked for another department across the county. Maybe she'd crossed paths with the mysterious Reese Perkins at some point.

"Will do. Later, Chief."

Pete gulped down the rest of his coffee before rising. He had a couple of other sources he could ask regarding Perkins. Zoe was one of them.

Pete found Zoe in the ambulance service's kitchen with the aroma of Italian herbs and sauce filling the small room.

"Whatever you're cooking smells great," he said.

She planted a hip against the counter and gave him a smile that would've seared whatever was in the oven. "I can't take credit. It's Tony's turn to cook, and he had to go out on a call. I'm simply making sure the meatloaf doesn't burn."

From deep in the building, a whoop went up.

"The rest of the crew's watching college football," Zoe said. "I guess the team of choice scored."

"Good. Looks like I have you all to myself."

The steaming sexy smile was back. "Always."

Pete's brain went someplace more appropriate for a man who was off duty. Unfortunately, Zoe was *on* duty. And he had a case to work on even if he was on his own dime. He cleared his throat.

Before he could ask her about Reese Perkins or Horace Pavelka, her expression clouded. "I had a visitor this afternoon."

"Oh? Who?"

"Lauren Sanders."

The name stirred jumbled memories from last winter. Pete had a tumultuous relationship with the news media. Lauren had at least earned his respect. "What's she doing in town?"

"Apparently, she's moving back to the area. She's trying to get a job on staff with the *Pittsburgh Reporter* by following Dr. Davis around."

The mental image struck Pete as funny. "Poor Lauren. There has to be an easier way to get a job."

Zoe suppressed a laugh. "Seriously. But that's not why she came to see me."

"The shooting?" he guessed.

"No."

The answer surprised him. "What then?"

She inhaled deeply. "Lauren wants to help me find my brother."

Not what Pete expected. At all. More memories flooded his brain. His thigh ached from the gunshot wound that had shattered his femur. Usually only the weather triggered the pain. But he didn't blame it on the cold and wet of November this time.

Except the man who'd shot him was dead.

Pete shook his head, clearing the ghosts that haunted him—and Zoe. "You mean the sibling your mother mentioned?"

"Lauren's already dug up a few details I never knew. The child was definitely a boy. And she found the mother's name."

"Melanie Wilson," Pete said without thinking.

The slow widening of Zoe's eyes, the stunned "O" of her mouth, jarred his brain into gear. Dammit. He'd never told her what he knew.

FIVE

Zoe felt the air being sucked from the kitchen, her lungs imploding, her foundation rocking. "You—how did—you know?"

Pete winced. "Sylvia. It's how I knew Jason lied."

"You never told me." The irony of the things she'd kept from Pete in the past wasn't lost on her. But he'd always been straight with her. Always.

He took a step toward her. "I started to. Right after—it all happened. After your mom called and told you about another sibling, I wanted to tell you. You cut me off. Said you weren't ready. Said you still needed to heal. So I kept it to myself."

Zoe's heart knotted at Pete's use of "another" sibling. They both knew there was only one. The one Lauren wanted to locate. And of course, Sylvia Bassi would know more details than anyone. Pete's former police secretary, currently one of the township supervisors, was privy to everyone's secrets. "What else did Sylvia tell you?"

"Not much. Your father and Melanie were in high school when it happened, so your sibling...brother would be around fifty. That's all I know." Pete closed the distance between them and tenderly palmed her cheek. "I'm sorry. I should've told you."

Zoe touched the hand on her face. "No. It's okay. I wasn't ready. I'm not sure I am now either."

"Ready or not, I think you need to let Lauren do this. She's good at what she does. Whatever comes of it, we'll handle the fallout."

Zoe fought back tears. *We'll* handle the fallout, he'd said. We.

She wasn't alone. "You're right."

His lips slanted into his lopsided smile. "Can I get that in writing? Maybe mark this date on the calendar?"

She jabbed him in his rock-solid abs. "Shut up."

They stood quietly, listening to the muffled sound of the football game seeping through the wall. Then Pete lowered his hand to his side. "Now, about Horace Pavelka..."

"Wait a second." Zoe opened the oven door. The burst of dry heat felt good on her face. She closed the door and checked the timer. "Come on. Let's go in the office."

A minute later, Zoe sat in the same spot Lauren had occupied earlier, one leg curled under her. Pete claimed the seat at the desk, swiveled so he faced Zoe and the window. She tried to gather her thoughts into some cohesive form as he waited.

"Horace and I graduated from the same class in high school. He was this timid boy. Everyone picked on him."

"You?"

The question startled her. "No. I liked him. He was sweet." She gazed into space, picturing him then with the short haircut his mother gave him, when all the other boys had longer hair, styled to look messy. "Some kids flat out bullied him. Called him awful names."

"Horse Ass?"

She looked at Pete. "That was one of the worst. Where'd you hear it?"

"From Grant Jennings. Today, when I interviewed him about the shooting."

"Grant and his brother are pigs." She should feel guilty for saying it, but she didn't. "Horace has been the victim of harassment all his life. The fact that he started carrying a shotgun in his car out of fear for his life doesn't surprise me. That something like this hasn't happened sooner...does."

Pete's eyes burned into hers. "Why do I get a feeling there's more between you and him."

She forced a grin. "Because you're good at what you do." She swallowed. Weighed out her words. "Horace was like a lot of bullied kids. Taking the abuse in silence, too afraid to take action. Except for one time." The memories rolled over her. "It was at a Friday night football home game. I was with a gang of kids but left them—I can't remember why. To go to the restroom or get something to eat. Who knows? I remember hearing voices coming from under the bleachers. Scared cries. And nasty, vicious laughter. This was before they installed the new lights at the field, so it was dark. But I could see a bunch of boys in a circle. And I could hear Horace in the middle of it, begging them to stop. Maybe I should've gone for help, but in that moment, there didn't seem to be time. I charged toward them, yelling."

"Alone?" Pete asked. "You went in alone?"

She winced. "Not one of my smarter moments."

"What happened?"

"They ignored me at first. I started shoving my way through, ordering them to stop. When I got to the center of the circle. Horace was on the ground. I could see he had either blood or mud—or both—all over him. They'd been kicking and beating him. One kid in particular was leading the mob and stood over Horace with some sort of stick. A broken broom handle maybe. He had it raised to hit Horace again." Zoe licked her suddenly dry lips. "I jumped in. Tried to take it off him. But he held on. Some of his buddies grabbed me. Pinned my arms behind my back. Then he—the guy with the stick—came after me."

A muscle in Pete's jaw popped. His voice was a soft growl when he asked, "What did he do?"

"I know what he intended to do. The look on his face, in his eyes...I've seen before. He moved in real close. I could smell the beer on his breath." She could still smell it as clearly as if he'd been in the ambulance service's office with them. "He put his hand on my face, then grabbed my hair."

Pete's fists clenched.

"But then he let go. I remember how surprised he looked right before he fell."

Pete scowled. "Fell?"

"Horace. He'd picked up the broom handle that Dennis dropped and hit him. Everyone had been looking at me, so they didn't see Horace get up." Zoe swallowed. "Horace saved me from I can only imagine what. But he paid dearly. They all turned on him. I knew I couldn't do anything to save him, so I ran and got help...which is what I should've done in the first place. By the time we got to him, the thugs had broken Horace's jaw, an arm, and several ribs."

"Good lord," Pete said under his breath. He fell silent. Then, jaw clenched, he met Zoe's gaze. "Wait. Did you say 'Dennis'?"

"Yeah. Dennis Culp was the ringleader that night."

Pete's eyes narrowed. "The victim and the shooter have a long history of animosity."

Zoe realized the implications of her story. "No. I mean yes, they go way back. But if you're thinking today's shooting was premeditated, you're wrong. If anything, it was the culmination of years of abuse."

Pete shook his head. "Do I think Horace went out and bought a shotgun because Culp beat him up twenty years ago? No. I think he knew what Culp was capable of. And considering the damage to Horace's car, he had a reason to be concerned."

Zoe blew out a relieved breath.

"Were the Jennings brothers there that night?"

"I don't think so. At least I don't recall. They were both several years behind me and Horace—and Dennis—in school. They didn't run with that crowd then."

"What about a man named Reese Perkins?"

"Reese Perkins?" She rolled the name through her memory and came up blank.

Pete must've read it in her eyes. "If not that night, how about lately? Does the name ring a bell?"

"No. I'm sorry. Who is he?"

"A ghost."

She looked at Pete, puzzled.

He gave her an apologetic smile. "Horace gave us the name.

Said Perkins was with Culp and the Jennings brothers this morning. I have one witness who mentioned a stranger with them, but we can't locate anything on him. Like I said—he's a ghost."

"Do you think he's using an alias?"

His smile warmed. "You want my job?"

"No. But let's face it. We've encountered a few people in the last year or so using false identities." Pete opened his mouth then closed it. Zoe knew who he was going to mention and was grateful he'd reconsidered. "Why don't you ask Horace?"

"I intend to." Pete stood. He crossed the room, leaned over and pressed a warm kiss to her lips. "Right after I thank him for what he did that night."

Zoe wanted nothing more than to wrap her arms around Pete and drag him onto the bench with her. Not very appropriate behavior given their current location in front of the picture window. Or the rest of her crew on the other side of the door. Her phone interrupted the moment. She retrieved the device from her pocket and checked the screen. Her stomach soured. "It's my mother."

Pete gave her a devilish grin. "Time for me to go."

"Coward."

He kissed her again, straightened, and seated his hat on his head as he slipped out the door.

Zoe swiped the green button. "Hello, Mom."

Kimberly Chambers Jackson's bluster scorched Zoe's ear all the way from Florida. "And just when the hell were you planning to tell me you'd gotten engaged?"

SIX

Monday morning dawned cold and damp. Pete arrived at the county jail in Brunswick before eight to find a handful of reporters gathered at the front door. He circled the block, found a spot in the official-personnel-only portion of the parking garage, and entered the jail through the prisoner intake door. At the sally port, he locked his firearms in one of the security bins before making his way inside.

Baronick waited for him at the main entrance. "Glad you could make it."

"Thank your sister. She agreed to cover for me." Pete looked around. "He hasn't been released yet?"

The detective checked his watch. "Should happen any minute now."

Pete glanced toward the front doors. "I'd like to get Horace out of here before certain parties hear that the DA declined to file charges against him."

"And by 'certain parties,' you mean the Jennings brothers."

It wasn't a question, and Pete didn't feel the need to reply.

One of the doors swung open. Zoe breezed in and headed for the security station.

"What are you doing here?" Baronick called to her.

"Same thing as you two."

Pete noticed while she still wore her EMS uniform, she'd emptied the pockets of her tactical trousers. Nothing set off alarms as she passed through the metal detector, and the guard waved her on.

"Aren't you still on duty?" Pete asked.

"My relief came in early." She eyed him. "What about you?"

He grinned. "Abby's relief is coming in late."

"You know," Baronick said, "I'm perfectly capable of releasing a prisoner without your help."

"I wanted to give Horace a ride home," Zoe said.

Pete shook his head. "I'm driving him back to Vance Township."

"But—"

Pete held up a hand to silence her. "Remember what we talked about on Saturday? I still need to question him."

Baronick looked puzzled. "About what?"

"Reese Perkins. Unless you can tell me something about the guy?"

"No," Baronick said. "Sorry. I use the same databases and social media sites as you. The name's an alias. Why do you care though? Everyone agrees Horace killed Dennis in self-defense. He's not facing charges. Why keep digging into this Perkins guy?"

Pete gave the question some thought. "Because something about him doesn't feel right."

"You listening to your notorious 'gut' again?"

"Maybe."

Behind them, a steel sliding door clanked and rumbled open. Horace shuffled out looking shell-shocked. Two nights in detention did that to a person, especially when he'd never been arrested before.

At the same time, the front door opened, and the Jennings brothers stormed through.

"What the hell's going on?" Grant demanded. "We heard on the news about that cold-blooded murderer being released."

"Dammit," Pete muttered. A scene including these two clowns was exactly what he'd hoped to avoid.

Baronick crossed to security, stiff arming a palm. "Do not let them in."

Horace glanced at the door he'd just passed through, probably considering if the holding cell was the safer option. Pete moved to shield him.

Zoe remained between the two parties, looking back and forth.

Grant pointed. "That man is a killer. He needs to be locked up, not set free."

A television news reporter and his cameraman squeezed inside behind the brothers. Baronick barked orders at all of them to step outside.

Horace whimpered.

Pete moved toward Zoe, who was watching the chaos, and placed a hand on her shoulder. "I'm taking Horace out the back." Pete considered whisking her off with them despite the sights and sounds between the steel door and the sally port at the intake entrance.

"Good. Go. I'll be fine." She looked at Horace. "I'll come by later, if that's okay."

He gave one quick nod, then met Pete's gaze.

"Have Baronick walk you to your car," Pete told her.

"I will. Now go."

The news crew had exited as ordered, but Grant continued his tirade. Pete turned to the guard next to the steel door and held up his ID. "Let us through."

The guard looked at the ID and at Pete. "Yes, sir." He radioed inside. "Open Door A."

Behind them, Grant shouted, "You won't get away with this. I'll see that you pay for murdering my friend."

Pete didn't need to tell Horace to stay close. If he'd been any closer, he'd have been in Pete's back pocket. They negotiated the hallway, past correctional officers, past holding cells, past arrestees awaiting their time in front of the judge. The clang of metal on metal—doors opening and closing—echoed throughout. The odor made him think of month-old dirty gym socks soaked in urine.

At the sally port, Pete retrieved his firearms from the locker.

Horace widened his eyes as Pete strapped the backup pistol to his ankle. "How were you gonna get those if we'd gone out the front?"

"We were never going out the front." Even if the Jennings brothers hadn't shown up, he had no plans to run Horace through the gauntlet of reporters.

"Oh."

Once in the parking garage, Pete was happy to find no lurkers around his Explorer. Horace slid into the passenger side, his gaze roaming over the small computer terminal, the switches for the lights and sirens, and the Remington Model 870 shotgun secured between the seats. "You okay?" Pete asked.

Horace slouched. "Not really. But I'm glad to be out of jail."

"I bet." Pete studied his passenger's face. The dark, puffy circles draped beneath haunted eyes. The creases carved in the soft flesh of his forehead. Horace carried the weight of having killed a man, on the heels of having spent his entire life a victim living his own personal hell. Had one night behind bars been any worse than the emotional prison in which he'd lived on a daily basis?

Pete started the SUV, eased out of the garage, and turned right, away from the front of the jail. Rerouting meant taking the long way through the city, but he didn't want the press or the Jennings brothers to spot his vehicle.

Horace dug in his coat pocket and came up with a cell phone, which he held up. "Do you mind if I make a call?"

"Not at all."

"Thanks. I want to let my girlfriend know I'm on my way home. She offered to give me a ride, but I didn't want her near that place."

"I understand."

A cold drizzle misted the windshield. Pete turned on the wipers and listened to the soft *whoosh, whoosh* filling the gaps in Horace's call.

"Hi, honey, it's me...no, I'm fine. Chief Adams is driving me home...It's fine. Really...Okay...I'll be there in a half hour or so...Yeah...Love you too. Bye." Horace ended the call but held the phone sandwiched between his hands. "Thanks. She's been a wreck over all this."

"No problem." Pete allowed Horace a few minutes of silence,

something he knew the guy hadn't received during his last two days in holding. Once they reached the outskirts of the county seat and the scenery shifted from houses to stretches of leafless trees on drab hillsides, Pete snuck a glance at his passenger. "You might want to stay somewhere else for a few days. Maybe your girlfriend's house."

"You mean because of Grant and Stanley?"

"Yeah."

Horace thought about it. "No. I don't want to put her in the middle of this any more than she already is."

"A hotel then? Some other friend's place?"

He shook his head. "I appreciate what you're telling me, Chief, but I really want to sleep in my own bed tonight."

Pete understood that too. "I'll boost patrols on your street. And if you see the Jennings boys hanging out or even driving past, call me."

"Okay."

"I mean it."

"I know. I will."

Once Pete whisked Horace away, Grant and Stanley Jennings had taken their demands for justice outside to the waiting media, most of whom ate it up. Zoe imagined the headlines. *Killer set free.* She waited with Wayne until they'd finally lost steam and dispersed.

"Thanks for walking me out," Zoe told Wayne as they headed for the public entrance to the parking garage. "Things got more intense than I expected."

"Things might be hot for your friend for a while."

She was afraid of that too.

"He should give some thought to a vacation trip." Wayne pulled up the collar of his dark wool coat. "Someplace warm."

Her phone vibrated in her pocket. She dug it out and found a text. "It's from Franklin."

"Does he want you to assist at an autopsy?"

"I hope not." After a full weekend on duty with the ambulance service, she wanted at least a few hours off. "He usually calls rather than texts." She thumbed the icon to open the message and read it out loud. "*Stop trying to help me.*"

"What's that about?" Wayne asked.

"I have no idea." She'd reply once she was in her truck.

They reached the row where she'd parked her multi-colored twenty-something-year-old Chevy pickup. Footsteps echoed off the concrete cave of the parking structure. She spotted the Jennings brothers advancing toward them and stuffed her phone in her pocket.

Wayne saw them too and swore under his breath.

"You," Grant bellowed. "We want to talk to you."

Zoe wasn't sure whether he meant her or Wayne. The detective took a subtle step to position himself between her and the brothers before striking a faux relaxed pose, his right foot and hip slightly back. She'd seen Pete take the same stance many times and knew he was keeping the side holding his weapon angled away from the aggressor.

Grant stormed up as close as he dared. "How could you let that murderer out on the street?"

"He killed our friend," Stanley said from beside his brother. "Where's the justice?"

Zoe moved to Wayne's left side. "You bullied Horace into protecting himself. Dennis had a baseball bat."

"And Horace had a shotgun." Grant took a step toward her. "Not a fair fight if you ask me."

Wayne countered, edging his shoulder in front of Zoe, while keeping his eyes on the brothers. "Have you ever been hit in the head with a baseball bat?" The detective snorted a short laugh. "Then again, maybe you have. The point is, we've got a slew of witnesses claiming you guys bullied Horace Pavelka on multiple occasions. Culp smashing his car, busting out his windows. Have you ever heard of Pennsylvania's stand-your-ground law? It states, and I quote, 'one can use deadly force, i.e. firing a gun, if he believes it's necessary to protect himself from death or serious bodily injury, such as when the other person displays or uses a gun or other item capable of inflicting death or serious bodily injury.' For the record, baseball bats have generally been found to be deadly weapons. Pavelka was fully within his rights to protect himself."

"Dennis wouldn't have hurt Horse Ass," Grant said, his voice lowered to a growl.

Zoe tried to move closer, but Wayne blocked her with his shoulder. "His name is Horace," she said.

Grant sneered at her. "You and him got a thing goin' on?"

Before Zoe could give in to her urge to choke the jerk, Wayne extended his arm in front of her. "Enough. Both of you." To Zoe, he whispered, "Cool it. You're playing into their trap." He raised his voice when he spoke to the brothers. "You need to back off and cool down."

"We'll cool down when that killer pays for what he done," Grant said. "And he will pay, mark my words. He's gonna get what's comin' to him, one way or another."

It was Wayne's turn to close the distance between them. "Be careful what you say in front of law enforcement."

The detective's towering presence either didn't intimidate Grant, or he was a better actor than Zoe would've guessed. Stanley, however, gripped his brother's coat and gave it a jerk.

"I'm done talkin'," Grant said. "I've said everything I came to say." He took two steps backward, pivoted, and, giving Stanley a shove, walked away.

Horace gazed out the passenger window, silent for most of the twenty-mile drive to Phillipsburg.

As they waited at the light to make the left onto Langstown Road, Pete brought up the subject he'd wanted to discuss all along. "You mentioned a fourth man on Saturday. Reese Perkins."

"Yeah."

"I haven't been able to track him down. Do you know where he lives?"

"No. Sorry."

The light changed to green, and Pete made the turn. "What do you know about him?"

"He's been running with Dennis and the Jennings brothers for about four or five months, I'd guess. He doesn't talk much. In fact, I don't think I've ever heard him utter a word. He...lurks. Stands off to the side and watches the others. Doesn't chime in but doesn't lift a finger to stop them either."

"How do you know his name?"

Horace's eyes narrowed in thought. "I'm not sure. I think my girlfriend told me."

The girlfriend who was supposedly awaiting Horace's return home. "Do you know anything at all about him?" Pete asked.

"Only what I've already told you."

"And he was there on Saturday?"

"Same as always. Just watching. And smiling. Like seeing Dennis and the Jennings boys intimidate me was great entertainment."

Pete maneuvered the winding climb up Langstown Hill to the town, made a right, then a left onto Horace's street. A deep blue Chevy Cruze was parked in his driveway. Pete pulled to the curb where the crime scene tape had been removed. "Mind if I come in and ask your girlfriend about Perkins?"

"Not at all."

Horace led the way up the wet driveway, through his side door, and into the biggest kitchen Pete had ever seen in a home.

Horace stepped out of his sneakers, leaving them next to a smaller pair of pink ones in a plastic tray next to the door. He noticed Pete checking out the sea of stainless steel. "Sweet, huh?"

A slender brunette, wearing tight jeans and a wide belt encrusted with rhinestones, appeared from the next room. She let out a cry and flung herself into Horace's arms. Pete smiled as the couple embraced. Horace might be a nerd with an unfortunate name, but he had a kitchen any chef would kill for and a cute girlfriend.

She realized they weren't alone and turned her tear-streaked face toward Pete. "Oh. Hello."

Horace was smiling for the first time since Pete had met him when he introduced Belinda Turner. She had one of those fresh girl-next-door faces. Pete had a feeling he'd seen her before but couldn't place where or when.

"Have we met?" he asked as he shook her hand.

Her eyes were clear, bright. Not evasive in the least. "No, I don't believe so."

Horace chuckled. "I would hope not."

It was Pete's turn to smile. "I do occasionally encounter people who aren't having the worst day of their life."

"I suppose you do." Horace looked at Belinda. "Chief Adams wanted to ask you about Reese Perkins."

"Oh?" Her girlish smile faded. "What about him?"

"Anything you can tell me would help. Do you know where he lives?"

She shook her head. "No."

"How about where he hangs out? Who are his friends?"

"He hangs out with Dennis Culp. Or did. And Grant and Stanley Jennings."

"Interesting. Both Grant and Stanley deny knowing him."

She blew a puff of air through pursed lips. "Those two lie about everything. They wouldn't know the truth if it bit them on the butt." Her cheeks reddened as soon as she said it. She lowered her face and apologized.

Pete contained his smile. "How'd you happen to meet Perkins?"

She looked up at Pete. All traces of warmth had vanished, and the blush deepened to crimson. She shot a glance at Horace before coming back to Pete. "I used to date Stanley. He introduced me to Reese."

There was no hint of surprise on Horace's face. In fact, he took her hand and gave it a squeeze.

That was where Pete had seen Belinda Turner before. The darker hair had thrown him, but she was the cute strawberry blonde in the photo with Stanley he'd seen at the Jennings brothers' house.

SEVEN

"Are you sure you're okay?" Wayne had walked Zoe the rest of the way to her truck despite her protests.

"I'm fine." It was only a partial lie. "I hope they don't try something else with Horace."

Wayne glanced in the direction they'd vanished. "I'll call Pete and tell him what happened. Plus, I'll alert county patrols and State Police. We'll all make added passes through Langstown."

She climbed into her truck, unconvinced.

"Don't worry. From everything I've learned, Culp was the ringleader of that bunch. Those brothers have always been all talk and no action. Little dogs with plenty of bark and no bite."

"I hope you're right. I've known a lot of little dogs who had no clue they were small." The only dog that had ever bit her was a Chihuahua.

"Don't worry," he repeated, firmer this time.

Zoe thanked him, closed the door, and started the old truck. The gas gauge registered under a quarter of a tank. She'd thought for sure she had over a half tank when she left Phillipsburg. The beast was becoming more of a gas guzzler by the month.

Wayne watched as she backed out of the space. When she shifted into drive, she heard a thump on the side of the truck and spotted him striding to her door. She powered down her window. "What?"

He pointed toward the rear of the pickup. "Your backup lights aren't working. Better get them checked."

"Great," she muttered. "And it's due for inspection."

"It's not gonna pass the way it is."

She managed a tired grin. "Are you gonna write me a ticket?"

"No." He stepped away and flashed his patented brilliant smile. "But Pete might. Drive safe."

After a stop at the farm to care for her horse and the boarders in her barn, Zoe climbed into her pickup and called Melvin Quinn, the new owner of Bud Kramer's Garage. He told her to bring it in anytime. He'd had some difficulties building the business up after the original owner's untimely demise, but he was a good mechanic. With any luck, he could diagnose and fix the taillight issue quickly. And cheaply.

Ten minutes later, she parked in front of the house she and Pete shared in Dillard. Signs asking voters to reelect Franklin Marshall as County Coroner adorned the lawns—signs that Zoe was responsible for. Across the road, someone had countered with a cluster of placards for Dr. Charles Davis. She tried to not take them as a personal affront. And failed.

Instead of going inside, Zoe stuffed her hands in her pockets for warmth, lowered her head against the drizzle, and walked down the street to Sylvia Bassi's door.

Besides her position on the board of supervisors, Sylvia served as everyone's surrogate grandmother and keeper of gossip. Although she used to resemble a female Pillsbury Doughboy, a heart attack last winter scared her into changing her lifestyle. She'd even completed the Mon County 5K a month ago. The newer, svelte version wore a long, oversized sweater and leggings as she answered Zoe's knock and ushered her in. Sylvia lacked her usual warm smile.

"What's wrong?" Zoe asked.

"You haven't seen the paper?"

"Not yet. Why? Is there something in it about Horace Pavelka?"

"Well, of course. He's the big news these days." Sylvia picked up her copy of the *Monongahela Review*. "But that's not what I'm talking about." She shoved the newspaper, neatly folded to display a story and photo, at Zoe.

The photo showed Dr. Charles Davis looking resplendent—and Zoe looking like a crazed idiot—in front of the ambulance garage on Saturday. "Oh, crap."

"Crap's a good word for it." Sylvia gestured for her to read the article.

Zoe flopped into one of the chairs at the kitchen table. "Dr. Charles Davis, candidate for the Monongahela County Coroner's Office, made several campaign stops in Phillipsburg Saturday, including the EMS garage where he spoke of his pledge to save the taxpayers' money by eliminating the need for a separate forensic pathologist. Joining in the debate was Zoe Chambers, one of Coroner Franklin Marshall's staunchest supporters and a deputy coroner in the office, who insisted that minimally trained civilian personnel were capable of doing the job as they have for years." She looked at Sylvia. "I never said this. It sounds like Davis wrote the article himself."

Sylvia plunked a cup of coffee in front of Zoe and took a seat across from her. "I knew it didn't sound like you."

Zoe thought of the text from Franklin. The one she'd forgotten to respond to after the confrontation in the parking garage. "This is what he meant," she mumbled.

"What who meant?"

"Never mind. Who's the reporter who wrote this piece of garbage?" She checked the byline and didn't recognize the name. Not Lauren Sanders. Zoe flipped the paper and slid it to the side. She had no interest in looking at that photo any longer.

"Sorry for ruining your day," Sylvia said.

"It was already headed south before I got here."

"Oh? Didn't they release the Pavelka boy?"

"They released him all right." Zoe told her about the Jennings brothers' rant at the jail and the confrontation in the parking garage. "Thank goodness Wayne Baronick was there."

"What's wrong with those two?" Sylvia huffed. "And in front of that Detective Moronic too."

Zoe choked on her coffee. "What did you call him?"

"You heard me. He's law enforcement so I'm glad he was with you. Doesn't mean I have to like him."

Zoe grabbed a napkin and pressed it to her mouth. "Better not call him that to his face." Although she'd love to see his expression if Sylvia ever did. Zoe lowered the napkin and gathered her composure, "I wanted to ask you about Melanie Wilson and my dad."

Sylvia inhaled. "Oh."

"Pete told me you knew about them."

She came forward, resting her forearms on the table. "I didn't know they had a child together. Not until Pete told me about your mother's phone call."

"Tell me what you do know."

Sylvia fell quiet. When she spoke again, her voice was low. "Gary—your dad—was a couple of years behind me in school. He was a handsome kid, junior varsity quarterback. All the girls were head-over-heels for him."

The dreamy, faraway look in her eyes wasn't lost on Zoe. "Even you?"

"Me? No. I was already in love with the man I later married. Now Melanie Wilson? She was a cheerleader and a tart and, shall we say, flaunted her wares."

Zoe choked again. "Flaunted her...?"

"You know exactly what I mean."

She did. She'd done her fair share of flaunting in her wild-child days.

"Apparently, a sixteen-year-old boy can only resist so much. I remember Melanie and her parents moved away. No one knew for sure why at the time."

"She was pregnant."

"So it would seem."

"With my brother."

"As I understand it, we don't know if the child was a boy or a girl."

"We do now." Zoe told her about Lauren and the envelope. "She gave me copies of the baby's birth certificate issued in Clarion and documentation of Melanie relinquishing her parental rights."

"Clarion." Sylvia rested her fingers lightly on her lips. "That's only about three hours north."

"That's where he was born. Doesn't mean he's still there."

Sylvia met Zoe's gaze. "What are you gonna do?"

"I'm not sure. Lauren offered to help me search for him. But we don't know anything. His name. Where he is."

"You have more than you did before." Sylvia reached across the table and touched Zoe's arm. "*He* might be looking for *you*."

She hadn't considered that possibility.

"Of course, Kimberly will probably have a cow if you tell her you're looking for her husband's illegitimate son."

"Mother thinks I already found him."

"You mean..."

"Jason. She sent me a box of photos of Dad to show him. I tried to explain, but she didn't want to hear about it."

Sylvia fell silent and lifted her coffee cup to her lips.

Zoe took a deep breath to clear her head. "Speaking of Mother, she called me the other day. Livid. Someone told her about my engagement. And by someone, I mean my dear cousin Patsy."

Sylvia lowered the cup. "You mean to tell me you've been engaged for over two months and never said anything to your mother?"

Zoe made a couple of failed attempts to explain, realized how whiny those explanations sounded, even to her, and simply said, "Yeah."

"Why not?"

She hiked an eyebrow at Sylvia. "It's Kimberly."

Sylvia thought about it. "Okay. But what did she say when she called you?"

"She wants to plan the wedding."

Sylvia's jaw went slack. "What?"

"Says it's her duty as mother of the bride." Zoe sipped her

coffee and wished she had something stronger in the cup. "She insists we have the ceremony in Florida."

"You have got to be kidding."

Zoe eyed Sylvia and again said, "It's Kimberly."

"What does Pete have to say?"

"I haven't had a chance to tell him yet."

"Are you going to do it?"

"No," Zoe said, while thinking, *Oh hell no.* "But you know how she is."

Sylvia grunted. "A blonde human steamroller." She met Zoe's gaze, an evil glint in her eye. "We have to come up with a plan."

Pete accepted Horace's offer of coffee. When Belinda suggested they move into the dining room, Pete looked down at his boots and the spotless ceramic tile floor. Horace insisted Pete not worry about it, but the nervous twitch at the corner of Horace's eye stirred Pete to vigorously wipe his feet on the welcome mat before proceeding.

Unlike the professional-grade kitchen, the dining room hadn't seen a remodel in probably thirty years. Still, the dark woodwork gleamed and the brass lighting fixture over the table shined like new.

Pete took a seat across from Belinda. "You dated Stanley Jennings?"

"For about six weeks. Yes." She glanced at Horace. "The only good thing about that relationship was meeting Horace."

"What can you tell me about your ex?"

"We met when we took an art class together."

"Art class?" Pete couldn't picture Stanley taking any kind of class, especially art.

She wrinkled her nose. "I found out later he only signed up because he heard there would be nude models. I think picking me up was a consolation prize. He was nice at first. Charming. Funny. But it wasn't too long before I saw through his façade."

"What happened?"

"At first, nothing big. Little things. He 'borrowed' money from me. Not a lot. But weeks passed, and he never repaid it. Kept making excuses. And then there were the lies. He broke a date. Told me he was sick, but a friend of mine saw him at a bar hitting on other women. And he had a mean streak. He'd say horrible things to me, then claim he was only joking around. He'd insult anyone who didn't agree with him." A rim of moisture appeared on her eyes as she looked at Horace. "But the worst was how he treated you."

"For instance?" Pete asked.

She lowered her gaze. "A lot of it was just childish. One time, we were in the grocery store. Stanley sneaked up behind Horace and shoved him into a display, knocking the whole thing over. Stanley said Horace was clumsy and tripped. And the name-calling." She shook her head. "I couldn't stand it anymore, so I broke up with him. I tracked Horace down and asked to meet him for coffee. He thought I was setting him up. But I talked him into it. I wanted to apologize for not doing anything to stop Stanley."

Horace squeezed her hand. "There's nothing you could've done."

"I know." She looked at Pete. "That was when Horace asked me out for the first time. We've been together ever since."

"I have to ask," Pete said. "Why did you stay with Stanley as long as you did?"

She grinned sheepishly and brushed a hand over her eyes. "I guess I'm a little slow. I let him fool me for too long. You have to understand, Stanley can be quite charming when it's to his benefit. He made promises he never fulfilled. It took me a while to finally see the truth."

Pete sipped his coffee. Damn. He needed to ask Horace what brand he used. To Belinda, he asked, "What about Reese Perkins. How does Stanley know him?"

"I'm not really sure. Stanley said they had a business deal together. The guy creeped me out. Never said very much, but he always seemed to be watching me. And not only me. I don't think he missed anything. He reminded me of a hawk looking for prey. And cold. He was...cold." She shivered.

"How so?"

She pondered the question. Made a few false starts, then said, "Stanley...and Grant and Dennis...are bullies. Reese Perkins?" She ran a tongue over her lips. "I'm only going by my feelings. I've never seen him do anything except watch."

"But?"

"I'm sure you've heard about kids who start out torturing animals and then they escalate? He reminded me of someone like that. I *think*—" She emphasized the word. "—he could kill someone and never feel a moment's regret."

The Jenningses' dump truck and lowboy remained unmoved from Pete's previous visit, but the pickup was gone, and no one answered his knock at the door. He sat in his Explorer and tried Stanley's phone, then Grant's. Both went to voicemail. Pete left messages.

When neither of them returned his call immediately, he headed out on patrol, planning to cruise the township roads for an hour or so. If he still hadn't heard from the brothers or received a dispatch by then, he'd go back to the station to catch up on paperwork.

He hated to wish ill on anyone, but he hoped someone requested assistance or needed an officer for something—anything—minor. Paperwork sucked.

The radio and his cell phone remained quiet for the first half hour. Pete decided to make a sweep past the brothers' residence, then drive through Langstown, specifically past Horace's house, and retreat to the stack of reports awaiting his attention on his desk.

His plan fell apart when his secretary's voice crackled over the speaker. "Unit Thirty, this is Vance Base. Do you copy?"

He unclipped the mic from his dashboard. "This is Unit Thirty."

"Respond to six-eighteen Second Street, Langstown. Report of shots fired."

Pete recognized the address. "Ten-four, Base. Call in County and State for backup."

"On it, Chief."

He switched on the lights and sirens. Six-eighteen Second Street. He'd been there less than an hour ago.

Horace Pavelka's residence.

EIGHT

'

Pete arrived first. Various scenarios scrolled through his mind. Hostage situation. Active shooter. Was the victim bleeding out inside the house? A few faces peered from windows of neighboring houses, but the sidewalks remained empty. So was Horace's driveway.

And Horace wasn't answering his phone.

Pete stepped out of his SUV.

Was a gun aimed at Pete at that very moment?

A screen door slammed nearby. Jan Gates appeared on her porch.

Pete pointed at her. "Get back in the house."

She waved a dismissive hand. "Whoever fired the gun is long gone."

"You saw them?"

"No."

"Then you can't know that."

"There was only the one shot. Then nothing. I'm sure he's gone."

"Please. Go inside. I'll get your statement later."

"Suit yourself." She shrugged and sauntered into her house.

Pete listened to the silence. No sirens. He keyed the mic clipped to his shoulder. "Vance Base, this is Unit Thirty."

"Go, Thirty."

"What's the ETA on my backup?"

"State Police are five minutes out. County's six."

Dammit. "Roger that." He should wait. But he did the math.

Considering the time since the 911 call had been made? Another five or six minutes could mean a helluva lot if a gunshot victim was bleeding out in that house.

He released his Glock from its holster and started up the driveway where Belinda Turner's Cruze had been parked. He climbed the three steps to the stoop at the side door. A peek through the sheer curtains covering the windows revealed nothing. No shooter. No body.

Keeping to one side, Pete tried the knob. The storm door opened with a soft click. He placed a foot to prevent it from swinging shut and wrapped his fingers around the entrance door's latch. It released as well. Had Horace, a terrified victim of bullying, left his doors unlocked?

Swallowing, Pete shoved the entrance door open and shouted, "Police! Throw out your weapon and move to where I can see you, hands up!"

Nothing. No movement. No sound.

Except for the distant whoop of sirens.

A glance down revealed no sneakers in the plastic tray and muddy boot tracks on the otherwise pristine floor.

Sidearm ready, and without disturbing the footprints, Pete eased into the kitchen. Around the center island.

Nothing.

"Horace," Pete shouted. "This is Pete Adams. You home?"

Silence.

Dead silence.

Pete left the kitchen, advancing to the hallway, which veered to his left. Three doors, all ajar. Was the gunman hiding back there? Pete's experience and gut suggested otherwise. The boot tracks grew steadily fainter. No sign of them in the hall. He took a long stride. Crossed into the living room to put a wall between him and any shooter lurking in one of the bedrooms.

He surveyed the long, narrow living room and imagined a chunk of it had been taken in the process of remodeling and expanding Horace's dream kitchen. Like the dining room, it boasted gleaming dark woodwork and brass lighting fixtures. Gun ready, Pete moved along the outer perimeter. He focused on a sofa positioned in the middle of the room, facing away from the front door.

Pete took one more step. No one behind the sofa.

He crossed to the door leading from the living room into the dining room where he'd shared coffee with Horace and Belinda a few hours earlier. In the same manner as he'd entered the house, Pete shouldered the wall. And took a quick look around the corner.

A man wearing mud-encrusted work boots sprawled facedown next to the table, a small, dark hole pierced the back of his jacket. A revolver lay on the table.

Pete dropped to his knees next to him and slipped his fingers into the groove at the victim's throat, searching for a pulse. Finding none.

The man had face-planted after being shot. The mop of sandy hair on the victim's head obscured a positive ID but ruled out Horace. Pete knew better than to move the body until the coroner gave the okay, but the logo on the back of the jacket narrowed the possibilities.

Jennings Brothers Construction.

Sylvia had agreed to pick Zoe up at Bud Kramer's Garage later that afternoon. Zoe took advantage of the free time to take a long, steamy shower. As she stepped out, wrapped in a bulky towel, she felt a cool draft. The bathroom door yawned open and two ginger tabbies watched her.

"Jade. Merlin. I'm perfectly capable getting a shower without your supervision," she told her cats.

Jade yawned.

Zoe slipped into clean jeans and a sweater before following the tabbies to the kitchen where she found the bowls half full. Merlin meowed.

Zoe pointed. "You have food."

Her phone burst into song, blasting out "Who Are You," the

tune she'd assigned to Franklin. Tired from the long weekend on duty, and comfortably toasty after her shower, she considered letting it go to voicemail. She answered, but with a growl.

"I need you to get up to Langstown," Franklin said. "There's been a shooting fatality, but I'm stuck in Marsdale investigating a traffic death."

"Langstown?" Had she been dropped into that movie about the same day repeating? "Again?"

"Same address. Different day. I'll join you if I can finish this up in time." He hung up.

Another shooting at Horace's house? A chill chased away the warmth of her shower. Had Grant and Stanley carried out their planned revenge?

A pair of Pennsylvania State Police vehicles blocked the street from traffic. Zoe held up her Coroner's Office ID. The trooper waved her through. The scene in front of Horace's house looked much as it had two days ago but without the body on the sidewalk. Or Horace perched in his car.

A trio of county PD squad cars joined Pete's SUV and a Vance Township cruiser at the curb in front of the house. Zoe parked her pickup behind the idling ambulance. She grabbed her bag and jogged toward the crime scene tape, which Abby Baronick lifted, allowing her to pass.

Two paramedics from C crew shuffled toward her, lugging their gear. Randy Nicholls met her gaze with a solemn shake of his head. "Nothing for us to do here," he said.

Pete waited at the side door, his face unreadable.

"Is it Horace?" she whispered as he let her in.

"No," he said without elaborating.

His answer should've eased her mind. It didn't. Zoe slipped a pair of disposable booties over her shoes and followed Pete through a kitchen that belonged in a restaurant. She gawked at the expanse of stainless steel, the professional-grade appliances, and the oversized mixers and bowls.

Pete must've noticed her gawking. "Haven't you been in here before?"

"No. But Horace was always happy when I saw him at the bakery. He was in his element. With his love of cooking, it makes sense to have a kitchen like this in his home."

"Watch your step." Pete indicated a series of yellow markers and a trail of boot prints on the floor. He led her to the doorway of the adjoining dining room and stopped. "He's all yours."

From her perspective, the table and chairs blocked most of her view. A body sprawled, facedown, feet toward her. She nodded at the revolver on the table. "That the murder weapon?"

"Would be my guess."

Zoe rummaged through her kit and came up with her camera. "Did you get your photos?"

"Yes, ma'am. Sketched the scene too."

She eyed Pete. He knew she hated being called "ma'am," but if he'd intended to annoy her, his face didn't reveal it. She raised the camera and started shooting orientation shots of the dining room and the body's position in it. As she lowered the camera to check the images on the screen, something small and sparkly at her feet caught her eye. "What's this?"

Pete moved closer.

Zoe knelt for a better look. "It looks like a diamond. Or a rhinestone."

"Probably a rhinestone. But don't touch it." He straightened and crossed the kitchen.

"I wasn't going to."

Pete returned with a numbered marker, which he placed next to the gem. "I think I know where it came from." He raised his phone to snap a photo.

"Oh?"

"Horace's girlfriend was here when I brought him home. She had on one of those belts with a bunch of stones on it."

"Horace has a girlfriend?"

"Belinda Turner," Pete said. "Know her?"

"No." Good for Horace, Zoe thought.

She left Pete to add the bit of bling to his notes and moved around the table toward the body, taking pictures as she approached. One good look confirmed the victim wasn't Horace. Too thin. Too much hair.

And Horace wouldn't have been caught dead in a Jennings Brothers Construction jacket. Literally.

"Is it Stanley or Grant?"

"Can't tell from this angle." Pete tipped his head as if the different perspective might help. "Except for the scar on Stanley's left cheek, they could be twins."

Only the right side of the victim's face was visible. Zoe refocused and snapped closer shots of the victim as he lay. A series of detailed shots, documenting the side of his face, the bullet hole in the jacket piercing the fabric dead center of the logo, and the position of his limbs. Then she set the camera aside and leaned in. "Single shot to the back. He fell forward. There likely isn't an exit wound, which explains the lack of blood. Death was instantaneous."

"The .38 revolver left on the table was fired once. County will run ballistics to confirm it was the weapon used."

"I don't want to turn the body. I'd prefer to transfer him facedown."

A painfully familiar voice behind them boomed, "At least you know to do that much."

Zoe didn't have to look to identify the new arrival. Dr. Charles Davis.

Pete intercepted him in the kitchen. "Who let you in here?"

"I did," Wayne Baronick said from the side door. Zoe couldn't see the detective from where she knelt, but if his voice was any indication, he wasn't happy. "The Crime Scene Unit just pulled up out front. Dr. Davis came with them."

"I was touring their van when the call came in," Davis said. "I thought I could be of assistance."

Pete continued to block his access to the body. "You're still a civilian and have no authority to be here. All you're doing is contaminating our crime scene."

Zoe wanted to hug Pete right then and there.

Davis huffed. "I would never. I simply intend to observe and offer much needed guidance."

"You can observe from the other side of the yellow tape. Outside. Detective? Escort Dr. Davis away from the crime scene please."

"Copy that, Chief."

Zoe pressed her lips together to keep from smiling. Wayne rarely played subordinate to Pete but sounded happy to do so now.

As the detective ushered a sputtering Dr. Davis outside, Pete returned to kneel next to Zoe. She whispered, "Thanks."

He grunted. "Marshall damned well better win reelection."

"Like I said, I don't want to roll the body, but let's turn his head and get an ID."

While Pete grasped the victim's shoulders and lifted slightly, Zoe rotated his head, turning his left, unmarred cheek up.

"It's Grant," Pete said.

She continued her examination as footsteps clomped across the floor behind them. She glanced over her shoulder.

Wayne appeared in the doorway between the kitchen and dining room. "Sorry about Davis. He's like trying to stop a runaway truck."

"You should've tried harder," Pete said.

"He might very well win the election. I'd rather not alienate him in case I have to work with him." Wayne gestured at the body. "What've we got?"

Pete climbed to his feet and brought him up to speed.

"Where's Pavelka?" Wayne asked.

"I cleared the rest of the house and put out a BOLO on him. Your county officers are questioning the neighbors."

Wayne looked at Pete. "Do you think Pavelka did this?"

"No," Zoe replied, fully aware the query hadn't been directed at her.

Pete narrowed his eyes at her. "You were at the jail this morning. Both Jennings brothers were fired up over his release."

She glanced at Wayne. Had he told Pete about their encounter in the parking garage? From his expression, she assumed not.

"Speaking of..." Wayne pointed at the body. "Where's the other brother?"

"Good question," Pete said. "From what I've seen, they're usually joined at the hip."

Wayne snorted a humorless laugh. "Not anymore." After a brief silence, he added, "The Jennings brothers came here to confront Pavelka. Maybe claim their pound of flesh. Pavelka shoots the one brother. The other—Stanley—grabs Pavelka and takes him...somewhere."

Pete looked around. "Maybe. But I doubt it. No sign of forced entry. Horace wouldn't have simply let them in. And I doubt Horace would've gone without a struggle. Nothing's out of place. Nothing knocked over." He paused. "Unless..."

"What?" Wayne asked.

"The girlfriend. She was here when I brought Horace home. Was still here when I left."

"Maybe Stanley took them both. Used the threat of harming the girl to get Pavelka to cooperate."

Zoe tipped her head toward the marker at the threshold. "If that rhinestone's hers, maybe there was a struggle and that's when she lost it."

"Or..." Pete left the thought hanging.

"Or what?" Wayne asked.

"Before she dated Horace, Belinda was involved with Stanley."

Zoe looked up at them, stunned.

"Do you think she was involved in this?" Wayne gazed at the body.

"I don't know," Pete said. "But I intend to add her to the BOLO."

"I know one thing for certain." Zoe stood and faced Pete and the detective. "Horace didn't shoot this guy."

"Did you find something?" Wayne asked.

"No injuries beyond the obvious cause of death."

"Then how do you know Horace didn't do this?"

"Grant was shot in the back." Zoe folded her arms. "If Horace had killed him, he'd have been facing him."

Pete grunted a response. "I agree," he said. "*If* Horace killed him in self-defense."

NINE

Jan Gates opened her door to Pete and stepped aside to let him in without a word. She'd traded the faded flannel for a sweater with holes in the elbows but, if Pete was to guess, hadn't brushed her hair in the two days since he'd last seen her. As before, she failed to offer him a seat.

He opened his notebook. "What can you tell me about what happened next door?"

"Not much." She studied him. "Is Horace dead?"

"We're not releasing the victim's identity pending notification of next of kin."

She grunted. "Nah. Ain't Horace. Must be Grant Jennings."

"What makes you say that?"

"Because I seen Grant go in the house right before I heard the shot. Seems only reasonable that one of them killed the other."

"Tell me exactly what you saw before the gunshot."

Jan shuffled across the room to pick up a pack of cigarettes. She tapped one out and clamped it between her fingers. "I heard a motor idling, so I looked outside and saw that pickup of theirs. The Jennings brothers, I mean. It was parked at the end of Horace's driveway. Grant climbed out and headed into the house."

"Do you remember what time this was?"

"The showcase was starting on my favorite game show, so probably quarter to noon."

Pete made a note. "What about Stanley?"

"He stayed in the truck. Next thing I knew, I heard the gunshot. Stanley sat there for a couple minutes. Maybe less. Then he burned rubber out of here."

"Did Grant have a gun?"

"Not that I saw. Could've had one in his pocket or tucked in his pants the way men do."

"What made you assume it was Grant and not Horace who was shot?"

She gave a bored shrug. "If Grant had shot Horace, Grant would've come out and took off with his brother. He wasn't the sort to stick around and admit to his crime. Not like Horace."

"Did you see Horace or anyone else come out of his house?"

"Nope. Just saw Grant go in and Stanley take off." Jan stuck the unlit cigarette between her thin lips.

Pete thought about what she'd told him. "How do you know it was Grant who went inside and Stanley who stayed in the truck? They look enough alike to be twins."

"Not if you're observant." She smirked around the dangling cigarette. "Grant's got a few pounds on Stanley. Walks with a more forceful stride. They're both blowhards, but Grant's the one more likely to take action."

"Sounds like you know them well."

"Anyone who's ever had the misfortune of dealing with those brothers could tell you the same thing. Me? Like I said. I'm observant."

"Did you happen to observe when Horace's girlfriend left?"

"Nope."

Pete studied Jan. So much for being observant.

She must've read his mind. "I don't spend my entire day looking out the window. If I hear something, I check it out. I saw you bring Horace home. The girl's car was there as I'm sure you know. But it was gone when Grant and Stanley showed up."

"Did you see anything else out of the ordinary?"

"Besides you and all the other cops showing up? Nope."

Pete tucked his notebook in his pocket. "Thanks for your help." He pointed at the cigarette still hanging from her mouth. "And thanks for not lighting up while I was here."

"Oh, I don't smoke anymore. Gave it up almost a year ago. Still like to keep them around though. What I don't have in the house is a lighter." She choked a gruff laugh. "I've never gotten desperate enough for a smoke to rub two sticks together."

Zoe helped Gene, the coroner's deputy in charge of transportation, wheel the cot carrying Grant Jennings' body to the van. Gene reminded Zoe of a sad basset hound. She wondered if he'd always looked like that or if he'd developed the expression as a result of driving dead bodies around.

Once the van disappeared at the end of the street, she surveyed the scene. Pete had gone to talk to one of the neighbors. Other officers canvassed the area, questioning residents and a group of gawkers. Wayne and the crime scene unit were doing their thing inside and around Horace's house.

"Care to ID the victim?"

Zoe turned to find Lauren standing behind her. The reporter's smile hinted she was kidding, but Zoe knew she'd gladly jot down any divulged tidbit. "Sorry. The victim's identity won't be released until after the family's been notified."

Lauren shrugged. "Can't blame a gal for trying. Detective Baronick has promised to issue a statement within the hour. Not that he ever gives much away." She looked after the departed coroner's van. "You going to the morgue?"

"Nope. Franklin'll be there by the time the body arrives. I have to take my truck to the garage." Zoe checked her watch. "Crap. I forgot to let Sylvia know I'd be late."

Lauren fell into step beside Zoe as she headed to her pickup, tapping out a text begging Sylvia's forgiveness.

"Have you given any more thought to what we talked about the other day?" Lauren asked.

"I have."

"And?"

Zoe stopped at her truck's door. A lump the size of a grapefruit rose into her throat. "I want to try to find him."

"Excellent."

"But I have to go. Can I call you later?"

Lauren handed her a business card. "Anytime."

Zoe pocketed the card and climbed into her pickup. She turned the key. The motor ground and churned but wouldn't start. "What the—" She looked at the dashboard. The gas gauge registered empty. "I know I needed to fill up, but I still had some in the tank."

"What's wrong?" Lauren asked.

Zoe heaved a sigh. "I'm out of gas." She dug her phone from her pocket and keyed in the number for Bud Kramer's Garage.

After explaining the situation to the secretary who answered, Melvin Quinn came on the line. "I could have one of my guys run a few gallons out to you, but it'd be just as easy to send a flatbed and give you a tow. Since you're coming here anyway."

She looked around at the legion of police vehicles jamming the street. "You'd have a hard time getting to me. But I'd appreciate the can of gas. And let Sylvia know what's going on, please."

"You got it."

Zoe hung up. Lauren remained outside her door, looking quizzical. "Looks like I do have some time to talk," Zoe said. "Where do we start?"

Pete returned to Horace's house. The crime scene techs continued to collect evidence. Tagalong Dr. Davis sat in their truck, his phone pressed to his ear. He spotted Pete and gave him a scorching glare.

Pete nodded his indifferent acknowledgement.

The coroner's wagon was gone, meaning the body was as well. Zoe's pickup remained where it had been. She and Lauren Sanders sat inside, engrossed in conversation.

Baronick trudged around the rear corner of the house and headed Pete's way. "Found something."

"Oh?"

"A trail behind the house leads up the hill through the woods. It's muddy as hell with all the rain we've had. But someone used it recently."

"How recently?"

"Very. We found a couple of useable footprints. They'd have been washed away in last night's rain, so had to have been made today."

"Footprints? Do they match the tracks inside the house?"

"No. Those appear to match the deceased. These don't have the heavy tread of a work boot. Probably made by a sneaker."

"Horace and his girlfriend wore sneakers."

"These are too big for a woman's shoe. I'm guessing a men's size ten."

"And I'm guessing that's what size Horace wears."

"Crime scene guys are making casts."

Pete reported what Jan Gates had seen. "She says she didn't notice Horace leave, but he could've easily slipped around back without her knowledge."

Baronick looked toward the house. "The Jennings brothers show up intending to make Pavelka pay for killing their friend. Stanley stays with the truck. Grant goes inside. Confronts Pavelka. One of them has a gun. Maybe Jennings brought it, and Pavelka took it from him. Or maybe Pavelka already had it. Either way, Pavelka shoots Jennings."

"In the back."

"Yeah." The detective paused. "Not self-defense this time. Instead of sticking around like he did on Saturday, he panics. Beats it out of the house and up the hill. Where's the trail lead?"

The trees, even without leaves, blocked the view, but Pete knew the lay of the land well enough. "Langstown Park."

Langstown Park consisted of a fenced playground, a handful of picnic tables, and a community hall, all of which were currently vacant. As was the parking lot. Pete stopped his SUV just off the road. Baronick pulled in next to him.

Pete didn't wait for the detective. He climbed out and strode toward the area where he guessed the footpath topped the hill.

Baronick trudged up behind Pete. "What'd you find?"

He pointed. The path, covered in soggy leaves, would've been nearly invisible except for the muddy skid marks. "I'll bet Horace and maybe some of his neighbors use this trail quite a bit in the summer. Shortcut to the park. But it doesn't look like it gets much traffic this time of year."

"Too muddy," Baronick said.

"And no reason to visit the park. Nothing going on."

"Unless you've recently killed a man and are making a run for it."

Pete gazed down through the trees. Pictured Horace stumbling, sliding, grabbing onto branches and underbrush as he scrambled up the hill. Pete turned his back to the woods, imagining the path their suspect had taken, across the grass to the paved lot. "He could have called someone to pick him up. Had them meet him here."

Baronick nodded. "That's what I would do. Who would he call?"

"His girlfriend."

"Belinda Turner." The detective looked toward Main Street. "She could've buzzed in here, he jumps in, off they go. I doubt anyone would've noticed."

"Maybe," Pete said. "I'll have someone question the residents across the road. One of them might've seen something."

"You've already put out a BOLO on the Turner woman's car." Baronick thumbed his phone. "I'll send one of my men to her house."

"You honestly believe you're going to find them there?"

"I like to think positive. Criminals have been known to be incredibly stupid."

Pete's mind returned to earlier in the day. His conversation with Horace on the drive home from jail. Horace and Belinda sitting at the dining room table. The label "criminals" didn't fit the couple Pete had spent time with. "You go ahead," he told Baronick. "I'm going to put out another BOLO. On Stanley Jennings."

TEN

The five-gallon can of gas barely nudged Zoe's fuel gauge, but it did get her down Langstown Hill and across Phillipsburg to Bud Kramer's Garage. She knew she should mention the lousy gas mileage to Melvin, but neither she nor her bank account wanted another repair bill. If she ignored the problem, maybe it would go away.

"It's about time," Sylvia huffed when Zoe entered the waiting area. "Melvin was getting ready to close up and kick me out."

"Sorry. I owe you."

"You better believe you owe me. Now get your business taken care of and let's get outta here. I'm tired of sitting, and I've read every outdated magazine they have in this place."

Zoe approached the sliding window separating the waiting room from the office. Melvin Quinn and another man in coveralls had their heads together, going over some forms on a clipboard.

Melvin looked up. "Ah. You made it."

"Finally. Thanks for the gas."

"No problem." He winked. "The price will be doubled and on your bill."

From behind Zoe, Sylvia snorted. "At least he's honest about gouging his customers."

The garage owner crossed to the window and plucked a form from the desk. "Verify all your contact information is current and initial the bottom."

She scanned the address—Pete's—and phone number, both correct. "How long do you think it'll take?"

"I should be able to get to it tomorrow. I'll call you with an estimate before I do anything."

"Thanks." She scrawled her initials.

The mechanic behind Melvin hung the clipboard he'd been studying on a peg. "Quittin' time, Boss. Okay if I head out?"

Melvin held up a finger. "Do you have your keys?" he asked Zoe.

"I left them in the ignition."

"Good." He turned to the mechanic. "Reese, do you mind pulling Ms. Chambers' Chevy pickup into bay two before you go?"

Reese? Zoe took a closer look at him. Tall. Dark-haired. A small gold stud in his pierced left ear. She guessed he was a few years younger than she was—probably about thirty. Her gaze snapped to his coveralls and the oval name badge stitched to the front. No last name. Just Reese. How many Reeses could there be in the area?

"No problem. See you tomorrow."

She waited until the mechanic shut the office door behind him before turning to Melvin. "Excuse me for asking, but what's that guy's last name?"

"Reese? It's Perkins. Why?"

Her pulse kicked up a notch. "I thought he looked like someone I knew," she lied.

"Nah." Melvin took the paperwork from her and attached it to another clipboard. "He's relatively new to the area. Came in a few months ago looking for work. Good mechanic."

Zoe glanced out the front window as Perkins climbed into her truck. "Guess it's not him then. Thanks." She wheeled and headed for the door.

"Let's go," Sylvia said.

Zoe stopped. "Not yet," she whispered. "Call Pete."

"What?"

Zoe shushed her. "Call Pete and tell him Reese Perkins is here."

She left Sylvia with her mouth hanging open and pushed through the door.

Perkins was turned away from her, backing the truck out of its spot. As soon as he completed the task of moving it inside, he'd be gone. Logic told her she'd learned where he worked. Pete could come by and question him tomorrow. Or the next day. But hadn't Pete referred to him as a ghost? What if she watched Perkins drive away and he vanished?

She had to keep him from leaving until Pete could get there.

Perkins eased the three-quarter-ton pickup toward the open door on the second bay. Zoe slipped in front of the first bay and waited. He glanced at her as he pulled into the garage, a puzzled look on his face. She ducked inside before he had a chance to lower the door.

Perkins climbed down from the truck's cab. "Is there a problem, ma'am?"

Ma'am? She choked down her annoyance with the term she'd been hearing more and more lately. "No. No problem."

He scowled, puzzled. "Then you need to leave. Only authorized personnel are permitted inside the garage."

Her mind raced. She needed to stall. "Maybe you could answer a few questions for me. About my truck."

"Talk to the boss."

"I would but I thought since you'll be the one actually working on it—"

"Look, lady. I'm off the clock." He moved toward her, hands up as though about to grab her shoulders. "You need to go."

She took a step back but stayed inside the bay. "You're new around here, aren't you?" she asked. "I'd have remembered if I'd seen you before. How about I buy you a cup of coffee and you can answer my mechanical questions."

"Not interested." This time Perkins did clamp down on her shoulders with a grip like an eagle's talons. "Out. Now."

He forced her back outside and released her. With his hand poised over the garage door opener, he sneered. "Does your fiancé know you go around inviting other men out for coffee?" He nodded toward her left hand.

The one with Pete's engagement ring on it.

The rumble of the door lowering saved her from having to answer. Miffed, she jogged back to Sylvia, who waited on the concrete step outside the office, her arms crossed.

"What the hell were you doing?" she demanded.

Zoe ignored the question. "Did you reach Pete?"

"Yes, but he said he's ten minutes away and is sending Kevin. What's going on? Who in blue blazes is Reese Perkins?"

"That's what we're trying to figure out." Zoe yanked the office door open to find Melvin headed toward it.

"Did you forget something?"

"Where'd Perkins go?"

Melvin glanced toward the door leading from the waiting area to the garage. "Probably out to his car. I was about to lock up. It's past closing time."

Zoe plowed past Sylvia at the front door as a red Dodge Ram pickup roared through the gate in the chain link fence protecting the vehicles parked behind the garage. Zoe launched off the step, sprinting after the truck. She might not be able to catch it, but she could at least get the plate number.

Perkins didn't stop or even slow before barreling onto the road. She watched as he squealed through the yellow traffic light and disappeared into town.

Sylvia's phone call reached Pete while he stood at Stanley Jennings' back door. Pete didn't expect an answer when he knocked and wasn't disappointed. From what he could tell, nothing had been touched since his last visit. The GMC was nowhere to be seen.

Hearing Reese Perkins was at Bud Kramer's Garage—although Sylvia knew nothing more and said she was merely relaying Zoe's message—gave Pete hope the day hadn't been a total waste.

By the time he arrived, his afternoon-shift officer, Kevin Piacenza, was already on the scene. Pete found Kevin, Melvin, Sylvia, and Zoe in the waiting area, but no one else who might have been the elusive Perkins.

"What's going on?" he asked.

Everyone but Sylvia responded, talking over each other.

Pete made a time-out signal with his hands. He studied their faces. "Zoe, you first."

She told him about learning Perkins worked on Melvin, explained how she'd tried to stall Perkins long enough for Pete to arrive, and concluded by telling of Perkins' hasty exit. "I got part of his plate number but couldn't make out the whole thing." She nodded at Kevin. "He just missed him. If I could've kept him here another few seconds, Kevin would've arrived in time to catch him."

Pete looked at his officer. "Your turn."

"We have a make and model of the vehicle and with Zoe's partial plate number, hopefully we can track him down."

"Good. Get on it."

"Copy that, Chief." Kevin pivoted and strode out the door.

Pete faced Melvin. "How long has Reese Perkins been working here?"

Melvin blushed. "A couple months. Honestly, I didn't know you guys were looking for him. I never would've harbored a fugitive if I did."

Pete dismissed his concern with a wave. "Perkins isn't a fugitive. At least not that I'm aware of. Right now, I simply want to question him as a witness." Pete thought of the second dead body. "Was Perkins here all day?"

"Yes, sir. I got here at eight. Reese was only a few minutes behind me. The only time he left was during his lunch break."

"What time was that?"

"He took off at eleven thirty."

"And how long was he gone?"

"Little less than an hour."

Which was right about the time Grant Jennings was being gunned down. "I'll need Mr. Perkins' address and phone number."

Melvin looked like he'd taken a long draw on a sour lemon.

"Something wrong?" Pete asked.

The garage owner's shoulders crept upward. "I have that

information and will give it to you, of course..."

"But?"

He squirmed. "Aw, hell. I guess you're gonna find out sooner or later anyway. I've been paying him under the table. Cash."

"Your idea or his?"

"His," Melvin said quickly. "I mean, he's the one who suggested it. Hinted that I could pay him more since I wouldn't be putting money into the government's pockets or into workman's comp."

And it helped Perkins fly under the radar. Pete wondered what else Perkins was keeping under wraps.

"I'm really sorry. This is the first and only time I've ever done that," Melvin sputtered.

Pete had his doubts. "I'm not the IRS. Get me whatever information you have on Reese Perkins. We'll forget the rest of the conversation."

Melvin's relief was palpable. "Thank you." He took a step toward the office. "I'll get that for you now."

Pete watched him scurry away and turned his attention to Zoe and Sylvia, zeroing in on Zoe. "What are you doing here anyway?"

She lowered her face. "My truck."

The multi-colored gas-guzzling monstrosity that he'd been trying to talk her into selling for years. "What's wrong with it now?"

"Backup light's out."

Relatively minor.

"And I was supposed to pick her up and give her a ride home," Sylvia said, glaring at Zoe. "Three hours ago." She turned the glare on Pete. "Since you're here and, according to the clock, you're off duty, you can take over as her chauffeur."

Without waiting for an answer, Sylvia stomped through the front door.

Zoe called a feeble "thanks" after her.

Melvin returned with a sheet of paper. "I wrote down the address and number Reese gave me." He handed it to Pete. "And about the other stuff?"

Pete gave him his best clueless expression. "What other stuff?"

Melvin's face split into a relieved smile. He looked at Zoe. "I'll get on your truck first thing in the morning."

Kevin stood at his cruiser in the parking lot as Melvin locked the door behind Pete and Zoe. "The plate comes back as stolen," the officer said. "It's supposed to belong to a black Subaru Outback registered to a Dorothy Aikman of Erie."

"That was no Subaru Outback," Zoe said. "It was a red late model Dodge Ram."

"Probably also stolen." Pete handed the sheet of paper Melvin had given him to his officer. "Call Brunswick PD and have them check this address. Also, keep an eye out for the truck."

Zoe scowled. "I thought you'd want to track him down yourself?"

"Sylvia ordered me to give you a ride home."

"I could go with you. Then we could both go home."

Pete aimed a thumb at Kevin, who was watching them, bemused. "Stuff like this is what I pay him for."

Zoe's scowl turned into a pout. Pete chuckled. To Kevin, he said, "If you manage to track Perkins down, give me a call. Same with Stanley Jennings, Horace Pavelka, and Belinda Turner."

Kevin studied the address Melvin Quinn had supplied. "We have a lot of local residents in the wind this evening."

"Yes, we do." Pete looked down at Zoe. "Let's get out of here. It's been a long day, and I'm off duty."

Zoe dumped the steaming spaghetti into a colander in the kitchen sink. "I talked to Lauren today. She's going to help me find my brother."

Pete stopped, one set of silverware on the table, the other still clutched in his hand. After a beat, he turned to face her. She waited for him to sarcastically point out how well that had gone last time. Instead, all he said was, "Okay."

"That's it?'"

"He's your brother. That makes it your decision."

"And you're my fiancé." She set the pot back on the stove and reached for the jar of sauce. "Like it or not, my decision involves you."

Pete gave her a lopsided grin. "Gotta be better than last time, right?"

And there it was. "Not funny."

"Look, we both know your missing brother isn't going to be anything like..." He hesitated. "...Jason. And I completely understand you wanting to locate him. I expected you'd have started looking months ago."

"You're okay with it then?"

"Yes, my darling. I'm more than okay with it. I'll even help, if I can. I have access to some databases, you know."

Zoe feigned horror. "I sure hope we don't find him in your criminal system."

Pete set the second set of silverware down. "Me too."

She poured the sauce in the hot pot. Pete moved to her side to take plates from the cabinet next to her. As she stirred, her mind wandered. She pictured their wedding day, a dream that changed with her varying whims. Outdoor ceremony at a park like her best friend's marriage a few months ago. A grandiose affair at one of the big churches in Brunswick with everyone from Monongahela County EMS, fire personnel, and law enforcement in their dress uniforms attending. Or the more frequent daydream of a country church wedding with only close friends in attendance.

In all of them, one part remained constant. She walked down the aisle alone. Her father had died when she was eight. She hadn't spoken to her stepdad in almost two years. More specifically, he hadn't spoken to her.

But in the present version of her dream wedding, her brother escorted her toward her groom. Except the brother she pictured was Jason.

"Zoe?" Pete's voice cut through the movie playing in her mind. "Are you okay?"

She blinked, bringing her fiancé and the simmering pot of marinara back into focus. From the concern in his eyes, she wondered if she was turning blue. "Yeah. Why?"

"The look on your face." He reached over and lowered the heat to the burner. "You were smiling, then you looked horrified."

She needed to contain her wedding fantasies to happier thoughts. And solitary moments. "I was thinking of Grant Jennings' homicide," she lied.

Pete nodded, apparently buying her cover story. "I'd like to know where Horace disappeared to. Hiding isn't going to help his case at all."

"Unless he's afraid for his own life."

"From what I've seen, when Horace Pavelka gets scared, people wind up in the morgue."

Zoe studied Pete's face, not liking what she saw. "Horace didn't shoot Grant."

"He shot Dennis Culp."

"Yes. Because Dennis was threatening him with a baseball bat. And he didn't run. He called 911 and turned himself in."

Pete met her gaze without a trace of a smile. "This time was different. Maybe Grant brought the gun with him. Forced his way into Horace's house. Maybe they struggled over the gun. Horace won. And he shot Grant."

"Grant was shot in the back."

"Which is what makes this time a lot different than the first. Hard to make a case for self-defense when the guy's walking away from you. Horace panics. He runs. Makes it up the hill to the park."

"Then what?"

Pete's forehead creased. "I don't know. Maybe he flagged down a ride. Maybe he walked to someone's house. Maybe his girlfriend picked him up and is helping him hide out."

Zoe thought about it and shook her head. "Horace wouldn't shoot Grant in the back. What about Stanley? He's in hiding too."

"A neighbor puts Stanley out front in the brothers' pickup at the time of the shooting. He took off after the gunshot when Grant didn't return."

Which supported Pete's hypothesis. Still, shooting Grant in the back? No. Not Horace.

Not without good reason.

Zoe retrieved the colander and poured the drained pasta into the pot with the bubbling sauce. As she stirred the mixture, she mused. Horace was missing. So was Stanley. Maybe Kevin would track one of them down. If not him, Seth or Abby later in the night.

If the police failed to locate any of them or come up with any answers by morning, Zoe would do some tracking of her own.

ELEVEN

Pete parked in front of his Vance Township police station Tuesday morning and cut the engine. Rain had started again overnight and fell in wind-driven sheets from a flat gray sky. Not eager to step out into the deluge, he remained in his SUV.

Zoe was up to something. After their discussion about Horace's guilt or innocence last night, she'd grown quiet. Pensive. When he asked her about her silence, she claimed she was thinking about the steps Lauren had suggested she take to find her brother. Pete knew better.

He gazed through the rain-streaked windshield at the warm lights glowing from inside the station. Taking a fortifying breath, he tugged on his ball cap and stepped out of the SUV.

He entered the station to find his secretary, Nancy, in her office engaged in a serious conversation with Seth and Abby. Shrugging out of his dripping coat, he eyed his two officers. "Did I miss something?"

"There was another burglary last night," Seth said. "Over in Marsdale this time."

Pete looked at Abby, who had worked for the Marsdale PD prior to taking the job with Vance Township. "Do you know the victims?"

"Yeah. Nice family. Good neighborhood. Similar MO to the other thefts."

"We're meeting with the task force as soon as we're done here," Seth added.

"Then let's do this." Pete gestured toward the hallway,

accepted a stack of pink call-back notes from Nancy's outstretched hand, and led the way to his office.

The two officers claimed seats in the visitors' chairs while Pete hung his coat on a hook and filled his mug from the Mr. Coffee machine in the corner. He lowered into his chair and glanced over Kevin's report on his desk. "Anything on our BOLOs?"

"Nothing," Abby said. "We drove past the Jennings place numerous times. No lights on in the house. No sign of their truck."

Seth pointed at the report in Pete's hands. "Kevin went to Belinda Turner's house, but no one answered when he knocked. Garage door was locked, and it's one of those that doesn't have windows, so no telling if her vehicle is inside. No lights on when we drove by later."

"And Horace Pavelka isn't answering his phone." Abby pressed her lips together in an exaggerated look of innocence. "I could ping it if you want."

"Not yet." Pete preferred to save illegal actions for times of desperation. "If he doesn't show up soon, I'll get a warrant."

The station's phone rang. He let Nancy get it.

"What about Reese Perkins?"

"No answer at the number Melvin Quinn gave you," Seth said. "The address is an apartment over a barber shop in Brunswick. Kevin requested one of their officers check it out."

"And?"

"No one home. Or if he was, he didn't let on. The building should be condemned. It's been cited a handful of times. Leaky roof. Exposed wires. That sort of thing. Absentee landlord. None of his neighbors admit to knowing anything about anybody."

"Anything else going on I should know about?"

"Locally, we had a couple of DUIs." Seth leaned back in his chair. "Investigated a home alarm on Ridge Road, but it turned out the family was dog sitting for a friend. Fido triggered their motion detectors. Otherwise, it was a quiet night."

Abby gave a short laugh. "The criminal element was busy burglarizing the home in Marsdale."

Pete's intercom buzzed. "Call on line one," Nancy said through the static. "It's Detective Baronick."

Abby rolled her eyes as Pete picked up the phone and punched the button. "To what do I owe the honor?"

"I thought you might be interested in the lab results from the Jennings homicide."

Pete glanced at his officers. "Abby and Seth are with me. I'm putting you on speaker." Pete pressed a button and replaced the handset in its cradle. "Go."

"First off, the muddy boot tracks throughout the house were a match to the victim. No surprise there. Second, the gun you found was definitely the murder weapon, and it was registered to Horace Pavelka."

So much for Grant bringing the gun with him.

"One odd thing though," Baronick said. "There weren't any prints on it."

"You mean other than Horace's?"

"I mean at all. Someone wiped it clean."

Pete rubbed his freshly shaven upper lip. "Why would he wipe his prints off the weapon and then leave it?"

"He probably wouldn't," Baronick replied. "But someone else might. If they were trying to make Pavelka look guilty."

"Unless Horace Pavelka's smart enough to want us to believe that," Pete mused.

There was a long silence on the line. "Maybe," Baronick said. He cleared his throat. "One last interesting tidbit. You know that rhinestone Zoe found on the floor?"

"Yeah."

"It's not a rhinestone. It's a diamond."

Seth blew a soft whistle. Abby shifted in her chair and scowled.

"Not a very good quality stone," Baronick went on, "but better than paste. Or cubic zirconium."

"It didn't likely come from the girlfriend's belt then."

"No. But did she have a ring? Or earrings?"

Pete pictured the girl sitting across Horace's dining room table from him. "Not that I noticed."

Baronick made a sound like he was stretching. "I'm heading over to the bakery. See if our missing suspect showed up for work this morning."

"Keep me posted." Pete ended the call and looked at his officers. "Abby? You have something on your mind?"

She'd been frowning into space but flinched at her name. "Maybe."

"Care to share with the class?"

"Later. After I confirm a few things."

Seth was studying her quizzically too but said nothing.

"All right," Pete said. "But don't keep any potential pieces to this puzzle quiet simply out of self-doubt."

She lifted her chin. "No, sir. It's not self-doubt. I simply want to narrow a broad range of possibilities, so I don't send the investigation off in a totally wrong direction."

"Fair enough." Pete turned to Seth. "Anything else?"

"No. That about covers our night."

"Then go meet with your task force."

As Seth and Abby vacated the office, Pete picked up his mug. Coffee, phone calls, paperwork. Then he'd tackle his primary objective of the day.

Find Horace Pavelka.

After driving an ambulance and a three-quarter-ton pickup, Zoe felt like her backside was dragging the ground in Sylvia's Escort. At least she'd agreed to loan Zoe the car. Initially, Sylvia had insisted on driving her around. Learning that Zoe wanted to be at her farm by seven a.m. changed her mind. Sylvia handed over the keys with orders to have the car back by noon. "I have a hair appointment in Phillipsburg at twelve thirty," she'd said. "And I don't intend to walk two miles in this rain."

Ordinarily, Zoe would've fed the horses and turned them out, but with the steady rain and wind, she cleaned the stalls, supplied the animals with abundant hay, filled the water buckets, and left them bedded down in their stalls.

She showered and changed clothes in the house. Still not quite in move-in condition, the once unlivable structure—a "gift" from her mother—was slowly shaping up. It had a furnace, hot and cold running water, an old but functioning bathroom, and a few pieces of thrift shop furnishings. The kitchen, however, lacked appliances. The drafty single-paned windows lacked curtains. And the bedroom lacked a bed.

Zoe's next stop was the county morgue located in the basement of the Brunswick Hospital. Competing signs, some touting Dr. Charles Davis for coroner, others asking for votes to reelect Franklin Marshall, dotted the lawns across the street from the hospital's rear entrance. The sight of the Davis for Coroner signs in yards flanking Franklin's own funeral home disheartened her. Traitors.

Franklin and Doc Abercrombie had already shed their butcher shop chic autopsy attire by the time Zoe entered the morgue's office.

"You're late," Franklin said without his usual heckling tone.

"As usual." Doc's voice contained enough snark for both of them.

In addition to downplaying his routine chastisement of her tardiness, Franklin appeared subdued in general. Aware of his health issues, Zoe asked, "You okay?"

He shot a glare her way. "Just peachy."

Well, at least his prickly attitude remained intact. She turned to Doc. "Find anything unexpected during the autopsy?"

"No. In fact both Grant Jennings' and Dennis Culp's autopsies were pretty *cut* and dried." Doc held her gaze and fought to restrain a grin while waiting for her reaction.

She hated to give it to him. "Ha," she said flatly. Morgue humor.

Franklin rolled his eyes. "Grant Jennings died from exsanguination. The bullet transected the descending aorta. It did a lot of other damage too, but none of that ultimately mattered. He bled out fast. Good job, by the way, keeping him prone to retain the blood loss inside the body."

"I have an excellent teacher."

Franklin huffed. "You'll need to start using past tense. The election's only a week away."

Zoe thought of the abundance of Davis for Coroner signs around the county, even next door to Franklin's business.

Doc elbowed the coroner. "Don't be such a defeatist."

"I'm not a defeatist. I'm a realist." Franklin looked at Zoe, his eyes as sad as she'd ever seen them. "And you better attend every autopsy you can from now on. You may not have the chance much longer."

Zoe pondered Franklin's words as she drove through town toward the bakery. She knew his suggestion to attend more autopsies was meant to expand her experience as much as possible. But Davis wasn't about to keep her on staff if he won the office, and she had no interest in applying for a position with another county.

She spotted Wayne Baronick's unmarked sedan across Main Street from the Brunswick Bakery. Was he waiting for Horace to come out? Or had Horace not shown up and Wayne was staking out the place in case he did? Either way, Zoe wanted to get to Horace first and was grateful to be driving Sylvia's car. An Escort was much less conspicuous than her ancient pickup with its mismatched door and tailgate. Zoe felt confident Wayne didn't notice her turning into the alley leading to the rear of the business.

The handful of spots near the rear entrance were filled. No one wanted to get drenched running into and out of the bakery. Zoe parked the Escort as close as she could, flipped her coat's hood up against the rain, and sloshed to the back door.

She stood for a minute to drip on the industrial runner strategically placed to catch snow, mud, and water from customers' feet. Then she made her way down the short hallway that opened into the showroom. Glass cases glistened in the bright lighting, displaying cookies, pastries, pies, and a wide variety of decorated cakes and cupcakes. The decadent aroma of baking sweets filled the air.

She gravitated toward a free-standing shelf display of wedding cake toppers, from the traditional bride and groom to carved and personalized crystal hearts. Horace had suggested a floral topping, mixing live flowers with his own edible creations.

Zoe hoped he'd still be able to design the masterpiece he had in mind. Looking around, she didn't see him behind any of the counters. She moved toward a window separating the sales floor from the bakery's kitchen, which allowed customers to watch the magic being made.

No Horace.

A glance out the front window revealed Wayne still sitting in his car across the street. At least he hadn't spotted her.

She waited in line at the cupcake counter where the owner waited on a woman in a long red raincoat. Once he'd boxed the woman's selection and sent her to the register, he smiled at Zoe. "How may I help you?"

"Um…" She hadn't planned to buy anything, but a paying customer might garner more cooperation. Cupcakes would make a nice thank you to Sylvia for the loan of the car, although she might not appreciate the temptation to wander from her new healthy lifestyle. "Give me three of the carrot cake ones. And three of the Death by Chocolate."

Her polar opposite choices brought a smile to his face.

As the owner transferred the cupcakes into a pink box, Zoe made an exaggerated point of looking around. "Horace has been designing my wedding cake."

The owner studied her. Recognition lit his face. "Yes, I remember seeing you in here speaking with him before. Congratulations."

"Thanks. I wanted to talk to him, but I don't see him around."

The smile vanished as he glanced toward the front window. And Wayne's car across the street. "Horace isn't here today." The owner closed the box's lid and tucked in the flaps. "There you go. You can pay up front."

Acting concerned, she chewed her lip. "I really needed to ask him something about my cake. And my wedding's only two weeks away." A brazen lie, but she was getting desperate. "Would you mind giving me his phone number? We've been talking a lot about this cake. I'm sure he wouldn't mind."

From the owner's dour expression, Zoe expected a flat-out no. Instead he slid the box toward her. "Wait here. I'll get it. And if you manage to reach him, tell him I understand about the problems he's having, but if he doesn't call me or come to work tomorrow, he's fired."

TWELVE

Baronick phoned Pete to report Horace hadn't shown up for work. His boss promised to call if he heard from him. It didn't take much digging to learn Belinda Turner worked the night shift at a manufacturing plant near Pittsburgh. She'd not only reported off last night but had taken the rest of the week off as well. Her supervisor told Pete she claimed to have the flu. Since a bug had been going around, the supervisor hadn't given it another thought.

Stanley Jennings' calls were going to voicemail. So far, he hadn't returned any of the messages Pete left.

Having no luck searching by phone, Pete decided to take the personal approach on his fourth person of interest.

He entered Bud Kramer's through an open garage door, ignoring the signs prohibiting unauthorized personnel. The hum of machinery and the high-pitched zip of an impact wrench made Pete's ears ring.

Zoe's truck was on the lift with Melvin and one other mechanic underneath. Pete approached. Rather than shout over the din, he waited until he caught the owner's eye.

Melvin waved, said something to his employee, and grabbed a rag to wipe his hands before stepping out from under the truck. "Hi, Chief. What can I do for you?"

Pete looked up at the Chevy's undercarriage. It showed evidence of its years. He wished like hell Zoe would sell the monstrosity. But that wasn't why he was there. "Where's Reese Perkins?"

Melvin huffed. "Didn't show up this morning, the son of a

bitch."

"Seems to be a lot of that going around," Pete muttered.

"What?"

"Never mind. Did he call?"

"Nope. It's damned disappointing. I thought I finally had a good, reliable employee."

Pete didn't mention the guy's appeal to be paid under the table. "I assume that means he didn't miss work as a rule."

"This is the first time. If he'd called and reported off, I'd have been cool with it. Like I said, Reese is a hard worker. But I have jobs lined up for him." He hoisted a thumb toward the Chevy above them. "Your girlfriend's truck for example. Being down a man is gonna put me a whole day behind."

Pete dug a business card from his pocket. "I'd appreciate a call if your good, reliable employee shows his face."

"You still want to question him about something he saw?"

Among other things. "Yep."

Melvin accepted the card and used it to point at a tool chest with a stainless-steel coffee Thermos perched on top. "He'll be back. He left his tools. Unless he's independently wealthy and can afford to replace the whole lot of them. I'll buzz you when I see him."

"I'd appreciate that." Pete studied the chest and the Thermos on top. "Is that his too?"

"Sure is."

"Mind if I borrow it?"

"Be my guest." Melvin excused himself and returned to Zoe's truck.

Pete wandered over to the abandoned beverage container. "Thank you, Mr. Perkins." He slipped on a pair of Nitrile gloves and gingerly picked up the Thermos, careful to avoid smudging any fingerprints his errant witness had left behind.

"Horace, it's Zoe. Again." She made her third attempt at reaching him at the number the bakery owner had given her. "Please call me.

You know all I want to do is help." She tried to come up with something more to entice a response, but she'd already passed along his boss' threat in an earlier message. Zoe ended the call as frustrated as ever.

She placed the phone on the kitchen table and picked at the carrot cake cupcake on her plate. When she'd returned Sylvia's car and offered the baked goods as a thank you gift, Sylvia had taken one look at the Death by Chocolate ones and declared her diet could go to hell. She'd claimed all three and sent Zoe home with only the healthier options.

She had to admit even the vegetable-based baked goods were scrumptious and turned her attention back to the genealogical site on her laptop.

Merlin, one of her two orange tabbies, sauntered across the room to sit next to her, looked up with demanding green eyes, and meowed. She scooped him into her lap only to have the cat climb onto her shoulder and wrap around her neck like a collar. "You happy now?" she asked.

His purr indicated he was.

A knock at the door startled her but not the feline. Merlin didn't budge when Zoe rose to answer the door.

Lauren Sanders stood on the porch, her wool coat glistening with rain. Zoe opened the storm door and stepped aside to let her in.

"Sorry I'm late." Lauren propped her umbrella in the corner and shucked off her coat. "I had to turn a story in to my editor." She spotted the cat. "Nice necklace. I see I should've taken my allergy meds before coming over."

"I could put them in the bedroom."

"I doubt that would help. Let's get some work done, and I'll get out of here."

Zoe lifted Merlin from her shoulders, deposited him on the floor, and returned to her laptop. "Would you like a cup of coffee and a cupcake?"

Lauren's already slightly red eyes widened. "Yes, please. What kind of cupcake?"

"Carrot cake."

The reporter's enthusiasm waned. "On second thought, I'll pass."

"They're actually pretty good." Chocolate would've been better. "I'll take coffee though." As Zoe poured, Lauren studied the laptop's screen. "You haven't made much progress."

Zoe choked a laugh. "I haven't made *any* progress. Oh, I've discovered I had a great-great-grandfather who fought in the Civil War. But that's not the direction I'm interested in." She placed a mug on the table, crossed to the recliner, and gathered an annoyed Jade under her arm.

After shooing both tabbies into the bedroom and closing the door, Zoe returned to find Lauren had moved one of the kitchen chairs next to Zoe's and was browsing the genealogical site.

"You haven't added Melanie Wilson yet."

Zoe reclaimed her chair. "I'm still trying to figure out what I'm doing."

Lauren reached into her satchel and pulled out a legal pad. "I have a friend in the courthouse and called in a favor. Got Melanie's birthdate." Lauren repositioned the computer. "Let's see what more we can find." She clicked a plus button and typed in the information they had about Melanie Wilson, connecting her to what Zoe had already entered regarding her father.

Zoe watched the reporter pecking at the keyboard. "Tell me something. Why are you doing this?"

Lauren wrinkled her nose, sniffed, and sneezed into the crook of her elbow. "What do you mean?"

Zoe stood to reach a box of tissues on top of the refrigerator. Sitting, she placed the box in front of Lauren. "Why are you helping me?"

She plucked one and pressed it to her nose. "You're wondering if there's a story in it for me?"

"The thought crossed my mind."

Lauren met Zoe's gaze. "You mentioned finding a great-great-grandfather who fought in the Civil War? I have ancestors who fought in the French and Indian War."

"This is a competition?"

"Not at all." Lauren faced the screen again, but Zoe had a feeling she was seeing more than names and dates. "When I was out of work after my big corruption story went bust, I was floundering. On a whim, I started researching my past. For something to do. But I got hooked." She glanced at Zoe, grinning. "It's addictive. When I found out you had a brother you hadn't known about, it triggered my curiosity. Besides, I'd run my family tree out as far as I could and needed a fix."

"You never did say how you found out about me having a brother."

The grin blossomed. "No, I didn't, did I? Okay, let's see where the search takes us." Sniffling, Lauren tapped the mousepad and pulled up a list of potential hints regarding Melanie's past.

After rejecting the first two as being different Melanie Wilsons, Zoe's phone rang. The screen identified Bud Kramer's Garage as the caller.

"I have to take this." With any luck, Melvin would tell her the problem was minor and inexpensive and her Chevy was ready to be picked up.

"Melvin Quinn here. I looked at your truck this morning." Something about his tone told her luck was not on her side.

"And?"

"You have a short in your wiring."

"But you can fix it? Run some new wires?"

A pause. "Sure, we can fix it. But we have to locate the short first."

"How long is that gonna take?"

"I can't say right now. I have one of my guys tracking it down."

"Okay..." She sensed there was more.

"We ran across another problem."

Crap. Sometimes she really hated being right. "What?"

"You ran out of gas because you have a leak."

Exactly what she hadn't wanted to hear. "Can you patch it?"

"Zoe, your truck is old. The gas lines are rotted out. If I patch one spot, it'll only be a matter of time before another leak crops up."

This really didn't sound good. "What needs to be done?"

"We have to drain what little gas is still in there. Drop the gas tank. And replace all the lines."

She cringed. "How much?"

A pained silence filled the air. When he spoke, he sounded apologetic. "Parts and labor will come to around five hundred dollars."

"Five—" Zoe stuttered. Choked. And swallowed. Her current, tightly stretched budget flashed like a warning sign inside her brain. The list of items she still needed for her farmhouse before she and Pete could move in. The expenses of a wedding, even a small one. What could she cut from either category? Did she really need a stove? Or a dress? Would Pete complain if she walked down the aisle in her jeans and barn boots?

"Zoe?" Melvin's voice filtered into her ear.

"I'm still here. Is that quote for both the wiring and the gas lines or only the—"

"Just the gas lines."

Crap.

"I can't quote you on the wiring until we figure out where the short is." Another pause. "Do you want me to go ahead with the repairs?"

What choice did she have? If she put gas in the tank only to have it drain back out, the truck would be useless. "How about if you change the gas lines but hold off on the wiring for now?"

There was a pause. "You do know your inspection is up next month, right?"

Double crap. "I forgot."

"It won't pass without backup lights."

She did some quick calculations. How much would payments on a new or even used vehicle be? Fixing up the old beast would be cheaper in the long run. "Go ahead."

"Look, I'll cut you a break as much as I can. Since taking this place over from Bud, business hasn't been great, and I really appreciate you sticking with me. Maybe we can even work out a plan to spread the payments out over a couple of months."

"I appreciate it." In truth, she doubted even spreading the bill out would be much help.

He promised to get back to her about the wiring ASAP. She ended the call and stared at her half-eaten cupcake, her appetite gone. Another sneeze brought her attention to Lauren, who looked like she'd come down with conjunctivitis.

"Oh my God. You need to get out of here."

Lauren pressed a wad of tissues to her face to muffle yet another sneeze. "I think you're right." She tapped the laptop's screen. "I also think I found our Melanie Wilson."

THIRTEEN

Pete succeeded in developing several usable prints from the slick stainless surface of the Thermos. He'd finished scanning them into his AFIS computer when Nancy appeared in the fingerprint lab's doorway.

"Chief, there's a report of a vehicle fire at the State Game Lands' parking area a mile west of Parson's Roadhouse. Fire and EMS are already en route."

Pete checked the computer for the as yet nonexistent results. Television shows always made him laugh at the speed in which results spewed out. In reality, it took considerably longer. "On my way."

By the time he arrived at the graveled lot, the blaze had been extinguished leaving a smoldering, blackened shell of a pickup truck.

Although afternoon temperatures crept into the sixties, driving rain continued to fall in torrents, leaving Pete to debate whether or not to don his rain poncho. Wearing it would keep the rain off but would create an internal steam bath. He opted to leave the wet weather gear behind, tugged on his cap, and stepped out of his SUV.

The EMS crew sat inside the ambulance. No patient to work on. Pete headed for the smoking pickup and spotted Vance Township Fire Chief Todd Onderick speaking with a pair of his firefighters.

"Chief. Good to see you." Onderick excused his men and extended a hand to Pete, who shook it.

"What've you got?"

Onderick nodded at the truck. "Abandoned. No one around or in it. Thank heavens. I'm betting we have a case of insurance fraud. Someone couldn't make their payments and lit it up rather than let the bank repo it."

Pete moved toward the front of the smoldering shell. "Not much left."

"Once it cools off, we should be able to give you a VIN."

Although a lot of the newer trucks shared a similar profile, a closer look at what was left of the grill answered one of Pete's questions. "Dodge."

"A 2019 Ram. That much I do know. My brother has one like it." Onderick grinned. "Only not as well done."

"Any idea what started the fire?"

"Not yet. It was fully involved by the time we arrived."

Pete looked around the lot. Gravel. A few weeds. And lots of standing water, either from the fire department's hoses or from the rain. No chance of finding much in the way of evidence.

A young firefighter jogged over to them. "Chief," he said to Onderick. Then he looked at Pete and hesitated. "Chief," he said again, obviously trying to decide if he should be more specific.

"What is it, Dom?" Onderick asked.

"Thought you'd wanna know. The license plate is missing."

"Really?" Onderick turned to Pete. "Seems odd if someone wanted to file an insurance claim stating his truck was stolen and torched."

"Maybe. Maybe not." And definitely not strange if someone torched his truck to hide evidence of foul play. "Do me a favor. Get me that VIN as soon as you can."

"Will do."

As Onderick and the young firefighter trudged away, Pete studied the truck. "I'd bet a month's salary that Dodge Ram used to be red."

"Thanks for the ride." Zoe exited Lauren's gray Chevy sedan at the farm. The November temperatures had been rising all day, but with the torrential rain and gusting winds, she still shivered.

"No problem." Lauren stepped out, popped open an umbrella, and pulled her leather satchel against her chest. "You're currently without transportation. I love horses. You need to feed your horses. And you don't have any cats here. It's a win all around."

Zoe dragged a backpack carrying her laptop and hotspot from the backseat, held it close to shield it from the rain, and slushed to the house.

Once inside, Lauren took in the ancient linoleum, the cheap kitchen cabinets with spaces that appliances once occupied, and the single-pane rain-streaked windows. "You're planning to live here?"

"You should've seen the place before we started working on it. At least I have heat and running water now." Zoe set the backpack on the floor next to a card table and a pair of folding chairs that served as temporary dining room furniture and retrieved the laptop from its case.

Once the computer and hotspot had booted up and connected, Lauren rubbed her palms together. "Now. Where were we?" She brought up the genealogy site and page they'd found while still at Pete's house. "Melanie Wilson." Lauren tapped the screen. "This is her. Born in Brunswick Hospital. Birthdate looks right. Went to school in Phillipsburg." Lauren scrolled through a short list of documents matching Melanie. "Looks like she married a Richard Henderson when she was twenty. Here's a death certificate for the husband. He died ten years ago. Melanie Wilson Henderson's last known residence is in Clarion."

"That's where she had the baby and put him up for adoption."

"Right." Lauren scanned the remaining information. "Melanie's parents are listed, both deceased, but nothing about a child." She clicked another document. "Oh, wait. Here we go."

Zoe's heart rate cranked up. "You found him?"

Lauren studied the screen, then heaved a loud sigh. "I thought maybe, but no. According to these records, Melanie gave birth to two children with her husband. Both daughters."

The chair creaked as Zoe flopped into it. "This site is useless."

"You need to send your DNA to see if you come up with a match."

"And if he hasn't already put himself in the system?"

"Then you'll hit another brick wall." Lauren turned in her chair to look at Zoe. "Have you filled out those forms for the Adoption Information Registry?"

"Yesterday. But I haven't submitted them yet." A rumbling motor outside drew Zoe's attention.

"You should get on that," Lauren said.

Through the window in the kitchen door, Zoe spotted a black SUV rolling into her driveway. "We have company."

"Oh? Who?"

"I have no idea." She stood and crossed to the door, peering out. The SUV looked like the kind the bad guys always drove on crime shows. Pete had been after her to install a security system. She'd added it to her to-do list. Right now, she wished she'd given it higher priority.

The vehicle pulled up beside Lauren's Chevy. Seconds ticked off, feeling like hours, before the passenger door opened.

And Kimberly Chambers Jackson stepped out.

By the time Pete returned to the station, the AFIS computer had kicked out a list of possible matches. With the help of a magnifying loop, he began the process of comparing the prints he'd lifted from Reese Perkins' Thermos to the ones the computer suggested.

The first four didn't quite mesh. The fifth one though...

To Pete's trained eye, the prints matched. The name didn't.

Christopher Lewis Nixon had a rap sheet that included a variety of burglary and theft charges. Shoplifting. Breaking and entering. Plus a handful of assault charges—both simple and aggravated—and a few drunk and disorderlies. He also boasted a half-dozen known aliases.

None of which were Reese Perkins.

He'd only served time once. Most of his cases resulted in dropped charges, making restitution, community service, or fines. Apparently, the guy had a hell of an attorney.

The Warsaw Avenue address in Erie was his last known address of record. Pete printed out Christopher Lewis Nixon's mug shot. While Pete had never laid eyes on him, Zoe had and would be able to confirm whether this was the same guy.

Pete's phone rang as he was closing the lab. Seth's number lit the screen.

"Chief, you need to get out here to the old Hill place on Mays Road." Seth's voice sounded more amused than stressed.

"The Hill place?" A long-abandoned and boarded-up house on a few acres of overgrown pastureland. "What's going on?"

"Well..." A pause. And was that a chuckle? "You have to see it to believe it."

"I'll be there in ten."

He made it in seven.

The house sat about a quarter mile off the road. Nature had reclaimed the driveway, except it showed signs of recent use in the form of muddy tire tracks. Pete hesitated before turning into the lane, but spotted Seth's personal vehicle, a new orange Jeep Wrangler, over halfway to the house. Three figures stood outside it, hunched against the rain. With a resigned sigh, Pete headed in.

Growing closer, he made out Seth in jeans and raingear as one of the figures. Although the smallest of the three was attired head to toe in camo Gore-Tex, Pete suspected it was Abby. Then he spotted the second vehicle.

A familiar beat-up GMC pickup was sunk axle deep in the muddy field next to the driveway. Which meant the third person in the trio was none other than the elusive Stanley Jennings.

Parking his SUV behind the Jeep, Pete stepped out, tugged on the bill of his ball cap to keep the rain off his face, and approached the soggy group. "Stanley," he said, putting some boom in his voice, "you're a hard man to track down."

The surviving Jennings brother slouched farther into his soaked flannel shirt but didn't reply.

Pete turned to his officers. "What happened?"

Seth exchanged a smirk with Abby before he stiffened his jaw. "We were driving around, checking out some of these abandoned properties, looking for possible hiding places for the loot from all the thefts." Seth lowered his face. When he lifted it again, a tinge of red flushed his cheeks. "I'd got to thinking about those burglaries last winter and them hiding stuff at..." His voice trailed off.

Pete filled in the blank. "At the farm that Zoe now owns."

"Yeah. I thought this ring might be using the same trick. It was a whim, but we're on our own time."

He looked from Seth to Abby. "This is what you two do for dates? Go out and try to find stolen merchandise?"

It was Abby's turn to lower her face but not before Pete caught her blushing.

"You were checking this property and stumbled across Mr. Jennings stuck in the mud?"

Stanley shoved his hands into his jeans pockets and appeared to retreat into his shell like a turtle.

Abby cleared her throat. "No. We were headed this way and came up behind Jennings' pickup truck a couple miles back. We decided to follow him. He must've recognized us and tried to rabbit."

"Apparently, he thought he could get in here and hide." Seth tipped his chin at the mud encrusted GMC. "He didn't make it."

Pete eyed Stanley, who still refused to look at any of them, then gazed toward the house. Mucky ruts marred the driveway with a swampy bypass around a rain-carved and water-filled ditch that transected the lane. It was the bypass which currently mired Jennings' GMC. "I'm guessing this isn't the first trip you've made in here, is it, Stanley?"

His eye twitched but he didn't say anything.

"We noticed that too," Abby said.

"We're wondering if our theory was right." Seth aimed a hard glare at Stanley. "And if maybe the Jennings brothers were part of our theft ring."

"I'd like to look inside that house," Abby mused.

Stanley's head lifted. The turtle coming out of its shell. "We aren't part of no burglary ring. This used to be our grandfather's place. I was usin' it to lay low for a while."

"Why are you laying low?" Pete asked.

Stanley's jaw quivered. "Because Horace Pavelka killed my brother and if he catches me, I'm next."

"What in heaven's name have you been doing? I gave you this farm almost a year ago, and you haven't done a damned thing with it." Kimberly, wearing a winter white fur coat that matched her sprayed-to-perfection updo, stood in the middle of the kitchen, her arms outspread.

"We have." Zoe hated the whiny pitch in her voice. "We had to completely replumb the house. New water heater. New furnace. New porch deck so we don't fall through."

Kimberly huffed. "No appliances. No furniture. No curtains."

"We'll use Pete's furniture. I can't very well move it here while we're still living there." Zoe aimed a glare at her cousin, Patsy, who had been behind the wheel of the black beast in the driveway. Questions roiled inside Zoe's head. *Why did you bring Mother here? Why didn't you warn me? Where the hell did you get that vehicle?*

Patsy Greene, who was in fact Kimberly's first cousin—a relationship she'd learned about less than two years ago—picked up on Zoe's displeasure and offered a sheepish grin.

Kimberly continued her inspection. She stomped one beige, mud-splattered boot. "This floor is hideous. You need ceramic tile." Looking toward the empty living room, she added. "Hardwood flooring in there. And paint. Or wallpaper." She shook her head and clucked. "Disgusting."

Zoe cocked a hip. "If you'd let me know you were coming, I'd have had the place all fixed up for you."

Kimberly huffed again. If she caught Zoe's sarcasm, she didn't react to it. Instead, her gaze settled on Lauren, who'd wisely chosen to sit quietly and observe. "Who are you?"

Lauren rose and started to introduce herself, but Kimberly cut her off with a wave. "Never mind." She pivoted to face Zoe. "We must firm up your wedding plans."

"Well, I—"

"I have most of the arrangements made."

Arrangements? "Mother? What have you done?"

Kimberly peeled off her beige gloves and beamed. "I've booked the Vinoy for the third Saturday in September."

"The Vinoy?" Zoe struggled to think of anyplace with that name in the Pittsburgh area.

"Yes. Only the best for my daughter's wedding."

"Where's the Vinoy?"

Kimberly fixed her with a look that teenagers give right before saying *duh*. "Why, it's in St. Petersburg, of course."

FOURTEEN

Plywood covered the windows and filled the space where a door should be. Other than the tire tracks leading to and from the yellow brick house, it appeared to have been unoccupied by human residents for decades.

Pete stomped his feet on the cracked concrete slab of a porch, dislodging some of the mud accumulated on the hike from where they had to leave their vehicles. Stanley worked his fingers into a gap between the plywood and the door jamb and it swung open enough to allow them through.

Seth clicked on a small flashlight and swept what they could see of the house. "Mind if we take a look around?"

Stanley dismissed him with a wave. "Knock yourself out."

Seth and Abby headed off to the right of the center hallway while Pete followed Stanley to the rear of the house, the *clomp* of their boots echoing in the hollow darkness. The place smelled musty. And empty.

"Wait here a minute." Stanley stepped through a threshold. Pete listened to his footsteps, then Stanley struck a match, touching the flame to the wick of a lantern. It flared to life, casting a glow across the room.

The kitchen reminded Pete of Zoe's except the cabinetry was better quality. The same empty spaces that should've held a refrigerator and a stove gaped at him. Pete stepped around a ventless propane heater to check out the meager supplies Stanley had spread next to a Coleman camp stove. A pot and skillet looked like something he'd picked out of someone's trash. Canned goods with an opener, plastic jugs of water, a jar of peanut butter, and a partial loaf of bread.

Stanley shuffled over to a stained sleeping bag on a flimsy cot and sat.

"How long have you been staying here?" Pete asked.

"Since yesterday morning." Stanley rested his elbows on his knees and studied his feet. "After Pavelka killed my brother, I knew I was next. I wasn't about to sit around waiting for Pavelka to show up and blast me too."

"Why would he come after you? After all, you and Grant went to Horace's house to confront him. Isn't that right?"

Stanley lifted his face. His eyes glistened in the dim light. "Grant wasn't armed. Pavelka had no cause to shoot him."

"Tell me what happened?"

"We was upset about Dennis. And about you cops settin' Pavelka free. We—Grant and me—needed to let Pavelka know he wasn't gonna get away with what he done. He was gonna pay."

"In other words, you threatened to kill him."

"No." Stanley squirmed. "We wouldn't have killed him. Grant wanted to scare him some. Put him in his place where he belonged."

Pete glared at Stanley. "And where did you feel he belonged? Cringing in fear?"

"Maybe."

"You and Grant went to his house. Then what?"

Stanley shrugged as if the answer was obvious. "Horace shot Grant."

"Before that."

"I don't know what you mean."

Pete sighed. "Did Grant knock on the door? Did he kick it in?"

"He knocked."

"And Horace let him in?"

"He let him in and then he shot him."

"Where were you when this was happening?"

The cot creaked under Stanley's shifting weight. "I was

watching from outside the window."

"Tell me exactly what you saw."

Stanley flung up his hands. "I told you."

"No, you didn't." Seth and Abby appeared in the doorway, but Pete kept his gaze on Stanley. "Take me through it step by step. Grant knocked. Horace opened the door and simply invited him in."

"Yeah." Stanley's voice sounded less sure.

"Then what? Horace offered him a piece of cake?"

"No. Don't be ridiculous." Even in the low light, Pete could see Stanley's eyes drift to the side. "They talked for a minute. Then Pavelka pulled out a gun and shot Grant."

"What kind of gun?"

"I dunno."

"A handgun? A shotgun? A hunting rifle?"

Stanley thought about it. "A shotgun?"

Pete crossed his arms. "You didn't see any of it, did you?"

"Yes, I did. I told you. Through the window."

"You didn't get out of the truck."

The cot squeaked again. "Well, no. But I heard the shot."

"Tell me what you did see."

Stanley's shoulders slumped. "Grant got out of the truck and told me to wait. He went to the door and knocked. Pavelka let him in. I sat there a few minutes and heard a gunshot. At first I thought—" He pressed his lips closed and looked away.

Pete filled in the blank. "At first you thought Grant shot Horace."

"I hoped." Probably the truest words he'd spoken that day. "But Grant didn't have a gun on him. That's the God's honest truth. We didn't realize Pavelka had another one. I started the truck and waited for Grant to come out. I expected we'd have to book it outta there. Except..." Stanley's voice quivered. "Except Grant didn't come out. So I called his phone. When he didn't answer, I knew right then and there. Pavelka had killed my brother just like he killed Dennis."

Stanley buried his face in his hands and wept, his agonized

sobs filling the quiet room. Pete left him to grieve and approached his officers, motioning them into the hallway.

"Did you find anything?" he asked sotto voce.

"Not unless you count bird droppings," Seth replied.

"Among other kinds." Abby shivered. "I need a hot shower."

"Did you check the basement?"

"No." Seth swung the flashlight beam around. "Any idea where the stairs are?"

"You want to be a detective," Pete said. "Detect."

As the pair headed off, he returned to Stanley, who was sniffling in the kitchen. "Tell me about Belinda."

Stanley wiped an arm across his face. "What about her?"

"Was she there when you and Grant arrived at Horace's house?"

"How the hell should I know?"

"Was her car in the driveway?"

Stanley thought about it. "No."

Pete crossed his arms. "You used to date Belinda Turner."

"So?"

"And now she's dating Horace."

Even in the low light and shadows cast by the propane lantern, Stanley's curled lip radiated his displeasure. "That's what I heard."

"Must've been hard for you. Seeing your girlfriend with another man. Especially one you thought so little of."

"Her loss."

"And Grant being the supportive brother probably wanted to make Horace pay for stealing her from you."

Stanley raised his face to Pete. "It wasn't like that. All we wanted was to scare the shit outta that pissant for killing Dennis. You're talking like Grant's the one who shot someone. Let me remind you, Chief, Horace Pavelka's the murderer. He's the one out to kill me too." Stanley smirked. "Maybe Belinda told him I was better in bed than him. Maybe that's what's got his panties in a wad."

Pete studied Stanley. With his rage barely controlled and his emotional balance off kilter, it was the perfect time to throw him a curveball. "Where's Reese Perkins?"

Even in the lantern light, the sudden paling of Stanley's face was obvious. "Wh-who?" he stuttered.

"Reese Perkins. The man who you and Grant Saturday morning when Dennis took a baseball bat to Horace's car."

"I don't know anyone by that name. There wasn't anyone else with us. Only me, Grant, and Dennis."

"And you've never heard of Perkins?"

"Nope."

"Funny. Belinda told me you and your brother had business dealings with him. The way she talked, he was around a lot."

Stanley's mouth opened but no sound came out. He brought a hand to his face and traced the scar with trembling fingers. He may have claimed to be scared of Horace, but he was flat-out petrified of Perkins.

"We found the truck Perkins had been driving," Pete said matter-of-factly. "The red Dodge? Burnt."

Stanley's head snapped up. "Is he dead?" He sounded entirely too hopeful.

"So you *do* know him."

Realizing his slip, Stanley went silent again. When he finally found his voice, he spoke in a whisper. "Don't you need to tell me I have the right to remain silent?"

"Only if I question you while detaining you." Pete gestured around the not-so-cozy kitchen. "We're sitting around your grandfather's house having a chat."

"Well, I'm done chatting."

"How about we talk more about Belinda? Where might she go if she wanted to hide out for a few days?"

"Belinda? Hide out?" Stanley snorted. "She got no reason to hide out. Miss Priss, goody two-shoes."

"What if she was hiding Horace?"

Stanley looked like he'd sucked on a lemon. "I have no idea."

"I think you do."

"You can think whatever you want."

Seth and Abby reappeared in the doorway. Seth gave a quick headshake. They hadn't found anything useful.

"Stand up," Pete said to Stanley.

"Huh?"

"I'm placing you under arrest."

"What? Why? I didn't do nothin'."

"You were present Saturday morning when Dennis was wielding his bat."

"That was Dennis. I was just hanging around. What are you gonna charge me with? Loitering?"

"Stanley, there's an entire litany of crimes I could charge you with. From stalking to harassment to making terroristic threats—"

"I ain't no terrorist—"

Pete glared at him and added, "How about conspiracy to commit murder?"

"I didn't murder no one. The only threat is Pavelka. He's the killer around here."

"Yet, you aren't doing a damned thing to help me find him. Or Reese Perkins."

Stanley looked down, his face the picture of inner conflict. Finally, he stood and extended his arms toward Pete, wrists together and ready for handcuffs. "Fine. Arrest me. I'll be safer in jail anyway."

The question was—safer from whom? Pete suspected Horace wasn't the threat Stanley most feared. "On second thought, Stanley, you're free to go."

He lowered his arms. "You're not locking me up?"

"Nope. I'm going to make sure the word gets out where you're staying though."

Stanley stiffened. "I'll move somewhere else."

"Really?" Pete looked around. "Frankly, I think if you had anyplace else to go, you'd have gone there already. No, if you leave here, you're going to be out on the street and easy to find. Maybe not by Horace. But definitely by someone with Perkins' resources."

Stanley's lower lip quivered. "You wouldn't."

"Bet me."

He heaved a ragged sigh. "What if I tell you where Belinda might go to hide?"

Bingo. "If your tip pans out, I may forget I ever saw you. If it doesn't..."

"I mean, I don't know for sure she's there. But I don't know anyplace else. Honest."

"Where?"

Stanley ran his tongue over his lips. "Belinda's family owns a fishing camp in Fayette County. She took me there last spring. It's kind of a dump."

Pete glanced around. If Stanley was comparing Belinda's family camp to this palace, all Pete could come up with was...it takes one to know one.

"And it's pretty isolated."

"Give me an address, Stanley. Fayette County covers a lot of ground."

"I remember the road," he whined. "Weird name. Ramcat. Three thirty-three Ramcat Road."

FIFTEEN

"St. Petersburg?" Zoe stuttered. "*Florida?*"

Kimberly glared at her. "No. Russia," she said sarcastically. "Of course, I mean Florida. Tom and I are planning to move there."

Another surprise, although much lower on the Chambers-Jackson shock meter. "You're moving from Sebastian?"

Kimberly peeled off her gloves. "We've decided we like the Gulf Coast better." She shrugged out of her coat and looked around for someplace to hang it. Finding nothing, she shoved it and the gloves at Patsy, who'd been standing quietly next to the door. "During one of our house-hunting expeditions, we stayed at the Vinoy. It's lovely. As soon as I heard my only child was getting married, I called and reserved space for next September."

Zoe folded her arms. "What if I don't want to get married in September?" In Florida. At the Vinoy.

"Don't be silly. When you're planning a big wedding, you're always limited by venue availability. I was lucky to be able to book it so soon. I think there was a cancellation."

Zoe pictured her mother browbeating whomever was in charge of events until they caved to her demands. "Big wedding? If we get married in Florida, most of our friends won't be able to attend."

"Tom and I have enough friends to fill the place. It'll be lovely."

"Lovely." Zoe threw Kimberly's new pet word back at her. "So this wedding is all about you." Zoe made no effort to hide her displeasure.

"We're paying for it. When *you* have a daughter, you can plan her wedding to suit you."

The words landed a sucker punch to the gut. Zoe wasn't sure which hurt worse. The knowledge that she'd never have a daughter—or a son—or the realization that her mother didn't know about her infertility.

Kimberly apparently took Zoe's silence as acceptance and crossed to the card table. Standing behind Lauren, Kimberly squinted at the laptop. "What are you doing?"

Before Lauren could reply, Zoe said, "Searching for my half-brother," knowing what a raw spot her father's high school fling was where her mother was concerned.

"I thought you already found him. I sent you photos of Gary to show him."

As usual, Kimberly won the emotional battle of words by landing another blow. Zoe had neither the desire nor the energy to explain to her mother what had happened last spring.

For once, Kimberly's limited attention span was a blessing. Instead of waiting for a response, she squinted harder at the screen. "Melanie Wilson." Contempt dripped from her words. Straightening, she turned on Zoe. "Why on earth would you want to find that bitch?"

The language shocked Zoe. Not that she'd never heard her mother swear, but Kimberly generally considered herself too genteel for such vulgarity. "Just because you'd prefer to forget my father ever lived doesn't mean I do."

Her mother's stunned reaction took Zoe by surprise. Kimberly's head lowered, and Zoe caught the shimmer of tears welling. "You're wrong," Kimberly whispered. She walked to the far side of the kitchen to gaze out the window.

Zoe shot a glance at Patsy, who maintained a poker face worthy of the Vance Township gang's weekly card game. Lauren hadn't budged, afraid to speak.

Kimberly brushed a hand across her cheek before facing them. "You're wrong," she repeated, her voice still soft. "I don't want to forget Gary. I could never forget Gary. He was the love of my life."

Zoe wondered what that made Tom but wasn't foolish enough

to ask.

Kimberly looked at her. "He gave me you. I realize we haven't always gotten along, but my heart beats in you. You're my only child." She choked. "It's more than I can stand to know you weren't *his* only—" She turned away again.

Long moments ticked away. Zoe realized her mouth hung open. Had she ever seen her mother this vulnerable before? Maybe. Right after Gary Chambers' accident. The loss had devastated both of them and should have driven mother and daughter together. Instead, Kimberly had clung to Tom Jackson, her late husband's best friend, for support. Eventually, they'd married. For years, Tom had been Zoe's champion, trying to heal her relationship with her mother...until Zoe's lack of trust had alienated him.

Zoe crossed the room, her boots the only sound. She hesitated, then touched her mother's shoulder. "I'm sorry."

Kimberly turned, her usually flawless makeup streaked. Her lips quivered into a feeble smile. "I am too."

Zoe considered hugging her mother. Waited for her mother to initiate the embrace or at least make some small move toward one. Instead, Kimberly sniffled, straightened, and returned her chin to its sanctimonious jut.

She cleared her throat and strutted past Zoe to the card table and her position behind Lauren. "What have you found?"

Lauren shot a questioning glance at Zoe.

She nodded, knowing Kimberly's curiosity in the search was as close to motherly concern as she was likely to get.

Lauren pointed at the screen and explained about Melanie's marriage to Richard Henderson and their daughters as well as her last known address. The reporter wisely left out the part of Melanie's life that took place prior to moving to Clarion.

"Nothing about the child she had with my husband?"

"No." Lauren chewed her lip. "I suggested Zoe send her DNA in to this genealogy site and send in paperwork to the Adoption Information Registry."

Kimberly looked at Zoe. "And have you?"

"Not yet."

Kimberly waved a hand as if shooing a fly. "Don't bother. That could take months to produce results."

Her mother's interest touched Zoe. For a moment. Then she realized Kimberly probably didn't want her to ever find answers.

"There's obviously a faster way."

Maybe Zoe was wrong about her mother. "Faster? How?"

Kimberly rolled her eyes. She extended a wide-open palm toward the laptop. "It says that trollop's most recent address is in Clarion. Go directly to the source. It's only a three-hour drive."

"She put the baby up for adoption," Zoe said. "I'm sure she doesn't know where he is."

Kimberly spun to face Zoe. "She was head-over-heels in love with your father. She may have given the child away, but I'll bet she never lost track of it."

Zoe looked at Lauren who shrugged. "Your mother has a point about one thing," the reporter said. "Clarion is only a three-hour drive. What could it hurt?"

"Exactly." Kimberly clapped her hands and rubbed them together. "What are we waiting for. Girls' road trip."

The implication sucked the air out of the room. "What are you suggesting?" Zoe asked.

Kimberly looked from Zoe to Lauren to Patsy. "My rental car is plenty big enough for the four of us. I haven't checked in at the hotel yet, so my luggage is already in the back. You girls need to throw together an overnight bag." She flashed the biggest smile Zoe had seen from her mother since...forever. "What are you waiting for? Let's go."

Pete showered, changed into clean jeans and a Steelers sweatshirt, and fed Zoe's demanding cats and still she wasn't home yet. He rummaged through the junk drawer to come up with a Pennsylvania roadmap, which he spread out on the kitchen table. He'd assigned Kevin the job of tracking down information on the Turner family's property in Fayette County, but curiosity drove Pete to do some preliminary scouting. Old school.

A friend had taken him fishing in Fayette years ago. He remembered the county, which touched Monongahela's eastern border, as rugged and beautiful in mid-summer. And he remembered hearing the weather forecast calling for several inches of snow in the Laurel Highlands but none locally. Otherwise, his knowledge of the area was sparse at best. What he did know was it fell well outside his jurisdiction.

The rumble of a car door slamming in front of his house drew his attention. He parted the curtains to see a gray sedan. Zoe leaned in the open passenger-side window to speak to the driver. Nodded. And stepped clear as the car pulled out.

When she entered the kitchen, she met his gaze with an expression he could only describe as shell-shocked. "Hi."

"What's wrong?" he asked.

She choked out a short laugh. "I don't even know where to begin."

He waited.

"My mother's in town."

That explained a lot. "To plan our wedding?"

Zoe dropped into the chair he kept next to the door. "For starters. Apparently, we're getting married in September in Florida."

Pete realized his mouth hung open. Kimberly had a way of doing that to people. "Oh."

One of the cats sauntered over to Zoe, who bent down and scooped it up. "I have to go out of town."

"Oh?" He expected her to say Kimberly was dragging her to Florida.

Instead, she said, "We're going to Clarion."

Definitely not what he expected. "Who's 'we'?"

"Mother, Patsy, Lauren, and me."

He pictured the foursome stuck in the same vehicle for the three-hour drive north. It wasn't a pretty image. "Should I alert the State Police?"

"Maybe."

"Why are you going to Clarion?"

Zoe stroked the cat in what was clearly an attempt to pacify her nerves. The cat soaked up the attention. "Lauren did some digging and found Melanie Wilson's last known address is in Clarion. Mother thinks Melanie might know where my brother is."

"But—"

Zoe stopped him with a raised hand. "It's Mother."

He'd had his own encounters with Kimberly Jackson. "Say no more. But all four of you?"

"I honestly don't know why my mother is suddenly so vested in helping me find my brother. The road trip was her idea. She basically ordered Patsy along as our driver."

"And referee."

"That too. Lauren happened to be there and is the one with the talent at researching, so Mother included her."

"Poor Lauren."

Zoe snorted. "I warned her. But if there happens to be a road rage homicide inside the car, she'll have the scoop."

He'd have chuckled except for the very real possibility. "Do you leave in the morning?"

"That would make too much sense. No, Kimberly wants to get started this evening. Lauren dropped me off to pack a bag while she goes home to do the same. And arrange for Marcus to stay with a friend. She's picking me up again in an hour."

An hour? "How long will you be gone?"

"Only a day. I hope." Zoe lowered the cat to the floor and rose. "I better get my stuff together." She noticed the map spread on the table. "Are you going somewhere too?"

"No." He thought about it. "Maybe." He told her about finding Stanley holed up in the abandoned house and his tip about the fishing camp.

She rested a finger on her lips as she studied the map. "That's rugged country."

"So is the area around Clarion."

She gave him a devilish grin. "Wanna swap?"

"Me? Spend a day in a car with your mother? She despises me."

Zoe's grin faded as she gazed at the map. "I tried calling Horace again this afternoon. He's still not answering. I'm worried." She turned away, paused, and faced Pete. "Any word on Perkins?"

"As a matter of fact..." Pete crossed to the antique wash stand beside the door and picked up the large envelope he'd placed there. He retrieved the mugshot and handed it to Zoe. "Is that the guy from the garage?"

She studied the photo. "That's him all right." Meeting Pete's gaze, she asked, "What was he arrested for?"

Pete started ticking off charges on his fingers. "Burglary, theft, criminal trespass—"

Zoe's phone interrupted the countdown. She checked caller ID and growled. "It's my mother."

He crossed his arms, waiting as she took the call. Kimberly's screech carried across the airwaves without being placed on speaker. The woman probably didn't even need the phone.

"Yes, Mom...I will...I am...Mom—"

Kimberly's rant cut Zoe off and earned an eyeroll.

"Okay...Yes...We'll be there in ten minutes. Bye." She ended the call with Kimberly still yammering.

"Ten minutes?"

"She made reservations at a bed and breakfast and wants to get there at a decent hour." Zoe made air quotes. "She's ordered Lauren and me back to the farm ASAP."

"Lauren just dropped you off two minutes ago."

Zoe raised an eyebrow at him. "You call Kimberly and tell her."

"No, thank you."

"I have to get packed." She returned the photo to him and stood on her tiptoes to plant a quick kiss on his lips. "Sorry I'm bugging out on you."

His gaze lingered on her retreating backside as she hurried through the living room. "So am I." Once she'd vanished into the hallway, he brought his attention back to the map on the table.

With Zoe heading out on a road trip, maybe he'd do the same thing. Different roads. Different objective. He picked up his phone and scrolled to his contacts, hitting the green call icon. "Abby? How would you feel about covering my day shift tomorrow?"

SIXTEEN

After almost three hours stuck in a vehicle with Kimberly, who alternately chattered about her plans for the wedding and griped about the late start they'd had and the lack of improvements made on the farm she'd gifted her ungrateful daughter, Zoe wanted nothing more than to lock herself in her room and decompress.

With Patsy at the wheel of the behemoth SUV, they cruised the streets of Clarion, following the guidance of the onboard GPS.

Kimberly reached across Patsy to flutter a manicured finger at a stately red brick Victorian. "That's it. Turn left here."

"I can't. It's a one-way street. No left turns."

Kimberly huffed. "There's no traffic. Make the turn."

Patsy ignored the demand. "I'll go around the block. It'll be fine."

Lauren leaned across the seat toward Zoe and whispered, "Your family trips when you were little must have been a blast."

"You have no idea." Lauren's remark set Zoe's memory rolling back to the two vacations she could recall. Kimberly had been different then. Self-absorbed, yes. But she'd been happy. With Zoe's dad around, everything was fun. His smile, his laughter infected everyone surrounding him. She remembered him scooping her mother into his arms and twirling her as she laughed. A bubbly laugh that Zoe hadn't heard since she was eight. Even Tom Jackson couldn't elicit that merriment from Kimberly.

At least not that Zoe was aware.

A series of right turns later, Patsy pulled into the parking area for the bed and breakfast.

Kimberly stepped out of the SUV and started for the house. "Be a love and bring my bags," she called over her shoulder.

At the rear of the car, Zoe exchanged looks with Patsy and Lauren.

"She wouldn't be referring to *me* as 'love,'" Lauren said. "We only met this afternoon."

"Does she mean *all* of her luggage?" Patsy mused.

Unlike Zoe and Lauren, who'd each packed a single overnight bag, Patsy had a roller bag and a small duffle from her flight home from Florida. Kimberly had two large suitcases, a massive carry-on, and what Zoe guessed was a makeup bag big enough to stock the Dior counter at a department store.

She eyed her cousin. "You know my mother. What do *you* think?"

"I say we take one, and if she wants more, she can come out and get it herself," Lauren said.

Zoe and Patsy looked at her, then at each other.

They divvied up Kimberly's luggage among their own and trudged like overburdened pack mules to the house.

Inside, Kimberly stood impatiently at the counter in the wide foyer. Zoe suspected the woman behind it had worn a genuine smile before Kimberly showed up, unlike the forced one currently plastered on her face.

"I'm sorry, ma'am," she said. "I told you on the phone that we only had three rooms available tonight."

"And I told you we needed four, including one with a king-sized bed for myself."

"We don't have any rooms with kings. Only doubles." She broadened her forced smile. "I've given you two single rooms and a third with two beds."

"That's unacceptable. I want to speak to the manager."

"Ma'am, I'm the owner. If you don't find our accommodations satisfactory, I can direct you to one of the hotels closer to the interstate."

Kimberly sniffed. "I already checked. They're all chains."

Zoe would've been happy with a chain hotel. However, driving back toward the interstate required lugging Kimberly's suitcase back to the SUV—did she have a dead body in there?—and meant being trapped in the vehicle with her again. "Mother, we're only here for one night. You're so slender, I'm sure the double bed will be plenty big. Patsy and I are fine sharing a room."

The "slender" comment worked. Kimberly rested a hand on one hip and lifted her chin as if posing. "I suppose you're right." She pivoted and headed for the staircase. "Bring my bags."

After the owner had shown them to their rooms, reminded them that breakfast would be served at seven, and distributed their keys, Kimberly slammed her door without a "goodnight." The owner gave Patsy, Lauren, and Zoe a pained, apologetic smile. "I hope you get a restful night's sleep."

"Me too," Zoe replied. Because she suspected it would be the only peaceful hours she'd have until she returned home.

When Pete left Vance Township Wednesday morning, the flat, gray sky had been tinged with pink. Innocuous-looking flurries, the first of the season, started floating on the air currents as he reached the Fayette County line. By the time he'd topped the summit on Route 40, an inch of the white stuff had accumulated on the grass. So far, the roads remained merely wet. He wondered if they were getting anything at all back home.

He also wondered about Zoe up in Clarion. She'd texted that they'd arrived safely but hadn't elaborated.

Following the guidance of his GPS, Pete took a left off 40 onto a winding, rolling road that would have been scenic even a week ago, before winds stripped the orange and gold leaves from the branches. A long downhill stretch of tight bends brought him to a stop sign on the edge of Ohiopyle. He remembered rafting here as a teen. Today, he was grateful the road hadn't glazed over, or the class-three rapids might have seemed like a walk in the park by comparison.

Instead of continuing down to the town's main street, he was directed to hang a right onto an even more treacherous, narrower road. One coated in a slick skiff of snow.

Whose brilliant idea was this?

Sugar Loaf Road was slimy enough, but Ramcat veered off to the left, down along what seemed to be little more than a driveway. Going was slow due to the snow and the gullies carved through the gravel and broken pavement.

Belinda Turner's family camp had to be along here somewhere. And if she wasn't there, Pete had wasted his morning.

Several of the camps edging the road looked like they'd been thrown together in an afternoon decades earlier. Nature was on the verge of reclaiming a few.

Pete checked the address Stanley had given him and squinted to see any identifying numbers on the shacks. He was getting close.

He braked in front of what he'd have taken for a storage shed had it not been for the numbers clearly labeling the slab wood-sided structure as the one he was seeking. A thin layer of snow-dusted gravel led from the road to the rear of the camp. No Chevy Cruze. No tire tracks in the snow. Pete nosed in far enough to be off the road and climbed out. The Pennsylvania mountain air was a good ten degrees colder than it'd been back home. Pulling his collar up against the chill, he picked his way across rocks and roots to a door that was the same shade of brown as the rest of the house.

No one responded to his knock. He tried the knob and was only mildly surprised when it clicked open. These old camps were often left unlocked for one simple reason: no one had anything of value to steal.

The interior of the cabin was dark, the gray daylight the only illumination. Pete flipped the switch next to the door. Nothing happened. The power had most likely been shut off long ago. The aroma of wood smoke masked the musty smell of abandonment.

He crossed the floor—the thump of his tactical boots the only sound—to a faded sofa, probably discarded and reclaimed for the camp. Next to it, dust coated a cheap-looking end table. He leaned down and squinted. The dust had been disturbed. A circle, possibly from a can of pop or a bottle of water, and a scuff as though someone had recently let their hand drape over the arm of the sofa, brushing a void in the coating.

Pete straightened. Sniffed. The wood smoke. He strode to the woodstove. Hovered a hand above it. Touched the cast iron surface. Cold. He squatted and opened the door. Picked up a poker and jabbed at the ashes. No embers.

He clicked his penlight and aimed the beam inside. No layer of dust either. And none on the small stack of wood piled next to the stove. Someone had been there all right. The smell of the now dead fire was too fresh.

A door led to a bedroom with a pair of bunk beds, all with faded spreads covering thin mattresses. Pete couldn't say for certain that any of them had been slept in. Nor could he say they hadn't.

He returned to the main room and crossed to the far side where a kitchen of sorts had been set up. The utility sink with a plain pipe faucet and what looked like a homemade counter was perfect for cleaning fish. He touched a bar of soap, which was smooth and free of dust but dry. He opened the cabinet door. Not even a can of beans. The beam of his penlight revealed specks. Mouse droppings. He considered using the soap himself.

Pete closed the cabinet and took one more look around the cabin. Belinda and Horace may have been here, but they were long gone now.

"There. That's it." Lauren reached from the backseat and tapped Patsy on the shoulder. "Stop here."

Patsy maneuvered the Navigator off the edge of the road next to a for sale sign.

"Uh-oh," Zoe said. "Are you sure this is the right address?"

Lauren looked at her notebook, then spun it around to show Zoe. "It's the one listed for Melanie Wilson Henderson on the genealogy site."

Zoe looked at Lauren's scrawls. They were on the right road, and the numbers matched the ones on the mailbox. But the one-story brick ranch house had the lonely look of abandonment. The yard hadn't been mowed in ages—the browned grass had grown tall and bent over, flattened. Like Zoe's heart. "She must have moved."

"Or died," Kimberly offered, sounding not at all sympathetic.

"Mother," Zoe protested.

"I doubt she's dead," Lauren said. "There would've been a death certificate listed."

Patsy turned to face the backseat passengers. "Now what?"

Zoe gazed out the window at the house. Now what, indeed. They'd driven all this way. Spent a very long night in a perfectly lovely bed and breakfast—one to which Zoe could never revisit after her mother's repeated demands to the owner for such things as room service at eleven last night and specific menu requests at the delicious breakfast offered this morning.

Kimberly poked Patsy in the arm. "Turn this thing around. Let's go home."

"Not yet." Zoe opened the door and stepped out of the massive SUV into a snow squall.

"What are you doing? Get back here."

She slammed the door, cutting off her mother's current tirade. They'd come this far. She wasn't about to go home without at least checking the place out.

The house didn't look any better close up. A long dead plant in a hanging basket swung from a hook on the front porch. The windows had been stripped of curtains or blinds. Zoe framed her face with cupped hands pressed to the glass for a better look inside. Nothing. No furniture. Nothing on the walls. Nothing covering the floors.

"Excuse me?"

She spun to find a gray-haired woman peering through the unkempt hedges bordering the yard.

"If you're interested in buying the house or getting a tour, I recommend you call the number on the real estate sign."

"I'm sorry." Zoe gave a woman a smile. "I didn't mean to trespass."

The woman didn't approach but pulled her coat tighter around her thin frame. "I keep an eye on the place since it's vacant. We had some problems when Melanie first moved out. Looters. Now, there's nothing left to loot, but the family doesn't want hoodlums breaking in and messing up the place."

Zoe wondered if she looked like a hoodlum. Especially with a seventy-five-thousand-dollar vehicle parked at the edge of the road. "I have no intention of looting or vandalizing anything. I was wondering what happened to Melanie. Did she—" Zoe hesitated. "Die?"

"No. Mercy, no." The woman relaxed and stepped fully into the overgrown yard. "Although, when you get to my age, you start to think dying isn't the worst thing that could happen. No, Melanie got to where her girls feared she wasn't safe living alone anymore. They moved her into a nursing home a couple of years ago."

"A nursing home? Do you happen to know the name of it?"

The woman scowled. Then held up one finger. "Wait here. I have it written down somewhere." She started to turn away but stopped. "Do you know Melanie?"

Zoe swallowed, her mouth suddenly dry. "I'm a friend of the family."

The woman accepted the partial lie, nodded, and vanished through the hedgerow.

After conferring with his map, Pete made his way down Ramcat Road, along the edge of the Youghiogheny River, and into the town of Confluence. Off season for fishermen, rafters, or kayakers, most of the town's eateries wore signs reading, "Closed. See you in April." Or May in a few cases. He did, however, locate a hole-in-the-wall establishment called the Turkey Foot Café with an open sign hanging on the door.

He hoped the name had more to do with the way the Laurel Hill, the Casselman, and the Youghiogheny merged than with the food offered. He needn't have worried. Turkey wasn't on the menu in any form.

His waitress, a fiftyish woman with gray hair pulled into a bun, wore a clean but threadbare apron over a flannel shirt and jeans. Her name tag identified her as Cindy. She filled a mug with coffee while reciting the specials. He took her recommendation. Meatloaf and gravy. "Make sure you save room for pie, sugar," she told him before whisking away to place his order. "It's the best around."

While Pete waited, he checked his phone, glad to see he now had a cell signal, something that he'd lost shortly after turning off Route 40. He called Abby, who reported all was quiet at home. And no, Vance Township wasn't getting snow. Just more rain. His next call was to Zoe, whose voice sounded strained.

"How's it going?" he asked.

"We found the house where Melanie used to live."

"Used to?"

"She's been moved to a nursing home. The neighbor lady gave me the name of the place, so we're headed there now."

Over the line, he could hear Kimberly's raised voice. "Be sure and remind him that he's responsible for buying the alcohol. He'll need to arrange everything with the bartender at the hotel."

Zoe's sigh filled his ear and his heart. "We're planning the wedding," she said.

No wonder she sounded stressed. "How are the four of you doing, trapped in the car together?"

"No blood has been shed. Yet. What about you? Any luck finding Horace?"

Cindy returned with his meal on a stoneware plate in one hand, a coffee pot in the other.

"No. I'll call you if I do." He wished her luck on her search, told her he loved her, and ended the call.

"You need anything else, sugar?" Cindy asked while topping off his coffee.

He was about to thank her and say no, but a thought occurred to him. "This place seems like the only one around that's open."

"Another restaurant across the river stays open all year too." She winked at him. "Our food's better."

Pete smiled at her. "I'm sure it is." He scrolled through his phone to bring up Belinda's photo and held it up to the waitress. "Have you seen this woman lately?"

Cindy dug a pair of reading glasses from her apron pocket and perched them on her nose before taking the phone to study the image. "I don't think so. Hang on a second." She searched the café. "Hey, Dottie. Come over here."

An older dark-haired woman, wearing the same style clothing and apron as Cindy, hobbled over to Pete's table. "What is it?"

Cindy handed her the phone. "Have you seen this gal?"

Dottie squinted at the screen. "Yeah. When was it? Let me think. Today's Wednesday? She was here Monday. Late afternoon. She and a fellow ordered supper. Chef salad for the girl. The daily special, beef stew, for the guy."

Pete reclaimed his phone, scrolled to the next photo—Horace—and handed it back. "Is this the guy?"

"That's him," Dottie said, nodding enthusiastically.

"You wouldn't happen to know where they went, would you?"

She returned Pete's phone. "No. But I can tell you they booked it outta here like their hair was on fire."

"Excuse me?"

"They were doin' like you. Checkin' their phones. You know, cell service is spotty around these parts, and we offer free Wi-Fi. They were only halfway through their meals when I figured they got a text or email or something because they up and left. Didn't ask for a doggy bag or nothin'. But they did leave cash. Enough to cover the tab and a nice tip."

"You didn't see which direction they went?"

"No, sir. It was the dinner crowd and all."

Disappointed, Pete thanked the women and stared at the steam rising from his plate. Monday. Horace and Belinda had come here right after the shooting with plans to hide out. Something they saw on their phones spooked them. They must have spent the night at the camp, which would explain the recent-but-cold fire in the stove, and then hit the road yesterday morning. Which gave them more than a twenty-four-hour head start on him.

He dug into his meatloaf—really good. Maybe Cindy was right about the pie too—and pondered the missing pair's next move. He knew what his was. Updating the Pennsylvania State Police and broadening the search. These two weren't hardened criminals. They couldn't stay hidden for long.

SEVENTEEN

The Willows looked more like another bed and breakfast than a nursing home. A farmhouse, much like the one Zoe once shared with Mr. and Mrs. Kroll, boasted new vinyl siding and a pair of modern additions. Had it not been for the sign at the end of the plowed driveway, she'd have thought it was simply another private residence.

Patsy steered the Navigator into one of the parking spaces reserved for visitors and cut the engine.

Zoe opened her door. "You all can wait in the car."

Kimberly barked a laugh. "And freeze? No way. We're coming with you."

Great.

"In a minute." She rifled through her handbag and came up with a compact, which she clicked open and squinted into. "My makeup's a mess. The lighting in that bathroom at the bed and breakfast was appalling. Couldn't they afford a decent lighting fixture?"

Lauren gave Zoe a sympathetic smile.

"Aren't you glad you came?" she asked the reporter.

"Actually, yes. I'm getting lots of material on dysfunctional families. I may write a feature article on the subject." She waggled her eyebrows. "Don't worry. I won't use your names."

Kimberly shot a glare at Lauren. "You aren't funny."

"I wasn't trying to be," she whispered to Zoe.

After Kimberly dabbed at her face and snapped the compact closed, they trooped to the front porch. Strategically placed hay bales supported colorful gourds and pumpkins without creating a hazard for wheelchairs or walkers. A half dozen rockers and several wicker chairs provided a lovely outdoor gathering spot, but with the cold and the snow, were currently unoccupied.

Zoe led the way into a center hallway atrium, which also might have felt like a private residence except for the receptionist seated at a reproduction antique desk and the trio of napping wheelchair-bound residents. Their presence labeled the Willows as a smaller version of the facility where Pete's dad lived.

The receptionist lifted her gaze from her paperwork. "May I help you?"

Kimberly moved toward the desk, but Zoe cut her off. "We're here to visit Melanie—" She almost said Wilson but remembered her married name. "Henderson."

The receptionist smiled. "I don't believe I've seen you before."

Fearing they'd be denied admission, Zoe shot a look at her mother—*be quiet*—and returned the receptionist's smile. "We're old friends up from Pittsburgh."

"How nice." She looked around and spotted an aide coming out of a room toward the rear of the house. "Kate, where's Miss Melanie right now?"

The aide paused. "She's in her room watching TV." Then she went on about her business.

The receptionist slid a book and a pen across the desk to Zoe. "Please sign in first." She aimed the pen at the staircase. "Miss Melanie's room is on the second floor. Number 203. If you prefer, you can use the elevator." She pointed toward the spot where the aide had been.

"The stairs will be fine."

Once they'd all signed the book, Zoe led the way upstairs, aware of her mother inspecting every aspect of the home.

"At least it doesn't stink in here like most of these places."

"Mother," Zoe hissed. "When have you ever been in an assisted living facility? They don't stink. At least the good ones don't."

Kimberly gave a dismissive huff.

Room 203's door stood open and the sound of televised voices drifted into the upstairs hallway. Zoe approached cautiously, still waiting for someone to dub them nosey frauds and toss them out. But the room was empty except for a frail gray-haired woman watching a soap opera from a recliner.

"Mrs. Henderson?" Zoe said. The woman didn't appear to hear. "Melanie?" Zoe said louder.

The woman's head snapped toward her. "Yes?" Her dark, confused eyes searched each of their faces.

"My name's Zoe Chambers." She strode toward her with a hand extended.

She'd hoped the mention of her last name might spark a reaction. It didn't. Melanie looked at Zoe's hand with the same puzzled expression.

Zoe'd seen that look on Pete's father's face. She withdrew the hand. "Melanie, we're from Vance Township."

No reaction.

"Phillipsburg?"

Nothing.

"My dad was Gary Chambers."

Melanie twitched. Her blank stare cleared as she met Zoe's gaze. "Gary? Is he here?"

Zoe ignored her mother's grunt and kept her eyes fixed on Melanie. "No, he's not."

"He's dead," Kimberly snapped.

Zoe spun to glare at her mother.

Patsy took Kimberly's arm. "Why don't we go downstairs and see if they have a snack bar or something. I'm hungry."

Kimberly shook her off. "I'm not. You go if you want."

Lauren stepped in front of Kimberly, blocking her view of Zoe and Zoe's of her. "What Patsy's trying to say nicely is we should leave and give Zoe and Melanie time alone."

Kimberly sidestepped Lauren and took a step closer to the woman in the recliner. Lauren blocked her with an arm, garnering Kimberly's wrath. "Take your hand off me."

Lauren did not.

Kimberly looked at Melanie, decades-old anger broiling behind her eyes. "Do you remember me? Huh? I'm Gary's *wife*."

Zoe wasn't sure which stunned her more. The fact that Kimberly appeared ready to deck the poor woman, or her referring to herself as Gary's wife, as if forty years had vanished into a time warp.

Melanie, however, never looked away from Zoe. Never acknowledged Kimberly's presence at all.

"Is there a problem?" A man about Zoe's age, wearing a suit and tie, stood in the doorway. "I'm Eric Bridges, the manager."

Crap. They really were gonna be tossed out.

Patsy stepped toward him with a smile and a handshake. Lauren again blocked Kimberly's advance and whispered something that Zoe couldn't hear. Whatever she'd said, the words appeared to sting.

"Fine," Kimberly muttered through a clenched jaw. She tipped her head to look at Zoe. "We'll be in the car. Don't be long." She wheeled and marched past Patsy and the manager, who watched her go, his mouth agape.

Lauren followed, pausing to apologize to him. "She's...difficult."

Zoe fought to keep from choking. Difficult? That was one word for her.

Patsy excused herself and trailed after the other two, leaving Zoe alone with Melanie and the confused manager.

He closed his mouth and turned expectantly to Zoe.

"I'm sorry about all that." She glanced at Melanie who was once again engrossed in the TV show. "I tried to get them to wait in the car."

"Can I help you with anything?"

"I doubt it." When he didn't move, Zoe gave him an abbreviated version of how her search for her half-brother had led her to Melanie.

Eric nodded. "Now I understand your mother's anger."

No, he didn't. But Zoe didn't correct him.

He tipped his head toward Melanie. "Did she respond to you?"

"She recognized my father's name." Or at least Zoe thought she had. Maybe she had another Gary in her life. Maybe "Gary" lived across the hall.

"Not surprising," Eric said. He crossed the room and knelt at Melanie's side. "She often rambles on about the past. She doesn't recognize her own daughters but talks about her childhood as if it was yesterday."

A spark of hope flickered. "You mean she might remember my dad?" And their son?

"You say they were in high school when this happened?"

"Yeah. They were sixteen, I believe."

Eric placed a gentle hand on the woman's arm. "Melanie?"

She turned her blank eyes on him.

He smiled. "Hi. I'm Eric."

Zoe felt certain he'd introduced himself to her many times in the past and noticed he didn't follow the introduction with *do you remember me?* She didn't. And with Alzheimer's patients, reminders that they should only produced stress and guilt.

"You went to high school with a friend of mine," he said. "Gary Chambers."

"Gary?" Melanie's befuddled expression grew thoughtful. And then she smiled. "He plays football." She reached up and fingered her hair, primping.

In that moment, Zoe pictured the girl Melanie Wilson had been. Sylvia had said she'd been pretty. Zoe didn't have to imagine too hard to believe it, visualizing the lines on her face as dimples, the gray in her hair as brunette, her milky brown eyes as the color of dark chocolate.

"That's right," Eric said while giving a questioning look to Zoe.

She realized he was wondering about her memory. Football. Zoe nodded, confirming he'd played. "And you're a cheerleader, right?" she asked, stepping into Melanie's past.

"Yes." The older woman's smile grew coquettish. "Phillipsburg Blue Demons. Go, team!" She raised a fist, clenching an invisible—to them—pompom.

"Go, Demons," Zoe echoed, remembering her own days of watching the Friday night games from the stands. A memory of that night beneath the bleachers...Dennis Culp and Horace...crowded out her current mission. She forced it aside with a mental note to try Horace's phone again as soon she was through here. "Tell me about Gary," she said.

Melanie's eyes met Zoe's with a scowl. "Why? He's my boyfriend. You can't have him."

Did Melanie see a younger Kimberly when she looked at Zoe?

"You're too old for him."

Zoe blanched at the realization Melanie, in her mind, was a teenager. Making Zoe old enough to be her mother.

Eric covered his smile with a hand. If Zoe had known him better, she'd have slugged him.

"She's a new teacher, Melanie," he said. "She's trying to learn about some of the students she'll be teaching."

"Oh."

When Melanie fell silent, Eric touched her arm. "You were going to tell us about Gary Chambers."

"I was? Gary Chambers? He plays football. Phillipsburg Demons. Go, team!"

A half hour later, Zoe, Eric, and Melanie had traveled the same circular route numerous times without progressing. One time, she mentioned he'd finally asked her out on a date, but her fragile memories disintegrated, never reaching any mention of teenaged sex or a pregnancy.

Or a child.

With Melanie focused on her soap opera, Eric and Zoe retreated to a corner of the room. "I'm sorry, Miss Chambers. I know you'd hoped to learn about your brother, but as you can see, she's not a great source of information most days."

Zoe looked at the woman her mother loathed and wondered if maybe Kimberly should've stayed to witness the conversation. "As soon as I heard she had Alzheimer's, I knew it was a longshot." Zoe thought about the brick wall blocking her search. "My mother believed Melanie might've tracked down her son," she mused out loud. Bringing her focus back to the manager, she asked, "What if she did more than that? What if she made contact?" The idea rekindled the spark of hope that this wasn't a total wasted effort. "Has a man ever come to see her? He'd be in his early fifties."

Eric stroked his chin. "I don't believe so. You can ask at the front desk, but I've never seen a man of that age visiting her. In fact, other than her doctor and her daughters, she doesn't get much company. That's why I came to check on you ladies. When I heard someone had asked about Melanie, I was curious."

Zoe thought of the scene he'd walked in on. "I assumed you wanted to break up the altercation my mother was creating."

He smiled. "That too."

She started to thank him for his time but stopped. "What about her daughters?"

"What about them?"

"If Melanie *had* tracked down her son, maybe they know about him."

Eric crossed his arms. "Miss Chambers, that's a big if. You admitted you're here on a whim. There's a very good chance Melanie preferred not to know anything about the child she gave up for adoption."

"I realize that. But we've driven all this way. I can't go home without exhausting the possibilities. Which, right now, is Melanie's daughters. Could you give me an address or a phone number for them?"

"I'm sorry. We take the privacy of our residents and their families very seriously. The best I can do is take your number and pass it along to them. If they want to get in touch, it'll be their choice."

And if they didn't, Zoe was back to square one.

EIGHTEEN

Pete arranged to meet with a trooper from the Pennsylvania State Police at the cabin on Ramcat Road.

"You're a little out of your jurisdiction." Trooper Duncan commented as they stood in the damp chill of the empty room.

Pete considered explaining how Horace had helped Zoe all those years ago, how he was supposed to bake their wedding cake, or how he'd been bullied all his life, garnering Pete's compassion. Instead, he said, "Yep."

"Care to tell me why?"

"Nope."

Duncan eyed him, then shrugged. "Fair enough." He tried the light switch, getting the same result as Pete had. "Most of these camps are seasonal. Rather than pay an electric bill, the owners shut off the power over the winter." The trooper hefted the five-cell flashlight he'd brought and shined the beam around the room. "Unless they use it for hunting as well as fishing."

"This camp looks like it hasn't been used for either the last few years."

Duncan grunted a response. He checked the woodstove, as Pete had done. Sniffed. And came to the same conclusion. "Someone was here a day or so ago."

"Yep."

The trooper retraced the steps Pete had taken earlier, sweeping the beam from the big flashlight around the cabin. "Any thoughts on where your suspects might have gone?"

"I hoped you might have some ideas. Do you know the Turner

family?"

"No."

Pete wasn't the only man of few words.

"Are you sure it was them who stayed here?" Duncan asked. "You probably noticed there's no lock on the door. Could've been anyone."

"I noticed. And no, I'm not sure." Stanley Jennings wasn't the most reliable informant Pete had ever used. This whole trip...this entire day...may have been a practice in futility. "Horace Pavelka's girlfriend's family supposedly owns this place. Horace and Belinda Turner are on the run. Seemed like a good spot to hide out."

Duncan nodded and swept the beam around the room one more time.

The light reflected off something under the couch and caught Pete's eye.

"I have the make, model, and license number of the girl's car," Duncan said. "I'll make sure it goes out to all law enforcement in Fayette County."

Pete moved toward the couch and gestured to the trooper. "Shine that light over here again."

"What have you got?" Duncan trailed after him lowering the beam to the floor as Pete dropped to one knee.

He wiggled his fingers into a pair of Nitrile gloves. Bent over. And reached into the shadows, coming up with a shattered cell phone. He held it on the flat of his palm as he turned to Duncan.

He let out a low whistle. "Someone didn't want to be reached."

Pete rolled it over. The battery cover was cracked, but the battery remained lodged inside. Pressing the power button, however, did nothing. "No dust. I'd bet it belongs to whoever stayed here."

"No bet." Duncan reached in his pocket coming up with an evidence bag. "I'll get it to our crime lab. If they were careless enough to leave the battery in place, they probably didn't bother wiping off their prints either."

Dammit. That was the problem with venturing outside of his

jurisdiction and bringing in the State boys. As sure as he was that Abby could bring the crushed phone back to life, he was in someone else's playground now.

Duncan must have read his mind and grinned. "I promise to take good care of your evidence, Chief. I'll be in touch as soon as we pull anything off it. At least we'll know for sure who camped here the other night."

Pete already knew. Horace wasn't a hardened criminal. He was on the run without a clue about how to stay off the grid, including the part about removing the battery.

Hopefully, he and Belinda wouldn't be smart enough to ditch the car either.

They returned to the cluster of fast food restaurants, chain stores, and motels near the interstate. Zoe watched Lauren set up her laptop at a table in one of the diners. Kimberly had retreated to the ladies' room. Patsy waited at the counter for their soup and sandwich orders.

"What do you hope to find?" Zoe asked, indicating the computer. She'd written this trip off as a waste of time and gasoline.

Lauren, however, gave her a mischievous grin. "I intend to find Melanie's daughters."

Doubtful, Zoe tipped her head to see the screen. "How? We don't even know their names."

"Oh ye of little faith." Lauren blew a quick raspberry. "I'm an investigative reporter."

Still skeptical, Zoe leaned back in the booth's bench seat and retrieved her phone from her hip pocket. "You investigate. I'm going to check in with Pete."

The call went straight to voicemail. "It's me. We've hit a dead end here. We're grabbing some lunch and then heading home. See you at suppertime." She paused before touching the red button and added, "Call me if you find Horace."

"We haven't hit a dead end," Lauren said.

Zoe set her phone on the table. "I'm beginning to think I never should've let you talk me into this search."

"Did you not hear me?" Lauren slid the laptop in front of Zoe. "Jessica and Amanda."

"What?" Zoe stared at a page on the same genealogy site they'd used before.

Lauren tapped the screen. "Melanie Wilson Henderson's two daughters are named Jessica and Amanda."

"They're probably married with different last names. And we don't have addresses or phone numbers for them."

Lauren reclaimed the laptop. "Give me a minute, will ya?"

Patsy arrived with two trays, one she placed in front of Zoe, the other she placed by the computer. "Thanks for the help carrying the food."

"I'm sorry." Zoe scooted to the edge of the seat.

Patsy flipped a hand at her. "Stay there. I've got it." She looked around. "Where's Kimberly?"

"Still in the restroom, I guess." Zoe looked toward the sandwich shop's windows and the parking lot. "She didn't take the car and abandon us, did she?"

Patsy laughed. "Kimberly? Drive?" She walked away, still laughing.

Zoe battled a grin. At one time, Patsy had idolized Zoe's mother. While she still got along better with her than Zoe did, Patsy clearly had come to see the woman had flaws.

"Jessica Blackstone."

Zoe looked at Lauren. "What?"

"Melanie's oldest daughter's married name is Jessica Blackstone." Lauren fingered the mousepad and tapped. "And her youngest, Amanda, is married to a guy with the last name Lyttle. With a 'Y.'"

Zoe's skepticism gave way to a sparkle of hope. "Does it show any contact information?"

"Patience, my dear."

Patsy returned with two more trays, which she placed across

from Zoe and Lauren. "What's going on?" she asked as she slid into the booth, leaving the end for Kimberly.

Zoe jabbed a thumb in Lauren's direction. "Miss Investigative Reporter is locating Melanie's daughters."

"Really?" Patsy took a bite of the dill pickle that came with her sandwich. "You can do that?"

Lauren glared at Patsy. "You people have no idea what I'm capable of." She spun the laptop to face Zoe. "Voila. Addresses and phone numbers for both women."

"What?" Kimberly stood over them, fists planted on her hips. "We are not going on any more wild goose chases." She lowered onto the bench seat with the grace of royalty.

Which was when Zoe noticed her mother's once again flawless eyeliner. "Did you completely redo your makeup in there?"

Kimberly squared her shoulders, but the corners of her lips twitched. "Not all of us were born natural beauties. Some of us have to work at it."

Zoe opened her mouth only to close it again. Had her mother just admitted to being less than perfect? Deciding against pressing the issue, she turned to Lauren. "How far are the daughters from here?"

"Give me a sec." Lauren pulled up a map. "Not far at all. We're about five miles from one. Ten from the other."

Kimberly opened her sandwich and picked several red onion rings from it. "We're going home. I've had enough of this scavenger hunt."

Zoe looked at her. "It was your idea to do this."

"And it wasn't one of my better ones." Kimberly delicately licked her fingers and put the sandwich back together. "I thought it would be nice to have some mother-daughter time. Plan your wedding. But..."

Zoe waited for her to finish. When she didn't, Zoe realized why. "You didn't really expect we'd find anything. That stuff you said about Melanie keeping track of her son? It was all a line of bull."

Kimberly fixed Zoe with the same hard glare she'd used when

Zoe had echoed a swear word she'd overheard as a seven-year-old. "Mind your manners, young lady." Jutting her jaw, Kimberly lowered her gaze to her sandwich. "It was not 'bull.' I thought she really might know. Maybe she did before she lost her memories. But her daughters? They're a waste of time."

"How can you be so sure?"

Kimberly's blue eyes came back up to Zoe's. "Because I wouldn't admit to you any lapses in judgment I had in high school. A mother wants to be a good role model to her daughter. Admitting to fooling around with the star quarterback isn't something she'd share."

The way she said it made Zoe wonder what "lapses in judgment" Kimberly'd had back then. However, now was not the time to press the issue. "We've come this far. I'm not going home without at least talking to them."

"It's *my* rental car. If I decide we're going home, that's what we're doing."

Patsy, who'd been silently eating her lunch, slammed a palm down on the table hard enough to draw the attention of nearby diners. "It's your rental car, but I'm the one driving it. If you insist on leaving now, you'll have to drive yourself. Alone. I'm staying to help Zoe. Even if we have to rent our own car to do it."

Kimberly's mouth opened, mirroring Zoe's. Patsy rarely went against Kimberly's wishes. More often than not, she was the one making excuses for Kimberly's bad behavior.

Lauren touched her fingers to her lips, but not before Zoe caught her grin. All three waited for Kimberly's reaction. Zoe suspected half the dining room waited as well.

Closing her mouth, Kimberly straightened. Still royalty. "Fine. Call the daughters."

"No," Patsy said before Zoe had the chance. "We're going to knock on their doors and ask them to their faces about their brother."

Zoe gave her cousin a grateful nod. "I want to look in their eyes to know if they're telling me the truth."

Kimberly huffed in exasperation. "Well then, hurry up and eat. I want to get back before dark."

Jessica Blackstone's address led them to a modest cement block home in an older neighborhood. The small yard backed up to a thick expanse of snowy forest. A white SUV was parked in a short, uncleared driveway in front of one of a pair of garage doors. Patsy maneuvered the Navigator next to it.

Kimberly was out of the vehicle before Zoe had a chance to stop her.

Zoe jogged through the four-inch accumulation of snow to catch up. "Mother, wait."

Kimberly ignored the order.

Zoe caught her arm as she reached toward the doorbell. "Stop it. Go back to the car and wait for me."

"I'll do no such thing. We're here to get information. I intend to see that you do."

Crap. Hurricane Kimberly was the last thing Zoe needed when dealing with sensitive matters. "Let me handle this my way."

"Your way will take too long. I don't intend on being stranded overnight in these mountains in this blizzard."

Zoe looked skyward. The soft snowflakes drifting to earth hardly constituted a blizzard. And if the Navigator couldn't handle a slushy road, Kimberly should demand a refund. "We're not going to be stranded. Go back to the car."

Patsy trudged up behind them. "Zoe's right. Kimberly, let's leave her to deal with this on her own."

Kimberly wheeled. "I'm only here to help."

The front door swung open, revealing a woman about Zoe's age wearing a dark turtleneck and a long sweater over faded jeans. She cracked the glass storm door wide enough to ask, "May I help you?"

Kimberly wheeled back. "Are you...?" She shot a raised eyebrow at Zoe. "What's her name?"

Zoe's fingers ached from clenching them. If she strangled her mother, no jury would convict her. She shouldered next to Kimberly on the small stoop and plastered her biggest smile on her face. "Jessica Blackstone?"

The woman looked from Zoe to Kimberly as if not sure who she should address. "Yes?"

Zoe extended a gloved hand. "My name's Zoe Chambers. You don't know me, but—"

"We're here to talk to you about your mother," Kimberly interrupted. "Did you know she slept with my husband when she was in high school?"

"*Mother*," Zoe snapped.

Jessica Blackstone planted a fist on her hip. "Excuse me?"

"I'm so sorry," Zoe sputtered. She grabbed Kimberly's arm and tried to drag her away from the door.

Kimberly shrugged her off. "The best way to get things accomplished quickly is to tackle them straight on." To Jessica, she said, "Well? Are you aware of your mother's promiscuous past, or aren't you?"

A second woman appeared at the door. The resemblance made it clear. This was Melanie's other daughter, offering backup to her sister, as if the house—and family—was under siege. "What's going on?"

From the fiery glint in Jessica's eyes, she didn't need any help. "Get off my property," she told Kimberly.

"I'm not going anywhere."

The second sister moved shoulder to shoulder with the first. "Yes, you are."

"Our mother is in a nursing home," Jessica said. "How dare you come to my house and trash her good name."

Kimberly barked a laugh. "Good name? That woman is nothing but a slu—"

Zoe cut between her mother and the sisters and took Kimberly by the shoulders. "Stop it."

Patsy seized Kimberly's arm. "You've helped enough. Let's go."

As Patsy dragged a sputtering Kimberly to the Navigator, Zoe faced the sisters. "I'm so sorry—" But they cut off her apology by slamming the door in her face.

NINETEEN

As Pete had expected, the snow transitioned to rain well before he crossed the Monongahela River and the county line.

He hated leaving the evidence and the case in State Trooper Duncan's hands, even though he knew the man and the PSP Crime Lab were more than capable.

Horace and Belinda had gone to Belinda's family's camp because it was familiar to her. Had it been simply an overnight stop on a planned journey elsewhere? Or had they intended to stay holed up there, only to be frightened into bolting?

Duncan had issued a statewide BOLO for the blue Cruze. No matter where they were headed, eventually they'd be found.

As the evening sky grew dark, Pete shifted his focus to the part of the investigation within his jurisdiction and control. Stanley Jennings was withholding information. Reese Perkins, or whatever name he was using now, had terrified Stanley into silence. Was Perkins still in the area? Or had he burnt his truck, procured other transportation, and moved back to Erie? If he was gone, maybe Stanley would relax enough to talk.

Pete tuned out the jumble of radio transmissions directed throughout the county from dispatch until a call aimed at his own officer snared his full attention.

"Control to Vance Thirty-one. Respond to 1498 Mays Road. Caller reports a shooting with one victim."

Kevin's voice replied over the radio. "Copy that, Control. Vance Thirty-one responding."

Pete knew the address. The old Hill place. He pulled up

Kevin's number on his phone.

"Hey, Chief. Where are you?"

"Between Brunswick and Vance Township. That Mays Road call you're responding to? That's where Stanley Jennings has been hiding out."

"I know."

"I'll meet you there. ETA, fifteen minutes."

"Copy that, Chief."

The rain finally stopped but night had closed in by the time Pete arrived. Red and blue strobes emanated from Kevin's cruiser, and an ambulance idled where Pete had been forced to stop earlier. Stanley's pickup remained mired in the mud. The emergency units' headlights shone on another car nose-down in the ditch. However, there was no one to be seen.

Pete again punched in Kevin's number.

"We're in the house," the officer answered. "The scene's secure. But you're gonna want to get in here."

Pete stepped out of his Explorer, grabbed his Maglite, and started toward the house. He paused at the car that had nosedived into the washout. A Chevy Cruze. Under the illumination of the flashlight beam, dark blue. He swore. Picked his way across the ditch. And broke into a run.

The plywood blocking the door had been ripped off, leaving the opening clear. Light and voices poured from the kitchen. Kevin leaned into the dark hallway as Pete approached.

"Chief?"

"What do we have?" But he reached the doorway before his officer could respond.

Two of Zoe's colleagues from the county EMS knelt over Stanley's sprawled form. His eyes were closed, his shirt cut open revealing a gunshot wound, upper chest. And a lot of blood.

The medics were frantically working on him but *not* doing CPR, which told Pete Stanley Jennings was alive. For the moment.

Pete surveyed the rest of the scene. Nothing knocked over. No sign of a struggle. Belinda Turner, her face streaked with tears, sat on a chair next to Kevin, her hands folded in her lap as if in prayer.

Except her hands, her arms, and her clothes were soaked with blood.

"Where's Horace?"

She looked up at Pete. "I don't know."

The owner of the bed and breakfast claimed she had no vacancies. Considering it was midweek and November, Zoe suspected the woman simply didn't wish to put up with Kimberly for a second night. They had no such problems securing lodging at one of the chain hotels near the interstate. At Kimberly's insistence, they checked in to a pair of adjoining rooms.

So they could discuss wedding plans. In theory.

"I don't see why you insist on spending another night in this Godforsaken town," Kimberly said from the doorway dividing the rooms.

"Because I'm not driving three hours in the dark in the snow," Patsy called from behind her.

Kimberly wheeled to address her cousin. "You're supposed to be on my side. Instead, all three of you ganged up on me, insisting we stay." She huffed. "If we'd left after lunch like I wanted to, we would've been home well before dark. We never should've bothered with those two girls."

"You should've stayed in the car like I asked and left them to me," Zoe muttered under her breath, forgetting her mother had the hearing of a dog.

"You'd have still been there, trying to pry out information they don't have." Kimberly lifted her chin. "I simply cut to the chase and established their lack of cooperation quicker."

"What you did was alienate Melanie's daughters." Zoe was convinced they did indeed have information. But they'd already had this argument in the Navigator.

Kimberly ignored her and studied her hand. "I'm over all this snow and cold and dry weather. My skin is drying up in front of my eyes. You three better be ready to leave first thing in the morning.

My flight to Florida departs Pittsburgh at three tomorrow."

Zoe glanced at Lauren, who knew the plan and smothered a conspiratorial grin. "We'll have you at the airport in plenty of time," Zoe said. The last thing she wanted was another night with her mother.

"You'd better." Kimberly continued scowling at her hands. "I'm going to put some lotion on these and then we're going out for dinner."

Zoe watched her mother retreat into the room she shared with Patsy, rose, and closed the door between them. She looked at Lauren. "You're sure you and Patsy can pull this off?"

Lauren leaned back on her bed, crossing her legs. "I'm positive. We'll keep your mother distracted if we have to tie her up and gag her."

"I found her next to the victim," Kevin told Pete. "She was trying to stop the bleeding. Says she's the one who called 911. I patted her down. No weapons. I haven't searched the rest of the house yet, but I haven't found the gun anywhere in the kitchen."

Pete kept his eyes on the woman who shivered, either from the damp and cold or because of the situation. Or both.

"I didn't handcuff her." Kevin aimed a thumb toward the front of the house. "Her car's stuck so she isn't going anywhere."

"That's fine." To Belinda, Pete again asked, "Where's Horace?"

"I told you I don't know."

He didn't buy it. "What happened here?"

"I don't know," she repeated. She tipped her head toward Stanley. "He was like that when I arrived. I called for help and tried to stop the bleeding." Her voice fractured. She lowered her head. "But there was so much...blood."

Pete gave her a minute to regain her composure. "That's your story?"

"I didn't shoot him," she wailed.

"I believe you. I think Horace did."

"No." She looked up at Pete, tears gleaming, but jaw set.

"Horace isn't with me. And he didn't shoot Stanley."

"If Horace isn't with you, why are you here?"

Belinda swiped at her tears, only succeeding in smudging her face with blood. "I needed to talk to him." She gestured at Stanley. "I wanted to find out what really happened at Horace's house when Grant was killed. You have to believe me, Chief Adams."

No, he didn't *have* to believe her. And didn't. Not all of it.

"Horace didn't shoot Grant. Someone's framing him. I thought Stanley might help me find out who."

The clomp of footsteps from the front of the house spun both Pete and Kevin toward the doorway, their hands on their service weapons.

A flashlight beam lit up the hallway. "Pete, it's Wayne Baronick," he called out.

Pete relaxed his hand. "That's a good way to get yourself shot, Detective."

Baronick strode into the kitchen. "That's why I identified myself. I have a couple uniforms outside. Crime scene unit's on its way." He looked at the paramedics. "What have we got?"

"Someone shot Stanley Jennings."

Baronick fixed Pete with a smirk. "I can see that much." He nodded at Belinda. "She do it?"

"Not according to her." Pete caught him up on what Belinda had already said. "She claims Horace wasn't with her."

"You don't believe her."

"Not for a minute."

Belinda shot a dark, tear-streaked glare at him.

"We need to search the rest of the house in case the gun is still here. I want a search of the surrounding area. Her car isn't going anywhere, so Horace is on foot. He couldn't have gotten far."

Baronick held up his phone. "I'll get the K-9 unit out here. We'll find him."

Once the detective had stepped into the hallway to place his call, Pete turned to Belinda. "We will find him. You could make it a lot easier on both of you by telling us what really happened."

Her chin quivered. "I already did."

The county medics had placed Stanley on a backboard and lifted him onto their stretcher. IV and oxygen tubes snaked from his arms and his face. "We could use a hand getting him outta here and into the ambulance," one of the medics said.

Pete looked at Kevin. "You go. I'll stay with her."

Once the room cleared, Pete faced Belinda. "Tell me what happened."

"I. Don't. Know."

"Tell me what you do know."

She chewed her lip, thinking.

"Where were you before you came here?"

Her forehead furrowed. Still thinking.

"Let me help. You were at your family's cabin in Fayette County."

That brought her eyes up to meet his. Her lips parted in a surprised "O."

"I know about the camp on Ramcat. I was just there."

More thinking. "I needed some time away."

"You needed a place to hide Horace," Pete corrected.

"No." Her voice pitched higher than her usual tone. "I was alone."

He decided to keep the smashed phone to himself for now. His ace in the hole. She'd called 911 for Stanley, so the phone he'd found had to be Horace's.

"The couple who ate at the Café in town wasn't you and Horace?"

She flinched ever so slightly. "No."

He'd play along for now. "Then what?"

"I decided if the police weren't going to search for who really killed Grant, I would. To clear Horace."

"And you thought Stanley would help you clear him."

"Yes."

"The funny thing is, I talked to Stanley earlier. The reason he was staying here was because he was terrified. He told me Horace killed his brother and was coming after him next."

"That's not true."

Pete turned and paced toward the smeared blood and debris of ripped sterile packaging, gazed at the mess, then faced Belinda. "If Horace didn't kill Grant and didn't attempt to kill Stanley, who do you think did?"

"I told you—"

"You don't know. But I asked who you *think* did it. You want to clear Horace, tell me where to look. You knew both brothers. Dated Stanley. You must have some thoughts about who would want them dead."

She pondered the question. "The only person I can think of who genuinely scares Stanley..." She looked Pete in the eye. "...is Reese Perkins."

TWENTY

Zoe had escaped her mother's ongoing wedding plan discussion Wednesday night by making a run to the hotel lobby for hot chocolate. Before filling a cup, she found a soft chair in a corner and called Pete to let him know she wouldn't be home. She told him about her exasperating day, and he told her about Stanley.

The need to return home and clear Horace almost drove her to cancel the plan she, Patsy, and Lauren had hatched. Almost.

By the next morning, the snow in Clarion had decided to take a break with a crystalline blue sky driving out the dismal gray clouds.

The "plan" called for a divide-and-conquer approach. Patsy had mentioned a high-end boutique in the Clarion Mall advertising a clearance sale with "drastic price cuts on their entire inventory of designer shoes." Zoe had no idea if there was a sale or even a high-end boutique, but the story snagged Kimberly's interest. Lauren deserved an Oscar for acting equally eager to check out the deals. The hard part involved persuading Kimberly they should walk the short distance to the mall. Patsy complained about her aching back and legs from all the driving and lack of activity, convincing even Zoe that she needed the exercise.

As soon as the three bargain hunters left the hotel, Zoe phoned the number she had for Jessica Blackstone. Thankful she answered and even more thankful she didn't hang up the moment Zoe explained who she was, Zoe apologized profusely for her mother's behavior. Once she promised to come alone, Jessica agreed to talk.

Twenty minutes later, Zoe parked in front of the same unassuming gray house with the same white SUV in the driveway, which had been cleared of snow since her previous visit.

The woman who answered Zoe's knock at the door was not Jessica Blackstone. Instead it was the one Zoe had assumed was the sister. She blocked the doorway, her stern expression and crossed arms adding to her gatekeeper persona. Zoe offered a hand, which she didn't accept.

"I'm Amanda Lyttle, Jessica's sister. I was here yesterday."

Zoe withdrew her hand. "I remember. I—"

"I'm not in favor of this meeting. That creature you had with you yesterday upset my sister. She has enough to deal with right now. I'll not have you adding to her stress."

The term "creature" stuck in Zoe's brain. While she couldn't argue about Kimberly's obnoxious performance yesterday, she was still Zoe's mother. "I have no intention of upsetting anyone. And I apologize for my mother's lack of tact—"

"She was rude."

"No argument. But I'm *not* my mother."

Amanda looked like she was debating whether to admit a wet, smelly dog into her sister's clean home. "Fine. But I'll end this meeting the moment things get out of hand."

"Agreed."

Amanda led her into a living room. Jessica was adding wood to a roaring fire in a massive stone fireplace. She turned to face Zoe and wiped her palms on her faded jeans before offering a hand to Zoe. "Please have a seat."

She did not, however, offer coffee or even a glass of water. The sisters' intention was clear. Deal with Zoe and get rid of her as soon as possible.

"I'm so sorry about your mother." Zoe fingered her engagement ring. "My fiancé's father has Alzheimer's too. It's a horrible disease."

The sisters exchanged a look.

"Thank you," Jessica said, her voice little more than a whisper.

"The reason I'm here is I recently learned I have a half-brother. From what I've been able to find..." Zoe licked her dry lips.

If Jessica or Amanda reacted badly to learning they also had the same half-brother, Zoe might find herself tossed out. She chose her words carefully. "I believe your mother and my father were high school sweethearts and perhaps had a child when your mother was a teenager."

Jessica nodded. "Scott."

Zoe's throat tightened. "Scott?"

"Our half-brother." Jessica glanced at Amanda. "Scott Nixon."

Zoe repeated the name to herself. Mouthed it. Conversations bounced inside her head. Fantasy introductions. *"This is my brother, Scott Nixon."*

"He tracked our mother down about ten months ago?" Amanda said, looking to her sister for confirmation of the length of time.

"About that," Jessica agreed.

Zoe struggled to find equilibrium. And breath to speak. "He tracked down your mother. But not his father? My father?"

"Mom told him his father had died years ago," Amanda said. "Scott was disappointed, but I guess he was just happy to have found us."

Zoe looked at her. Was she being smug? Having Melanie for a mother and Amanda and Jessica for sisters was more than enough. He didn't need more. He didn't need a third sister.

He didn't need Zoe.

Or was she projecting her fears of rejection on these two women?

"Is he—does he—" Zoe stuttered. Paused. Settled her frantic mind. "Is he from around here?"

"No," Amanda said.

An all-too-familiar vacuum opened in Zoe's chest.

"He lives in Erie," Jessica said.

Zoe inhaled. "Erie?" A couple more hours west and north by the interstate. "Do you have his phone number? Address?"

Jessica appeared about to rise, perhaps to say, *"Yes, I'll get it for you."*

But Amanda placed a hand on her sister's shoulder to keep her seated. "I'm not sure we should give out his information."

For the first time, Zoe wished she'd brought Kimberly along. Her mother would have browbeat the info from them, which was exactly what Zoe wanted to do. She unclenched fists she hadn't realized she'd made. Took a breath. "He's *my* brother too. Maybe he'd like to know he has family on our father's side. Did anyone even bother to tell him our father had another child?"

Jessica opened her mouth, but Amanda's hand visibly tightened on her shoulder. "No."

Jessica glared at her sister and pushed the hand away. "We didn't know," she said to Zoe. "And if Mom knew, she never told us."

"But now you do. Don't you think Scott would want to know too?"

Amanda shrugged. "Maybe."

"Please. At least give me his phone number." Zoe felt the heat and dampness of tears welling and swiped a hand across her eye. Bad enough she was pleading. She refused to cry in front of these two. "If he blows me off, fine. But at least I can tell him I exist."

Amanda stood firm. "How do we even know you're who you say you are?"

"What?" Maybe she should've taken Lauren's advice and sent in a DNA sample. "Do you want to see my driver's license?"

Amanda shook her head. "I'm sure the name you gave us is yours. But this whole story about your father being the man our mother had a relationship with? You could've made it all up."

"For what purpose?" Was Scott rich? "Look. Your mother clearly told you about her affair with my dad. His name was Gary *Chambers*. My name is Zoe *Chambers—*"

Amanda cut her off. "Mom never told us his name."

Zoe didn't believe her. "But when Scott came looking for her, he must have known his father's name too. He must have mentioned it."

"Not to us."

Zoe's hands were clenched again, and this time, she kept them that way. "I'm from the same town where your mother went to high school with him." A thought struck her. "The birth certificate's available online. I've seen it. It doesn't give the child's name but states a baby boy was born to Melanie Wilson and Gary Chambers here in Clarion. Look it up if you don't believe me."

"We believe—" Jessica started only to have Amanda's hand come down on her shoulder again.

"Even if all this is true, I'm still not comfortable handing out Scott's contact information."

As much as Zoe wanted to reach out to her brother now rather than later, she could tell Amanda, for whatever her reasons, wasn't about to bend. "How about you give him my phone number? Then if he's interested, it'll be up to him to call me."

"No," Amanda replied.

But Jessica shot a defiant glare at her sister. "Yes," she said firmly before facing Zoe. "Yes. I'll do that."

After a late and unproductive night, Pete arrived back at the station early. Nancy already had the coffee made—bless her—and told him Seth and Abby were in the bullpen, working on reports. With a fresh cup in hand, Pete bypassed his office to check in with his midnight shifters.

He pulled out a chair from Kevin's currently empty desk and sat. "Give me an update."

"Quiet night," Seth said. "A couple of drunk and disorderlies at Rodeo's. A traffic collision with only minor injuries. And a reported prowler over in Elm Grove. Turned out to be one of the Arnold boys sneaking around his girlfriend's house."

Abby grinned. "Young love."

"Sara O'Brien?" When they both nodded, Pete added, "He's lucky her dad didn't give him a dose of birdshot."

"I told him that," Seth said.

"How's the burglary task force going?"

"There haven't been any more break-ins since Monday night." Abby sounded disappointed. "Maybe our ring has moved on."

"Or is laying low for a while," Seth said. "Maybe we were getting too close for comfort."

"Anything on Pavelka?" Pete asked. The dogs had come up blank last night.

"Nope. No sightings."

Maybe Belinda was telling the truth about going to see Stanley alone. But if that was the case, who shot him? They hadn't found a gun on her, in the house, or in her car. She could've ditched it anywhere though.

The bells on the front door derailed Pete's thoughts. "Finish your reports and get out of here." He rose and headed toward the front of the station.

Baronick, looking uncharacteristically weary, stood at Nancy's window. Pete gestured to him and stepped into his office.

Once the detective settled into the guest chair, Pete met his tired gaze. "Well?"

"As of a half hour ago, Stanley Jennings was in surgery. The bullet did a helluva lot of damage internally."

Not to mention all the blood he'd lost. "Anything new on Pavelka?"

"You were there last night. The dogs didn't get a hit on his scent except in the girl's car. And we don't know how recently he'd been in it."

"Yes, we do. The waitresses in Confluence placed them together on Monday evening."

"Which the Turner girl denies."

"She's lying."

"Probably." Baronick's phone rang. He glanced at the screen. "This might be something," he said before answering. The brief call produced a couple of uh-huhs and okays. "Thanks." He ended the call. "She's definitely lying. That was the Pennsylvania State Police Crime Lab. The smashed phone you found in the cabin? It was Pavelka's all right."

"Did they get anything off it?"

"Not yet. Whoever broke it did a good job."

Pete wished he'd kept it. He'd put money on Abby being able to unlock the phone's secrets. "Where's Belinda Turner now?" The last time he saw her, Baronick was placing her in the backseat of one of the county patrol vehicles.

"We let her go."

Not the reply Pete had expected. "Why? We know she's been harboring a murder suspect."

"And she wasn't about to give him up." Baronick flashed his veneered smile. "Voluntarily."

Pete leaned back. "You're having her tailed."

"Oh, yeah. We put her in a taxi since her car's out of commission. He drove her home, which is where she remains."

"Didn't go to work today?"

"Apparently not. Sooner or later, she's gonna lead us to her boyfriend."

Pete fingered his upper lip. "If Horace wasn't at Stanley's house, who shot him? The girl?"

"We swabbed her hands for gunshot residue. She was clean. She either didn't fire a weapon or—"

"Or she wore gloves."

"Which we didn't find at the scene. Nor did we find the gun. But my men are still out at the property searching."

Pete met Baronick's gaze and held it. "What about Reese Perkins?"

The detective huffed. "Or whatever he's calling himself today. We still have the BOLO on him."

Perkins was once again a ghost in the wind. Pete rocked forward in his chair, bracing his forearms on his desk. "Belinda said Stanley was terrified of the guy. When I mentioned Perkins to Grant last Saturday, he denied knowing him, but I had the impression he was terrified of him too."

"Considering his rap sheet, they had good reason to be scared. Perkins is one bad dude."

"Let's hope Stanley gets out of surgery soon and can tell us who shot him. And why."

Baronick's phone rang again. He answered and listened. This

time there were no uh-huhs, although his expression spoke volumes. None of it was good. "Thanks for letting me know." The detective stuffed his phone in his coat pocket and looked at Pete. "You can quit hoping for an ID from Stanley Jennings. He died ten minutes ago."

TWENTY-ONE

"I can't believe you did this to me." Kimberly, clutching a tissue, stormed through the door between the two rooms, her face a vivid shade of cardiac red. She'd been back and forth through that doorway at least a dozen times in the past ten minutes.

Zoe sat on the edge of one of the hotel beds next to Patsy. Both had their hands folded in their laps. Lauren relaxed against a mound of pillows on the other bed, her legs stretched out. Without the familial ties to Kimberly, Lauren was merely an impartial observer. Or so she probably thought. Kimberly, however, appeared on the verge of strangling all three of them.

"I didn't do anything to *you*." Zoe kept her voice in the low tone she'd use with a patient having an emotional breakdown. "I needed to speak to Melanie's daughters on my own."

Kimberly opened her mouth but instead of continuing to rail at them, she gave a short gasp, then a second. And sneezed. "Damn allergies," she muttered and dabbed her nose before jabbing a finger in Zoe's direction. "You went behind my back. And *you*." She aimed the digit alternately at Patsy and Lauren. "You conspired with her to keep me from finding out."

"You're just angry because there wasn't really a shoe sale," Patsy said.

Kimberly wheeled on her. "You lied to me. You, whom I've had to my home and treated like family."

"She *is* family," Zoe said.

She might as well have thrown gasoline on a fire. "Not anymore." Kimberly spun and stomped to the other room. And sneezed again.

Zoe took a deep breath, knowing the silence settling over them was temporary. Kimberly would be back.

Zoe looked at her cousin. "She didn't mean it."

Patsy's cheeks were paler than usual. "Yes, she did." She met Zoe's gaze and managed a weak grin. "But she'll get over it."

"Yes, she will." Zoe elbowed her. "She has to if she wants a ride home."

"Which brings me to the next topic. What do we do now?"

Lauren sat up and swung her feet to the floor. "We wait for the brother's phone call, that's what."

Kimberly, still sniffling and raging, reappeared in the doorway, as Zoe had known she would. "We most certainly will *not*. My flight to Florida leaves this afternoon." She looked at her watch. "We need to go *now*."

Zoe squirmed. As much as she hated to admit it, her mother was right. They had a three-hour drive home. She glanced through the window at the fat snowflakes once again falling. If the roads were bad, it might take even longer. But she was so close to finding her brother. Breaking off the search now ripped at her heart.

"Check out is in an hour," Patsy said. "We could give it a little more time."

Kimberly homed in on her again. "More time? Did you not hear me? I have a plane to catch."

Lauren acted as if Kimberly wasn't in the room. "We have a name now. I can get on my computer and find an address for him."

Zoe started to object but closed her mouth. Was she desperate enough to lurk outside his house? Become a stalker? "No. I'll wait for his call." But she filed away the idea for future use.

"Okay," Lauren said. "We could head to Erie. That way when he does call, we'll already be there."

"And if he doesn't call?" Kimberly planted her fists on her hips. "Do you suggest we simply hang around until this man decides he wants to contact you? It's Erie. In November." She waved at the window. "In a snowstorm. I may have lived in Florida for decades, but I do remember lake effect snow."

Her mother had a point. Scott had made no attempt to track Zoe down before. Maybe he had no interest in talking to her now.

Lauren stood and approached Kimberly. "There's another option."

Hurricane Kimberly turned her gale-force bluster on the reporter. "And what might that be?"

"We split up." Lauren pointed at Kimberly and Patsy. "You two head home. Zoe and I'll rent a car and go on to Erie to find her brother."

"That's the stupidest idea yet."

"Why?" Lauren demanded. "Because it's not yours?"

The room fell silent, all the air sucked out of the eye of the hurricane. Zoe waited for Kimberly to flatten Lauren verbally if not physically.

For what felt like an eternity, the only sound was the soft *tick* of ice crystals tapping on the window. When Kimberly again spoke, her voice was quieter. "No. Because I was always taught you leave the dance with whomever brought you. We all came together. We stay together." She looked at Zoe. "If you insist on continuing this wild goose chase..." Kimberly stood taller and lifted her chin. "I'll reschedule my flight."

Zoe stared at her mother. Who was this woman?

"Yes." Lauren fist pumped. "Let's finish packing." She scurried toward the bathroom. Patsy jumped to her feet and headed to the other room.

Zoe continued to study Kimberly. Although her eyes remained red, the flush had seeped from her face as had the furor, replaced by resignation. Her mother had conceded to this quest even though she had a valid point. There was no guarantee that Scott wanted to be contacted by a previously unknown sibling.

"No," Zoe said.

Lauren backpedaled. "What? Why not?"

Zoe shook her head. "I mean, yes. Let's finish packing. But we're not going to Erie. We're going home."

*   *   *

The county crime scene truck blocked access to the Hill property well short of the ditch that had claimed Belinda's car. Pete left his Explorer at the end of the lane and hiked in. Baronick and a pair of techs surveyed the quagmire where Stanley's pickup had been stuck.

"Mud wrestling, anyone?" Pete asked.

"Too cold," Baronick replied. "What are you doing here? We've got this."

"I'm on my way to Brunswick for Stanley's autopsy." And to stop at Belinda Turner's house and break the news about her ex-boyfriend's demise. In the late morning daylight, the lane leading to the ditch appeared more churned than yesterday. "How many vehicles have been in here?"

A crime scene tech straightened from looking at the mud. "Hard to tell. All the rain did a number on the tracks. Nothing's well enough defined to even photograph, let alone make a cast. Same with boot prints."

"Outside at least." Baronick elbowed Pete. "Inside is another matter."

Instead of following the worn path to the front porch, they picked their way through flattened grass that hadn't seen a mower in years. Still, they couldn't avoid the mud once they reached the house. Before entering, Pete retrieved a pair of boot covers he'd stuffed in his coat pocket. He'd contaminated the scene enough last night. Baronick slipped on his own disposable booties.

The hallway was one big smear of dried mud. "Looks like an army traipsed through here," Pete muttered.

"They did. You and your officers. EMS. The victim. The Turner girl."

"And the killer."

"Assuming that's someone other than Turner."

"Have you located the murder weapon?"

Baronick made a sour face. "No."

"You're comparing shoe prints to those you know were here?"

"Yep. Speaking of, we'll need yours before you leave."

Pete watched a tech photographing the floor. "You think you're going to be able to sort through that mess?"

"Our forensics team is good. Damn good." Baronick gestured for Pete to follow him.

Shouldering the wall to avoid stepping on the evidence, they continued to the kitchen where emergency lighting filled the room. Prying the wood from the windows would've risked further contaminating an already devastated crime scene. A pair of techs worked the room, one examining the countertop, the other stooped over the dried pool of Stanley's blood.

"How's it going?" the detective asked.

The tech by the spot where Stanley had bled out straightened and pointed. "It's easier to get usable boot prints in the blood than the mud. Fewer people approached the body. We still have to eliminate the known prints though."

"How many different types of shoes have you found?" Pete asked, silently making his own count. Belinda, Kevin, two medics, his own, and... "Six?"

"Yep." Baronick named the five Pete had thought of and Stanley.

Pete shook his head. "The victim isn't going to walk through his own blood and leave tracks."

"Point taken." Baronick frowned. "Who's the sixth person?"

Pete held his gaze. "The shooter."

Zoe slung the last of her mother's suitcases into the Navigator after calling Pete to let him know they were headed home. His news about Stanley Jennings' death should've stirred more sympathy than it did. Instead, her main concern was Horace. Pete hadn't come out and said it, but he obviously believed Horace was responsible for both brothers' murders. Now that the search for Scott was simmering on a back burner, she needed to find the missing baker and clear his name.

Kimberly sashayed out of the hotel, paused to sneeze and dab her nose, then fluttered a sheet of paper. "The bill's paid. Let's get on the road, girls."

Zoe lowered the liftgate and climbed into the backseat with Lauren, who looked more dejected than she. "Hey," Zoe said to her. "I appreciate your effort. At least I know who my brother is now."

With Kimberly cradling a box of tissues in the front passenger seat, Patsy settled behind the wheel. "I hope they've plowed the interstate."

"If it's any comfort, Pete said there's no snow back home."

"Good." Kimberly blew her nose. "I don't want weather delaying my flight."

As they pulled out of the hotel's parking lot, Zoe's phone rang. Not one of the tunes she assigned her regular contacts. She retrieved the cell from her pocket and checked the screen. The name sucked the air from the vehicle.

Scott Nixon.

She flipped the phone toward Lauren to show her the caller ID.

"Stop the car," the reporter demanded.

As Patsy braked and Kimberly started screeching her displeasure, Zoe plugged one ear and swiped the green button. "Hello?"

The pause was long enough to raise Zoe's fear the call had been dropped. Or she'd hallucinated it. But a soft, masculine voice identified himself as Scott and said, "I was given this number and told you were looking for me."

Zoe's mouth went dry. She swallowed. "My name's Zoe Chambers. My father was Gary Chambers. I believe he was your father too."

After another lengthy silence, he said, "I didn't realize my father had any other children."

"Just me." She winced at the too perky squeak to her voice. "At least as far as I know." She winced again at her babbling and shot a glance at a glowering Kimberly, glad her mother wasn't privy to both sides of the conversation.

"I'd like to meet you. Talk to you. About our father," Scott said.

Zoe closed her eyes, surprised at the rush of heat behind her lids. "I'd like that too."

"I'm in Erie right now. Where are you?"

"In Clarion, but we were about to head back to Pittsburgh."

The storm brewing on Kimberly's face threatened to wipe her off the face of the earth if she changed plans.

Zoe thought of her work schedule—on duty Monday, Wednesday, and Friday of the coming week. "I could drive back up next Saturday."

"That won't work. I'm leaving for Arizona in the morning. I keep a place there November through April."

Kimberly must have read Zoe's eyes. "No," she said firmly. "No, no, no."

"What's that?" Scott asked.

"Nothing." Zoe glared at her mother. "We can be in Erie in a couple of hours. How about I meet you for dinner?"

From beside her, Lauren whooped. Kimberly pivoted forward and pounded a fist against the dash. Patsy remained silent, her lips pressed into a thin, pale line.

"Would it be all right if you came to my house?" he asked. "I still have a lot of last-minute packing to do. I make a mean lasagna."

"That'd be great." Zoe braced the phone between her shoulder and ear, dug a notebook and pen from her purse, and jotted down the address he gave her. "I'll see you soon."

Kimberly continued to chant, "No, no, no, no," while shaking her head as Zoe ended the call.

She reached forward and placed a hand on her mother's shoulder. "It's okay. We'll do what Lauren suggested. You and Patsy go to Pittsburgh so you can catch your flight. Lauren and I will rent a car and go on to Erie."

Kimberly twisted in her seat to fix Zoe with a venomous stare. "You don't know this man and yet you're going to his house?"

"He's packing to leave for Arizona in the morning."

Kimberly gave an exaggerated eyeroll. "His travel plans carry more weight than mine, I see."

"Mother, I told you, go back with Patsy."

"I'm not leaving my only child to meet with some stranger in a strange city."

"I've been to Erie before."

"That's beside the point."

"I'll have Lauren with me."

Kimberly shifted her fierce eyes to the reporter. "It's her fault we're here in the first place. She's the one who put you on this snipe hunt."

Zoe decided against reminding her mother that *she* had suggested the girls' road trip. "It's because of Lauren I now know who my brother is."

Kimberly threw both hands up in exasperation. "That's what I said. It's her fault. And I'll personally hold her accountable when this all blows up in your face."

Behind them, a car honked its horn. Patsy powered down her window enough to wave him past. "Make up your minds," she said as she zipped the window closed again. "We can't keep sitting here."

Zoe held Kimberly's ferocious gaze, determined not to cave to her mother's game of chicken. To her surprise, Kimberly's eyes softened. And she sneezed.

She wiped her nose furiously and exhaled a frustrated breath. "Fine. We go to Erie."

Patsy looked at her. "All of us?"

"*All* of us." Kimberly faced forward. "I'll have to eat the penalties for changing flights. Besides, I probably shouldn't be flying with this cold."

Patsy shot a surprised look at Zoe before shifting the Navigator into gear. "All righty then. We're going to Erie."

TWENTY-TWO

Belinda Turner's address was a single-story red-brick house on the northern edge of the county seat, one of a string of similar residences built in the fifties. Pete recognized an unmarked county PD car parked at the edge of the road within easy view.

Belinda's driveway was empty—her car had yet to be hauled out of the ditch, and Horace's was still in impound—but lights shined through the windows, suggesting someone was home.

She answered the doorbell wearing sweatpants, a superhero t-shirt, a pink bathrobe, and slippers that looked like monster feet with claws. Worry lines creased her pale face. "Have you found Horace?"

"Not yet. You could help us with that."

"I've told you. I don't know where he is."

Pete still didn't believe her. "May I come in?"

She stepped aside. Not defiant but not welcoming either.

Pete removed his hat and wiped his feet on the worn welcome mat before crossing the threshold.

"Coffee?" she asked.

"No, thank you."

She pulled her robe closed and folded her arms to keep it that way. "Any word on Stanley?"

"That's why I'm here. There's no easy way to say this. I'm sorry to tell you, Stanley died in surgery this morning."

Her jaw tensed. She looked away and blinked, but Pete didn't notice any telltale gleam of tears. When she brought her gaze back, her eyes remained lowered, not meeting his but focusing somewhere around his throat, as if she hadn't the energy to lift them any higher. "I'm sorry to hear that."

"Belinda, if you know where Horace is, it'd be in everyone's best interest to tell me now."

"Everyone's?" She shook her head. "Not his."

"I like Horace."

She looked skeptical.

"I do. I'd rather be the one to bring him in than have some overeager SWAT team bust down his door and drag him out."

The mental image he painted produced a sheen in Belinda's eyes that Stanley's death hadn't.

Pete kept his voice gentle. "Where is he?"

Her lips parted. Closed. Myriad emotions played across her face until she lowered it, blocking his view. "I don't know."

He'd suspected she was lying before. Now he knew without a doubt. He also knew she wasn't going to tell him. "All right." He retrieved a business card from his pocket and held it out. "If he happens to get in touch with you, give him my number."

She took the card without looking at it.

"Tell him I know what he did for Zoe. And I owe him."

That lifted her eyes up to his. From her puzzled expression, he assumed Horace had never shared the story of that night beneath the bleachers. If nothing else, her curiosity might entice her into contacting her elusive boyfriend.

Back in his SUV, Pete pulled up Baronick's number. When the detective answered, Pete said, "I need you to do something."

"What?"

"Get a warrant."

"For what?"

"I want a tap placed on Belinda Turner's phone."

"I'm way ahead of you. It's already in place."

"Good. Unless I miss my guess, she's going to be making a call to our missing suspect very soon."

As Pete turned onto Flannigan Avenue and approached the parking garage entrance of Brunswick Hospital—the one leading to the morgue in the basement—he wondered if someone was offering a sale on campaign signs. Specifically, those touting Dr. Charles Davis for County Coroner. Zoe had been keeping up with counterdemands to reelect Franklin Marshall, but someone had more than doubled the number of Davis placards edging the street.

A small crowd gathered on the sidewalk in front of the funeral home. From the midst of the group, Dr. Davis stepped into the street and raised a hand at Pete, who powered down the passenger window.

The candidate moved to the side of the vehicle. "Chief Adams. I assume you plan to attend the autopsy of Mr. Stanley Jennings."

"I do."

"Good." He raised his voice so the others—especially the reporters, Pete surmised—could hear him. "I'm glad to know at least one man of integrity will be overseeing the procedure."

Man of integrity? "What do you want, Dr. Davis?"

"I wanted to be present for the autopsy, but that self-righteous excuse of a medical expert had hospital security remove me from the grounds."

Pete wondered if Davis referred to Coroner Marshall or Doc Abercrombie but not enough to ask. "I'm glad to see you're complying."

From Davis' clenched jaw, Pete surmised he hadn't provided the hoped-for response. "It would behoove Mr. Marshall—" Davis cranked up the volume again. "—and the good people of Monongahela County to allow me access to the current morgue in order to make the transfer of authority proceed in a seamless fashion."

"I wasn't aware the election had already taken place," Pete said, boosting the sarcasm level. "Or that you won."

"Don't be snide, Chief Adams. It's not becoming of a peace officer," Davis said with a sneer. "The election's only five days away."

"I'm surprised you don't have it down to hours and minutes."

From Davis' reaction, Pete suspected he did. Perhaps even seconds. The pathologist wagged a finger through the window. "You'd be prudent to show me a degree of respect. We'll be working together soon enough."

"I'll show you respect when you've earned it." Pete jabbed the button to power up the window.

Davis withdrew his hand, cradling it as if Pete had come close to amputating it, and stepped clear. Pete wheeled away from the curb and made the hard left into the parking structure.

He parked in one of the spaces reserved for authorized vehicles and breezed through the automatic doors, his footsteps echoing down the empty hallway. While the public areas of the hospital had seen multiple remodels over the years, the basement retained the same beige block walls and industrial grade floor tiles as had been installed decades earlier. Davis wasn't entirely wrong about the county morgue needing an update, but he was entirely wrong about the competency of the staff. Pete had worked with the best during his days with the Pittsburgh Bureau of Police. Marshall and Doc were equally skilled, efficient, and dedicated.

And they were already working over Stanley Jennings' body.

Pete slipped into a pair of disposable biohazard coveralls and entered the autopsy suite.

Marshall glanced up and nodded a greeting but remained at Doc's side. Zoe's absence slammed Pete. He pictured her standing between the two men. Pictured the curves of her back and hips, which would've been hidden by scrubs and a waterproof apron had she had been there. At least she'd be home in a few hours. Her search hadn't been as fruitful as she'd hoped, according to the phone call she'd made earlier. Pete wasn't entirely saddened by the news. If another family member showed up and broke her heart all over again...

He shook off the memories and regrets from last spring and crossed to the autopsy table. The "Y" incision had already been made, the ribcage opened, and the internal organs within the chest removed. "Find anything?"

"Quite a bit," Franklin Marshall said. "There was a single gunshot wound—entry only—just below the sternum." The coroner jabbed a thumb into his own solar plexus to indicate the location. "Stippling around the wound indicated—"

"Stanley allowed the shooter to get close," Pete mused out loud.

"He was shot from roughly a foot away."

Doc Abercrombie leaned farther over the body, peering inside. "The bullet nicked the liver, then transected the aorta." He reached into the cavity with a large pair of forceps. When he straightened, he held the instrument up, revealing a mangled chunk of metal in its grasp. "And lodged in the spine."

Pete squinted at what was left of the bullet. "Small caliber."

"Yes." Doc dropped it into a stainless-steel pan with a *clink*. "My guess would be a .22."

Pete suspected the lab would agree. "Small weapon. Easy to conceal."

"I can also tell you what we didn't find." Marshall met Pete's gaze. "On physical examination, there were no defensive wounds. No bruising of the knuckles. Or anywhere else for that matter. No skin under the fingernails."

Which, combined with the close range of the gunshot, suggested he wasn't afraid of his killer, ruling out Horace and Perkins, both of whom apparently terrified Stanley.

It did not, however, rule out Belinda Turner.

The trip from Clarion to Erie should've taken three hours. It took over five. The early winter snowstorm intensified by the mile as did Kimberly's cold symptoms. By the time they passed the Mill Creek Mall at the southernmost edge of the city, traffic had slowed to a crawl, and white-outs limited vision to mere yards. Taillights in front of them were blurry red ghosts cautioning them to back off.

"I can't believe I'm in the middle of a blizzard when I should be on a plane to Florida," Kimberly grumbled through a handful of tissues.

"You didn't have to come," Zoe said.

Versions of this conversation had played on a loop for the last ninety minutes. This time, Lauren abandoned her support of the plan and stared out her window at the snow instead.

Lately, Patsy hadn't said much either as her knuckles whitened on the steering wheel.

Afraid Pete would hear Kimberly's tirade in the background if Zoe called, she sent a text stating her brother had called and they were on their way to meet him. *Staying over one more night*, she typed, intentionally leaving out the part about the "one more night" being in Erie.

She did, however, phone Scott to let him know they were running late. Her attempt to shush Kimberly had the opposite effect.

"I will *not* be quiet. Look at the roads. This is madness."

"Will you puh-leeze shut up," Patsy snapped. "It's hard enough to focus on driving without having to listen to you."

Kimberly turned to her. "Excuse me? Whose side are you on?"

"I'm on the side of getting us there in one piece."

In the midst of the squawking, the call connected. "It's me. Zoe," she said into the phone, wishing she could mute the argument. "I wanted to let you know we're running behind schedule. The roads are slippery."

He chuckled and she immediately liked his voice. A beacon of warmth on a blustery evening. "I'm not surprised, although from the sounds of it, I thought you'd stopped at a sports bar."

Zoe shot a dark look at her mother, but Kimberly was too busy ranting at Patsy to notice. "Sorry about that."

"Hey, seriously, if you want to pull off and get a room somewhere, we can meet first thing tomorrow instead. I'll leave for Arizona a little late is all."

Zoe gazed out the window at the cluster of barely visible hotels and the exit ramp they'd already passed. "Too late. We're almost there."

"Then I'll see you when I see you. Be careful."

As Zoe ended the call, Kimberly aimed her phone's screen at the backseat. "Have you seen the weather forecast? They're calling for a foot of lake effect snow. If we don't die on the roads tonight, we'll be stranded here until spring."

"They do have road crews in Erie," Lauren said.

Zoe had to bite her lip to keep from smiling at the reporter's voice of reason.

Kimberly glared in Lauren's direction. "This is all your fault. I hold you personally responsible if anything happens to my girls."

Zoe caught a glimpse of Patsy's eyes looking at her from the rearview mirror. They were Kimberly's "girls"? Kimberly was actually concerned for more than her own skin? She must be really sick.

Kimberly continued to rant for the next half hour while they exited the interstate and ventured over lesser traveled—and unplowed—side streets. Lauren spotted the house numbers attached to a porch with its light on. "That must be it."

Patsy eased the Navigator to the curb. "We'll wait here."

"We'll do no such thing." Kimberly released her seatbelt. "I'm not letting my daughter go into a strange house alone."

Zoe hopped out of the backseat and placed both hands on Kimberly's door before she could open it.

The window lowered. "What are you doing?"

"You turned Melanie's daughters against me before I had a chance to talk to them. I'll not have you alienating my brother too."

"Face it, Kimberly," Patsy said. "You don't make the best first impression. Besides, you're sick."

"I am not," Kimberly sputtered.

"Speaking of..." Zoe looked beyond her mother to Patsy. "Why don't you go find a hotel. Get checked in. And then you can come back and pick me up. We should be done with supper by then."

"No way are we—we—" Kimberly's face contorted as she sneezed. And swore. "We aren't leaving you."

Patsy reached across the center console to touch Kimberly's

arm. "Zoe has a point. You sound awful." She lifted her hand to place it to Kimberly's forehead. "My God. You're burning up."

"You'd have her walk into that house with a man none of us knows from Adam?" Kimberly's voice suddenly sounded weak. "Alone? Are you all insane? Do you have any idea what could happen to her? That man could be a psychopath for all we know."

"He's my brother."

Kimberly fixed her with bloodshot, watery eyes. "He's a stranger."

Zoe stared at her mother and realized her concern was genuine. Those weren't tears of anger or even fever gleaming on her over-mascaraed lashes. They were tears of fear.

"Tell you what," Lauren said. "How about I go in with her. I've dealt with a lot of crazies in my line of work and have developed a sixth sense about these things. I'll get her out in a heartbeat if I pick up any weird vibes."

"But if we're gone—"

"I'll call an Uber."

Kimberly shifted to study Lauren for several silent moments. After a glance at Patsy, who nodded her consent, Kimberly again faced Zoe. "Fine." She shook a finger at her. "But you be careful."

Grateful that her mother knew nothing about what had happened with Jason last spring, Zoe smiled. "I will. I promise."

TWENTY-THREE

Zoe and Lauren watched the Navigator's taillights fade into the veil of snow as it drove away.

"I hope this is the right address," Lauren said.

"Me too. But I wasn't about to have them wait until I got to the door. Mother would've changed her mind about butting out."

Lauren snorted. "By the way, we need to stop at a pharmacy and load up on cold remedies. We're bound to come down with whatever bug she has."

"First things first." Zoe headed toward the front porch along a recently shoveled sidewalk and climbed the salted steps. Scott must have prepared for her arrival. At the door, she froze. Would this meeting be awkward? Two total strangers forced into an uncomfortable dance? Or would she immediately bond with him? The way she had with Jason.

The memory curdled her stomach.

"You okay?" Lauren asked from behind her.

Zoe drew a deep breath of cold air. "I'll have to get back to you on that." She glanced over her shoulder at the reporter. "I'm glad you're here."

Lauren gave her a comforting smile. "Don't worry. I'm a good judge of character. If you get all googly-eyed over your brother, but I think he's a serial killer, I'll let you know."

"Good." Zoe didn't voice the rest of her thought. *Because I'm a lousy judge of character.* She raised a fist and knocked.

The inner door swung open to reveal a wiry man with thinning tousled brown hair, a tight smile framed by a trimmed gray-tinged beard, and dark eyes. The storm door immediately fogged. Before her view of him vanished, he pushed it open. "You must be Zoe."

"I am. And you must be Scott."

The lines at the corners of his eyes crinkled. "I am," he echoed with a note of humor. He stepped clear. "Come in. Please."

Zoe introduced Lauren as they stepped inside a small, sparsely decorated living room filled with delectable aromas coming from the kitchen. "Lauren's been helping me try to find you."

"Good." He stuffed his hands into his jeans' pockets. "I'm glad." After an uneasy moment of staring at each other, he grinned. "Sorry. I never expected to hear I had another sister." He gestured at a gray microfiber sofa. "Please. Have a seat."

Once Zoe and Lauren settled into the overstuffed couch and Scott perched on the edge of a matching chair, they fell back into the awkward silence. Zoe searched his face for some hint of familiarity. Her father had been blond, like she was. His eyes had been blue, like hers. He'd been tall, or at least he'd seemed so to an adoring eight-year-old. Scott had his mother's brown hair and eyes. His height was average. Taller than Zoe, shorter than Pete.

Zoe recalled her first meeting with Jason, whose fair hair and eyes so reminded her of her dad. She remembered their instant connection. The embrace. The joyful tears.

The horrible end.

She blinked. Maybe a rocky start would result in a better long-term relationship. "Did you find Melanie, or did she find you?"

He cleared his throat. "I found her. I've always known I was adopted. My parents were great. But Mom...my adoptive mother...passed away five years ago, and Dad died last December. I felt..." He struggled for the words. "Lost. Adrift. They'd always been uncomfortable with the idea of me tracking down my birth parents, but after they were gone..." Scott leaned forward, hands folded, elbows braced on his knees, his gaze on the floor between his feet.

"My dad—" Zoe hesitated. Should she say *our* dad? No. Not yet. "My dad was killed when I was eight. I know what you mean about being adrift."

Scott lifted his eyes to hers. "They do tend to offer us an anchor, don't they? Dads, I mean."

She nodded, afraid to speak, the decades-old memories suddenly fresh. The wounds raw.

"I started searching and located Melanie. My birth mother." Scott straightened and gazed across the room. "I was eager to meet her. To connect to my history." He smiled sadly. "And then I found out she had Alzheimer's and my father had died years ago. At least she was still clear enough back then to tell me that much. It was a real kick in the head. Except for Jess and Amanda. Sisters. I'd never had siblings before, so that was kinda cool."

Zoe fought the burst of heat behind her eyes. "So you never bothered to track down any more of your family." She hated the jealousy that spilled from her heart into her voice.

Scott looked at her, stunned. "No. No, that's not it at all. When I found my father had died so long ago, I assumed he never had any more kids. It was a stupid assumption, obviously." He scooted to the edge of his chair and reached a hand toward Zoe. "I'm sorry."

She studied the open palm. Grasped it.

In the next moment, he'd stood and pulled her up and into his arms. The scruff of his beard brushed the side of her forehead as she buried her face into his shoulder, inhaling the scent of some masculine, woodsy soap. The lump in her throat bust in a choking sob.

This—was her brother.

Lauren cleared her throat. "If you'll excuse me, this is my cue to go use the bathroom."

He drew Zoe back, looked down at her, and smiled. A real smile, revealing teeth and a hint of dimples through the beard for the first time. Not her dad's smile. But a nice one, nonetheless. Without taking his eyes from Zoe, he said to Lauren, "Upstairs. Last door on the right."

As she clomped up the steps, she called down, "Smells like something's burning."

Scott sniffed. His smile vanished, replaced by panic. "Damn. The lasagna." He released Zoe and bolted into the next room.

She laughed. "I like my pasta well done." She scooped up her purse and raked through it, coming up with her phone. "If you don't mind, I'm gonna call home and let my fiancé know I'm okay."

"Fiancé?" Scott said from the other room. "Congratulations. And no, I don't mind at all. Dinner will be ready in about five minutes."

She scrolled to Pete's number. Before she could press the green button, she heard footsteps at the front door. Scott hadn't mentioned additional company for dinner. The storm door squeaked open.

Instead of knocking, the new arrival barreled in. "Hey, Dad—" He saw Zoe. And froze.

She stared at the man. His dark eyes. The light glinting off the stud in his left ear. Recognition froze the core of her brain.

"You," he said, his voice low and accusatory.

Zoe swallowed. Hard. What the hell was Reese Perkins doing here?

Pete's phone rang as he sat at his desk, writing out the affidavit to request a search warrant for Belinda Turner's home. He checked the screen, hoping to see Zoe's name. She'd texted him earlier to say she was spending another night in Clarion, but he still longed to hear her voice.

The name on caller ID, however, was Abby's.

"What've you got?" he asked.

"I'm at the Jennings brothers' house. I think you need to see this."

Ten minutes later, he pulled into the driveway and parked behind the county CSU's truck. Although neither brother had died here, their property was still considered a secondary crime scene.

He made his way around the police vehicles and under the yellow tape. Abby met him inside the same back door he'd used when he interviewed Grant Jennings almost a week ago. Crime scene techs worked in the living room where they'd talked.

"I'm surprised you're still here," Pete said to his officer. "What's going on?"

Abby gestured for him to follow her. "While we were going through the house, I found something." She led him to a door and a staircase to the basement.

He followed her down the steps. The space had been finished into a game room, complete with a pool table, leather sectional sofa, and large screen TV. A door stood open with several county officers swarming around it.

"There's a storage room down here with boxes of stuff," Abby said. "At first glance, it looked like they'd packed to move or go to a flea market or something. But when we started opening the boxes, some of the contents rang a bell with me. I pulled up the list of merchandise stolen over the last several months that we compiled for the burglary task force, and guess what?"

Pete studied the boxes, some open, some still stacked, and the officers going through them. "It matched."

"Uh-huh." A broad grin spread across her face. "I've been inventorying the contents of that room. Everything in there is on the list."

"The Jennings brothers were your burglars."

"Which explains why there haven't been any break-ins in the last few days."

"I'll bet Culp was part of it too."

"That's my guess."

"Good work, Abby."

"That's not all." She shifted eagerly from foot to foot. "Some of the stolen items on my list are still missing. Namely, the jewelry."

"They probably fenced the smaller stuff."

"I've already contacted the local pawn shops. But remember the diamond Zoe found at Horace Pavelka's residence after Grant's homicide?"

He did.

"Something about it had been bugging me, and now I know why. A pair of diamond earrings was reported stolen in one of the thefts." Abby's smile widened. "At the time I took the report, the victim, an older lady, mentioned they'd been a gift from her late husband...and said one of the settings was loose. She'd been meaning to take the earrings to a jeweler. Just hadn't gotten around to it."

Pete rolled the new information around his brain. "Someone in Horace's house was wearing those earrings."

"Or one of them. The one with the loose setting. Grant, maybe?"

Pete shook his head. "I'll have to check, but I don't remember Grant having any piercings. And he didn't seem like the diamond type."

Abby tipped her head and gave him a look. "*Everyone's* the diamond type, Chief."

"Maybe. But you know who I believe definitely *is* the diamond type?"

She raised a questioning eyebrow.

"Belinda Turner."

Perkins reached toward his waistband and in one fluid, practiced movement, brought a gun out and aimed at Zoe. With his other hand, he snatched the cell phone from her hand.

She'd looked down the barrel of firearms before, but this time felt more deadly.

Her eyes glued to the muzzle of the weapon, she heard rather than saw Scott come into the room behind her.

"Hey, son, guess who—" The footsteps stopped. "Christopher, what the hell are you doing?"

Christopher?

"I was gonna ask you the same question," Perkins said. "What's she doing here?"

"She's my half-sister."

Perkins snorted. "No, she's not. She's a cop here to bust me."

What? "No," Zoe sputtered.

"Shut up." Perkins brought the pistol closer to her face. She instinctively drew back.

"A cop?" Scott asked. "What are you talking about?"

"She's a cop from Monongahela County." Perkins glared at her. "I didn't put it together until I saw you chasing me in the parking lot and then spotted your partner coming the other way."

Kevin. He'd pulled in at Bud Kramer's less than a minute after Perkins sped away. Zoe tried to choke out a denial, but words wouldn't come.

"How'd you manage to tail me here?"

"I didn't." Her mind whirled out of control. Perkins had called out "Dad" when he came through the door. Scott had called him "son." Had she walked into a crime family? *Her* family? Her knees weakened. Not again.

"What'd she do?" Perkins sneered. "Tell you she was long-lost kin? And you bought it?"

Scott's footsteps and the creak of the floor told her he was approaching. Coming around beside her. Still, she couldn't force her eyes away from the gun. Scott appeared in her peripheral vision and moved to stand next to his son. He put a hand on Perkins' arm. "That's not necessary. Put the gun down."

He didn't.

"Is what he said true?" Scott asked Zoe. "Was this story about your father a lie?"

"No." She forced her gaze away from the pistol and focused on Scott's eyes. He looked sad. Disappointed. Not lethal like Perkins. "I'm not a cop. I'm a paramedic and a deputy coroner. I had no idea he was your son. Or that he was in Erie."

"Liar." Perkins stepped closer, his face inches from hers. The gun pressed into her solar plexus and forced her breath from her.

She stared into his dark eyes. "If I was a cop, don't you think I'd have arrested you then?"

His jaw twitched. A flash of doubt?

She turned to Scott. "I'm not lying to you. My dad was Gary Chambers. Last spring, I found out I had a sibling. It's taken me until now to track down your mother. And you."

The gun dug deeper into her gut. "Shut up." Perkins glanced at his father. "You're not buying this, are you?"

Scott held her gaze. She silently pleaded with him to believe her. "I'm not a cop. If I was, I'd have a gun. I don't. You can search me."

Perkins nodded. "Do it."

Zoe wished she could read Scott's eyes. She raised both arms.

Perkins moved back enough to allow his father to step in front of her. Scott brought both hands against her sides. She closed her eyes, cringing as he patted her down with a thoroughness that led her to wonder if he'd been a cop himself. Or a TSA agent.

"She's clean."

Perkins returned to his previous position, his face inches from hers, his tobacco-laden breath choking her. "Are you wearing a wire?"

"No," she said firmly.

His lip curled in a smirk as his gaze lowered to her chest. "Take off your shirt."

The thought of standing in front of two men...her brother and his son...stripped to her bra, choked her.

Scott reached over, blocking his son. "No. I told you. She's clean."

Zoe looked at her brother. Did he believe her? Or was he merely a decent enough human being that he wouldn't let his creep of a son have his way with her.

"Besides," Scott said. "With modern technology, they don't need to wear wires anymore." He gestured to Zoe's phone still clenched in Perkins' left hand.

So much for him believing her.

Perkins looked down at the phone. He dropped it to the floor. And crushed it under one heel. He brought those dark, soulless eyes back to hers. "Where's your partner?"

Crap. She was sure he meant Kevin, but she'd forgotten Lauren was still upstairs. Zoe looked at Scott.

He never met her gaze, keeping his on his son. "She came alone."

"Like hell. She probably has backup positioned outside." Perkins glanced toward the window. "We have to get out of here."

"You go," Scott said. "I'll keep her here while you get away."

Zoe plastered on her best poker face, hoping Perkins wouldn't read her gratitude.

"No," he said. "You stay if you want. She goes with me."

TWENTY-FOUR

"What do you mean, Belinda Turner's missing?" Pete demanded. He once again stood in front of Horace's girlfriend's house. Temperatures tanked as the day's rainclouds had cleared at dusk, revealing a star-filled sky. "I thought you had men watching her."

Baronick and a pair of county uniforms had beaten Pete there. "I did." The detective glared at the officers, who wore the hang-dog look of abject failure. "Care to explain to Chief Adams what happened?"

They looked at each other. Pete expected them to throw a game of rock-paper-scissors to determine which one should share. He saved them the trouble and stood in front of the officer with the name tag Kissell. "You. Talk."

He swallowed. "We received the call to take Ms. Turner into custody and hold her until the warrant arrived to search her house. We knocked on the door, but no one answered."

Pete silenced him with a hand. "I get it. She's gone. What I want to know is how she got away when she has no vehicle, made no phone calls, and you two were surveilling her house?"

Kissell swallowed again. "I don't know, sir."

Pete shifted his gaze to Baronick. "Detective?"

He held up a folded paper. "We have a warrant to search for the earrings, one of which is minus a stone. Maybe we'll find the evidence inside as well as something to show where she went." He grinned. "After all. Those earrings are small. They could be anywhere."

Pete understood. "And we'll look *everywhere*." If there was evidence of Horace and Belinda's crimes in that house, he'd find it.

But an hour later, he hadn't. Belinda's jewelry box held a massive collection of costume stuff. Gaudy fake gems and cheap necklaces and bracelets. The kind of stuff sold in low-end box stores. They searched every drawer, every container, every space that might hold the tiny diamond studs. Pete even checked the ice cube trays in her freezer.

Baronick, Pete, and one of the uniforms reconvened in the living room. The detective shook his head. "Nothing."

Pete swore. He looked at the officer. "Where's your partner?"

"He said he had an idea and went to check it out. Said he'd be back in a few minutes."

"From where?" Pete asked.

"I don't know, sir."

Baronick fixed him with a dark glare. "How long ago?"

Before the officer could reply, Officer Kissell strode through the door. "I know how she got out without us seeing her."

"How?" Baronick asked.

"While I was searching the basement, I noticed the door leading into the backyard. I thought, if it was me, I'd slip out and into the woods. There's a bar about a quarter mile from here." He grinned. "So I ran over to the bar and asked around. One of the guys remembered seeing the Turner woman a couple hours ago. She claimed her car wouldn't start and she needed to get to the hospital to see a friend. One of the regulars offered to give her a ride."

"The hospital?" Baronick said. "Pavelka got hurt?"

"Maybe," Pete replied. "Get someone over there now." To the officer, he asked, "Did you get the name of the guy who gave her the lift?"

"Yes, sir." He produced a slip of paper. "Name, phone number, and address."

Baronick took the note. "Good work, Kissell."

Pete's phone rang. Lauren Sanders' name came up on the screen, and he immediately sensed trouble. Why the hell was Lauren calling him instead of Zoe? He excused himself and headed for the kitchen. He hit the green button. "Lauren?"

"Pete, Zoe's in big trouble," the reporter whispered, her voice so soft, he had to strain to hear.

He plugged his other ear. "What kind of trouble? Where are you?"

"I'm upstairs in her brother's house. They're downstairs. He's got a gun."

The breath in Pete's body leeched out, replaced by ice. Not again. "Her brother has a gun?"

"No. Reese Perkins."

"Reese Perkins?"

"Yeah. Look, I have to find a way out of here before they come for me too. I'll call you back as soon as I can."

"Wait. Where in Clarion are you? Give me an address. I'll call State Police."

"Not Clarion," she whispered, her voice raspy. "Erie."

The line went dead.

"Lauren?" he said. "*Lauren!*" As if shouting might reconnect the dropped call.

"What about Reese Perkins?"

Pete wheeled to find Baronick at the doorway. "He's got Zoe. In Erie."

The detective's face paled. "Let's go. I'll drive."

Zoe sprawled across the backseat of a crew-cab pickup, her arms bound behind her with duct tape. Attempts to break or even loosen it failed. She tried to sit up only to have Perkins aim the gun at her again with orders to "Stay down."

Did he not want her to know where he was taking her? Not that it mattered. The snow fell so hard and steady, all she'd been able to see was a white veil. Besides, a nagging voice inside her head kept reminding her—she'd seen his face. She knew who he was. Sort of. There was nothing to stop him from killing her. Unless...

"I wasn't lying about being your dad's sister."

"Shut up."

"My father slept with your dad's birth mother when they were in high school."

"So what? He didn't want anything to do with either of them. That Melanie woman didn't want my dad. Why should either of us care about you?"

"I'm your aunt."

"Aunt." He snorted. "You're nothing more than an ant at a picnic. You know what I do to those kinds of ants, don't you?"

She could guess.

"I squash them like the bugs they are."

So much for developing a familial bond. "He called you Christopher."

"Shut up."

"That's your real name?"

"I'm not telling you again. Shut. Up."

Her shoulders started to cramp. She squirmed in search of a position to relieve the stress on them. The inside of the truck lit up from the headlights of a vehicle coming the other way. The diamond stud in Perkins' ear caught the light. "Nice earring," she said.

Perkins twisted in the driver's seat, bringing the gun around. "What part of shut up don't you understand?"

She felt the truck's forward movement shift. Perkins jerked around to face front, grabbing for the steering wheel. The rear of the pickup arced toward the edge of the road. Perkins swore. Cranked the steering wheel. But the truck skidded into a spin. Zoe closed her eyes. Waited for impact. Or for the thing to go into a roll. Without benefit of a seatbelt, she'd become a ragdoll, tossed around the cab, bashing off the roof. The windows. The seats...

Headlights shone into the cab, revolving like the beam from a lighthouse. Except it was the truck spinning. Tilting.

Then a jolt.

Zoe was flung from the backseat onto the floor. And the pickup lurched to a stop.

Pete's call to Zoe went directly to voicemail. As did his calls to Lauren and Kimberly. "Dammit."

Baronick pushed his unmarked Dodge Challenger well over the posted speed limit north on I-79. "I can't believe you don't have a name for Zoe's brother," the detective muttered. "I've got the state police looking for her, but Erie's a fair-sized city. It'd help if we had a starting point."

"The last time we spoke, she didn't know his name. Hell, I'm not even sure this guy *is* her brother. He could be bait in Reese Perkins' trap."

"And Perkins has at least ten aliases."

One of which had an address on record. Pete mentally kicked himself. He yanked his notebook from his pocket and flipped through the pages. Found it. "Have them try Warsaw Avenue." He read the house number to Baronick. "It's the last known address for Christopher Lewis Nixon a.k.a. Reese Perkins."

While Baronick phoned the PSP in Erie, Pete stared at the road in front of them. The detective maneuvered one-handed through northbound interstate traffic, keeping the pedal mashed to the floor and his phone to his ear. Still, Pete pressed his right foot into the passenger-side floorboards as if he could coax even more speed from the Challenger.

Inside his head, he replayed Lauren's frantic call. *Zoe's in big trouble.* Reese Perkins thought she was a cop. And he had a gun. How the hell had he tracked her down? And why? If he believed she was a cop, why not stay as far away as possible?

And what were Zoe and Lauren doing in Erie? They were supposed to be in Clarion. Zoe'd texted they were spending another night, but no mention of Erie.

Baronick ended his call and tossed the phone onto the center console. "State and Erie City Police are on it. They'll let us know as soon as they check the place out."

Pete grunted.

Baronick swung the Challenger across three lanes to the far right as they neared Cranberry, avoiding the slower traffic making the left-hand exit onto Route 19. At the same time, the first snowflakes began to drift into the headlight beams. "We have another problem," he said.

Pete looked at him.

"They're having an early winter snowstorm. A lot of the roads are unpassable. Once we get north of I-80, the going's gonna be rough."

"Dammit. We should've brought my Explorer."

"We didn't know. And my Challenger's faster."

"Until it gets stuck in a snowdrift." He should've checked the weather forecast.

"Look at it this way," Baronick said, "the snow'll slow Perkins down too. If we're lucky, he'll be the one stuck in a drift."

Pain seared through Zoe's shoulder. She been tossed onto the floor, hands still bound behind her. Had she dislocated her shoulder? Torn something? She couldn't tell but knew it wasn't good. She'd had no luck loosening the tape before. Now, attempts at freeing her hands were impossible. On the plus side, she was very much alive. Being dead wouldn't hurt this bad.

From the front seat, Reese produced an encyclopedic string of profanities as the ignition ground but refused to fire.

Slowing her breath to control what felt like knives slicing through her right arm, she assessed her situation. The truck had stalled. From its slant, she assumed it had ended its spin, nosed into a ditch. There had been no hard impact, telling her the other vehicle missed them. She was stuck in a snowstorm with a killer who believed she was a cop. And she had a badly injured shoulder.

Groaning, she squirmed, struggling to move into a more comfortable position.

"Shut up," Reese growled.

The truck's starter sputtered and turned over but still didn't fire. The stench of gasoline wafted into the cab.

"You've flooded it," Zoe said.

In the low light provided by the dashboard instruments, she saw him pivot. Saw his gun aimed at her face. "If I want your opinion, I'll ask for it."

She decided replying wasn't a good idea.

He turned away from her and again attempted to restart the truck. This time he kept at it. Zoe held her breath. The engine was either going to start or the battery would go dead with the effort. She wasn't sure which was better for her. After a good ten seconds, the engine sputtered and caught. It didn't sound healthy, but the thing was running.

She heard Reese sigh.

The interior of the pickup lightened. Another vehicle approached. Pulled alongside. Stopped. This might be her chance to get help.

Except Reese slipped his right hand between the front seats and jammed his gun into her hip. He powered down his window. "Hi."

"Hello there," a male voice said from the other vehicle. "Looks like you could use some help."

Zoe wanted to scream. Didn't dare. She had no doubt Reese would shoot her. Either now or later. He planned to kill her. But if she cried out for help, he'd also shoot the unwitting Good Samaritan. He'd leave them, dead or dying, and take off in the other car.

Reese laughed. A genuine-sounding laugh. "It does, doesn't it? But I'm good. I work for a garage and they're sending a tow truck."

Half-truth. The garage he worked for was a hundred and fifty miles south.

"Do you want me to wait with you?" the Good Samaritan asked.

"Thanks, but there's no need. I'd hate to see you get stranded out here just to keep me company. I'll be fine."

"Okey dokey then. Stay safe."

"You too." Reese powered up the window as Zoe's potential

savior drove away. Reese twisted in the seat to look at her. "Good girl. You might live to see the morning after all."

TWENTY-FIVE

After what felt like hours and a lot of jamming the gearshift into reverse, revving the engine, rocking, shifting into drive, revving, and rocking—over and over—the pickup leveled and regained footing. From the front seat, Reese muttered something that sounded victorious as they once again rolled down the road.

Zoe strained to roll onto her left side, but the movement and the position sent hot daggers slicing into her right shoulder. She bit back a yelp knowing it would only bring renewed threats from Reese. She refused to give in to whimpering. Refused to give him the satisfaction. Instead, she chewed her lip and continued to search for a position on the floor that hurt less.

She needed to hurt less. To free her brain of being totally consumed by her shoulder in order to think clearly. To plan.

No one knew where she was. Hell, *she* didn't know where she was. They'd been driving for what? An hour? Two? Time was a blur. From the backseat floor, she couldn't see a road sign. Or even the road. Streetlights and the rare passing vehicle's headlights revealed it was still snowing. A lot.

She tried to judge their speed. They weren't going fast. The tire sounds were muffled. The roads were snow covered.

Where was he taking her?

It didn't matter.

No one knew where she was.

Pete thought she was in Clarion. Patsy and Kimberly? They must have realized by now that she was missing.

Lauren. What had happened to Lauren? Scott hadn't told

Reese about her. Had flat-out lied about another person in the house. Zoe could hug him for that. Except he hadn't done a thing to stop his murderous son from walking her out at gunpoint.

Reese Perkins was Scott's son. Her nephew. Was it possible that he was the stone-cold killer who'd murdered Grant and Stanley Jennings, leaving Horace to take the blame? Or had he killed Horace too? Maybe Horace wasn't missing. Maybe he was dead.

The thought brought a rush of heat to her eyes.

A jolt—a pothole—drove new knives of pain slicing through her shoulder. She breathed deeply, forcing the agony down. Forced her mind to focus elsewhere.

Given half a chance, she needed to use whatever she could to free herself. To escape. Her arms were restricted. But her legs weren't.

As she plotted, considered her options, the truck slowed. She strained, trying to see something to let her know where they were. From her angle, all she could make out was black sky streaked with white. Reese steered hard to the right. Tires ground and churned. The truck lurched. Bounced. Rocked. Wherever they were, the snow was deeper. Unplowed. The pickup crawled forward. Stopped.

Reese shifted into park. Cut the engine. He half turned in her direction. "End of the road."

Her heart stilled. This was it.

He stepped out. A wall of cold air rolled into the truck. The cold amplified when he yanked open the back door and icy pellets stung her cheeks. He grabbed her by the collar of her coat and jerked her up, dragging her across the floor. The pain in her shoulder drew blinding tears. Drove all thoughts of escape into the distant reaches of consciousness.

By the time she found her breath, she was standing beside the truck, ankle deep in a flat sea of white, the only illumination the truck's headlamps and half a dozen weak lights atop poles dotting the empty parking lot. Fifty yards away, blacker than the black night, a massive shadow of a structure. An abandoned factory? Warehouse?

Reese prodded her with the gun. "Move."

Zoe staggered forward a step. Hesitated.

He prodded her harder. "*Move.*"

She took another step. And another. The building was huge. And dark. Empty. As was the parking lot. She shot a look in the direction they'd come. Made out deep tire tracks leading from the truck into the night. One of the overhead lights caught a hint of a chain link fence. There must be a road beyond. But no cars moved along it. No sounds, even muffled ones, of traffic. Only the wind moaning, reminding her of her aloneness.

Reese intended to walk her into that abandoned structure like cattle to the slaughter. No doubt with the same result in mind. He'd shoot her and leave her. It would be days...weeks...longer...before anyone found her body. Pete would never give up looking, but it would be too late.

The cold numbed her shoulder. And her toes.

But not her brain.

She stopped. Inhaled.

He jammed the muzzle of his gun into her back. "Don't make me tell you again. Move."

"No." Before he could react, she wheeled toward him. Slammed her good shoulder into the arm holding the weapon, knocking it away from her. Threw her weight into him. Instead of forcing him off his feet, he merely staggered.

"Bitch," he hissed, bringing the gun around.

She headbutted him. Her forehead to his nose. A move she'd seen in the movies which had given her a headache just watching it. But that headache was nothing like the real one. Flashbulbs popped behind her eyes. However, the move had the desired effect. Reese bellowed. Dropped the gun. And grabbed for his nose, which she could tell—even in the low light—she'd bloodied.

What she couldn't see was where the gun had gone. As Reese screamed epithets at her, she kicked at the snow. Pictured herself finding the gun, squatting and grabbing it with her hands taped behind her, and running. But the pistol had sunk beneath the blanket of white and no amount of scrapping with her booted foot could locate it.

She took off, loping toward the truck. If she couldn't find the gun, she hoped he couldn't either. The snow sucked at her feet. Behind her, Reese continued to hurl a litany of curse words. She expected to hear a shot. Expected to feel the burn of the bullet piercing her back. Expected it to be the last thing she ever heard or felt.

She reached the truck's driver's door. Now what? She hoped he'd left the keys in the ignition. But first things first. Her hands were still bound. Even with her back to the vehicle, she couldn't reach the latch. She risked a glance toward Reese. He was on his knees, searching for his dropped weapon.

She needed to free her hands.

She looked around. The wheel well had one of those smooth skirts. Probably not sharp enough to cut through duct tape. But the bumper...

Zoe plowed her way to the rear of the vehicle. Squatted. Maneuvered her wrists into the small gap between the truck's back fender and the chrome bumper. The pain in her shoulder nearly drove her all the way onto her knees. She bit her lip. And sawed. With each breath, with each stroke, she silently chanted, *Ignore the pain. Ignore the pain. Ignore the pain.*

She glanced at Reese. Still on all fours. Still searching.

The tape started to tear. She felt it rip. *Ignore the pain.* She doubled her effort. Pressed harder into the edge of the bumper. The tape gave a little. Then a little more. One last slice. And her arms were free.

She wanted to rub them, especially the right one, to massage away the cramping. But no time.

Reese held something in his hands.

Zoe stumbled to the driver's door. It was unlocked.

She glanced over her shoulder. Reese was on his feet. Turning her way.

She yanked the door open and scrambled in. Slammed the door.

Reese trudged toward her, his arms at his sides. Did he have the gun?

Heart pounding, she reached for the ignition. And fingered air.

She looked out the window. Reese was close enough for her to see his bloody nose. His lips parted in a fiendish grin revealing predatory teeth. He held up one finger. The truck's key fob dangling from it.

Crap.

He raised his other hand. Zoe again gazed down the barrel of the gun. "Come out of there," he said.

The wind whipped his words away, but she could read his lips. She looked around the cab, searching for options. Weapons. Found none. Ideas. She was fresh out.

Reese jerked the door open. "I said, come out of there."

She looked at the gun. Looked beyond him to the shadowy structure. He was going to kill her, either here or there. There, she might never be found. Her body would be left to decompose. Here, she'd at least leave blood evidence for Pete and the crime scene unit to find. They'd be able to track who killed her.

Reese wouldn't get away with it. Pete would see that justice was served.

"No," she said.

Reese glared at her. "What?"

"I said, no. If you're gonna shoot me, you're gonna have to do it right here." She was amazed how steady her voice sounded.

His face softened. "I'm not gonna shoot you."

She choked a laugh. Made a point of looking at the gun.

The glare returned. "I'm serious. I don't want to have to shoot you. I need to stash you here to give me time to get away. I'm gonna take you inside, out of the weather, and tie you up. Once I'm safely out of town, I'll call my father and tell him where you are. If you're his sister like you said you are, he'll come and free you. If he's found out you're a cop like *I* say you are...well, maybe he'll free you and maybe he won't."

Reese held her gaze. She studied him. Searched his dark eyes for some sign of honesty. Goodness. Truthfulness. She wanted to believe him. Wanted to trust what he said.

She wanted to live.

"You're my nephew," she said, her voice no longer steady. "We're family."

"Which is why I don't want to shoot you. I want to give my dad time to find out if you're telling the truth." Reese continued to hold her gaze.

Zoe continued to study him.

He pocketed the key fob. "Here's how this is gonna play out." He held up one finger. "You go with me into the warehouse. I tie you up. Dad confirms you're his sister and comes to release you." He held up two fingers. "Or Dad confirms you're a cop trying to arrest his son, and he leaves you to rot. But, being resourceful, you'll have lots of time to get loose. In the meantime, I'll be long gone."

Another angle struck her. "Aren't you putting your father in a hell of a position? You're making him an accomplice. You might be long gone, but he'll still be here facing the police. Facing charges. Because of you."

If her words had any impact on Perkins, he didn't show it. He held up three fingers, and his voice grew menacing. "Or you refuse to come out of my truck, and I shoot you where you sit and drag your body in there for the rats to eat."

Zoe didn't like the third option at all. The first two were reasonable, especially since she knew she wasn't a cop. Would Scott go to the trouble to confirm her story? He'd seemed like a good guy.

Right up to the point where he did nothing to stop his son from kidnapping her.

Somewhere in her consciousness, a voice screamed. She could identify Reese. No way would he risk leaving her alive.

She didn't want to die. Resisting at this point seemed to guarantee her death.

And rats chewing on her.

She shivered. Shoved the screaming voice down into the darkest part of her mind and covered it with the slightest glimmer of hope.

Because that was all she had.

"All right." She pivoted in the seat and slid down.

"Smart move." He grabbed her right arm and spun her to face the truck. It felt like he was ripping her shoulder from her torso.

She yelped.

"Oh, shut up. I didn't hurt you."

Maybe not intentionally. Not yet. But the pain nearly dropped her to her knees.

He reached into the cab and came up with a roll of duct tape. Forced her wrists together and once again bound them behind her. He jerked her around to face him, retrieved the handgun he'd stuck into his waistband, and gestured with it. "Walk."

Reese had been here before. Of that, Zoe was certain. He marched her directly to a door, which screeched open without the benefit of a key. If she could work free from whatever restraints he used on her, she should be able to get out the same way.

Provided he kept to his word and didn't shoot her.

"Inside," he ordered.

Zoe stepped through the door into total blackness. She stopped, blind, uncertain.

Reese jabbed her in the ribs with the gun muzzle. "Keep going."

"I can't see."

She heard a muffled sound, then a small beam from his phone lit the area in front of her. Concrete floor stretched out into the darkness. Nothing to fall into. Nothing to bump into. He nudged her again. "Move."

She obeyed, her concern shifting from what was before her to the gun behind her and the man holding it.

A shadowy image came into view. A support post or pillar of some sort. Reese grabbed her left arm and steered her toward it. Something about it raised the hairs on the back of Zoe's neck even before the phone's flashlight revealed what she was seeing.

A large metal loop hung from the pillar, reminding her of the rings she'd installed at her barn. Convenient for tying the horses for being saddled or groomed. This one held a length of chain.

She stopped.

Reese shoved her the last few yards.

A closer look at the setup did nothing to ease the terror seeping deeper into her bones than the cold. Not one, but two chains were anchored into what appeared to be a concrete support, which was thick enough she couldn't have reached all the way around it. At the end of each chain, a shackle.

She'd walked into a scene from a bad horror movie.

Not only had Reese been there before, she wasn't the first person he'd chained up in this place. At least there wasn't a corpse already occupying the restraints. Nor was there any blood that she could see. If he'd shot anyone here, she saw no evidence of it.

And she had no intention of being the first. Or of letting him clamp those heavy cuffs on her.

Zoe snapped her head back, blindly targeting his already bloodied, possibly broken, nose. But he anticipated the move and dodged the blow.

He laughed, a harsh, vindictive sound, and spun her toward him. "Not very original. I never took you for a one-trick pony—"

She shifted her weight to one foot—and kneed him in the groin with every ounce of force she could muster.

He gasped. Doubled over. The phone clattered to the concrete floor, its tiny light extinguished, plunging the warehouse into total blackness.

Free, Zoe bolted into the dark, trying to remember where the door was.

It didn't take long before she realized exactly how dark it was, and how lost she was. She stopped. Willed her eyes to adjust to the total absence of light. Strained to hear footsteps telling her whether Reese still followed her. She knew he had to be. But she heard only the howl of the wind outside.

Which way to the door? She'd walked straight...how far? Then he'd steered her slightly to the left. She'd broken away from the right. Meaning, she needed to go...

She had no idea.

Find the wall, she thought. Then she'd feel her way along it until she located the door. The plan would've worked better if she could extend her hands in front of her. With her arms restricted, she'd have to hope she didn't find the wall with her face.

Still no sounds of footsteps. Or wheezing through a bloodied nose. Zoe eased forward into the black void. Tried to judge how close she must be getting. How many steps had it taken her to get to the pillar?

Why the hell hadn't she counted?

She figured she must be getting near. Was she simply guessing? Or was she using some sixth sense? Human sonar. She slowed. Slid one foot forward, waiting to toe the wall. Then sliding the other one forward. Two steps. Three steps. Four.

She kicked something solid. Leaned her good shoulder toward it and touched cold, hard, brick. Found it.

A sound. A scrape. Nearby. She froze. Held her breath. Listened. Outside, the wind wailed. Had she imagined the sound? Seconds ticked into a minute. Nothing. It must've been the wind.

Which direction to the door? She was down to two choices. Fifty-fifty. She'd gambled on much steeper odds playing poker. But this time the only thing in the pot was her life.

She set her left shoulder against the wall and started forward. Slowly, listening.

After what seemed like a mile, the surface changed. She turned her back to it, using her numb hands to explore. Instead of rough brick, she touched smooth steel. The door. Facing the inner blackness of the warehouse, she slid her fingers to the push bar latch. Clung to it as if her life depended on it. Which it did. She paused again to listen. Where had Reese gone? Surely she hadn't knocked him unconscious.

Hearing nothing, sensing nothing, she threw herself back against the bar, which released with a loud metallic click. The door swung out into a blast of wind-driven snow, letting in a stream of light from the parking lot.

A stream of light that fell upon the bloodied and furious face of

Reese Perkins.

TWENTY-SIX

The news of the snowstorm hadn't been exaggerated. Once Pete and Baronick got north of I-80, the roads grew treacherous. Instead of pedal-to-the-metal speeds, they were forced to creep along with other cars and semis. A long stream of red taillights stretched in front of them.

Pete thumped the armrest with one fist. "I'm ready to get out and walk."

Baronick glanced over at him, his face as tense as Pete had ever seen it. "If I thought we'd actually make it on foot, I'd be right with you."

The detective's phone rang. He snatched it from the console. "Detective Baronick."

Pete listened to half of the conversation, which consisted of a string of uh-huhs.

Baronick's expression started out hopeful but faded to disappointed. "Keep me posted as soon as you know anything...ETA? I have no idea at this point..." Disappointment morphed to frustration. "Great. Just great," he said, sarcasm oozing from his words. After a thank you that carried minimal gratitude, he ended the call.

"Well?" Pete asked.

Baronick growled a sigh. "They searched the address you gave them for Christopher Nixon. No one was there. They said it looked about as personal as a cheap motel room. Except for one photo of what appeared to be him as a kid on a fishing boat with a man they think is his dad. They did some digging and learned Nixon's father, one Scott Nixon, also lives in Erie. No one was home at his address either. They're questioning his neighbors, one of whom said he'd had a lot of company coming and going earlier this evening."

"Company?"

"Yeah, but he couldn't be more specific. Apparently, he was engrossed in Thursday Night Football and wasn't paying attention to what was going on outside."

A lot of company. Could the son be one of his visitors? Could Zoe?

"I know what you're thinking," Baronick said. "But he might've had his buddies over to watch the game too."

"Maybe." Pete keyed Zoe's number into his phone for the gazillionth time. Voicemail again. He tried Lauren's and Kimberly's phones with the same result.

Dammit.

"Who are you trying to call?" Baronick asked. "Besides Zoe."

"Her mother and Lauren Sanders. They were all on this road trip together."

"Voicemail?"

"Yeah." He didn't like it. None of it.

"This storm might be playing havoc with the cellular signals."

"Maybe." Pete wasn't buying it.

"It was only the three of them?"

"Four. Zoe's cousin, Patsy, is with them, but I don't have her number."

"What's her last name?"

"Greene."

Baronick picked up his phone and grinned. "With an 'e' on the end?"

"Yeah." What was he up to?

The detective placed a call. Seconds ticked by. "Josie? Hey. It's Wayne. Remember that favor you owe me? I'm cashing it in."

A few minutes later, Baronick read Patsy's number to Pete, who keyed it in. He hit send as the detective thanked his source and ended the call.

The ringback tones played in Pete's ear. Once. Twice. Three

times. He waited for the automated voice to come and tell him the party he was trying to reach was not available.

"Hello?" Patsy sounded desperate.

"Where's Zoe?" he demanded.

"Pete?" He heard the tears in her voice. "I don't know. I don't know where any of them are." She started to pour out how they'd tracked down Zoe's brother. How she and Kimberly had left Zoe and Lauren at his house and had gone to check in at the hotel. "I took a shower and when I came out, Kimberly had left a note saying she was taking the car keys because Zoe had been kidnapped." Patsy paused to catch a ragged breath. "I haven't heard from any of them since."

Pete pieced together the fragments of Patsy's story. "You left Zoe at her brother's house?"

"Scott's house. Yeah."

"Scott?" What were the odds? "You don't mean Scott *Nixon*?"

"Yeah."

Pete looked over at Baronick. "Scott Nixon is Zoe's brother."

Reese grabbed Zoe's right arm and wrenched it. She cried out, convinced the limb was tearing free from her shoulder.

"What's wrong?" He hissed into her ear. "Did you hurt yourself?"

So much for believing she could hide her injury from him.

"I'd shoot you, but then I'd be putting you out of your misery." He yanked her away from the door.

As it swung shut, she was once again in total darkness. Except for the fireworks popping inside her skull.

He propelled her across the room with a death grip on her arm. The only thought able to surface through the fiery hell of pain was *I'm going to die.*

This was it. She'd botched all attempts at escape. No one knew where she was. Reese knew of her weakness—her Achilles shoulder—and would torture her with it.

As before, he clicked on his phone's flashlight to guide them to the pillar. Unlike before, he didn't afford her the opportunity to resist.

"Sit." He punctuated the growled order with a twist of her arm.

She yelped and dropped to her knees on the cold, filthy cement floor.

He dragged her around until her back was against the equally cold post.

As Reese worked with the chains, Zoe let her head fall forward, battling to corral her tears. She'd already revealed her physical weakness to him. She refused to give him the satisfaction of knowing how terrified she was.

He locked the shackles around her wrists. She heard a soft click—a sound she recognized as a pocketknife opening. With one quick slice, her wrists were freed from the tape, relieving the tension on her shoulder.

"See? Isn't that better?" he said, his voice taunting.

She didn't lift her face. Was he going to shoot her? Probably not. There was no need.

"Remember, I told you I planned to leave it up to my dad to rescue you if your story checked out?"

It would. He was her brother. It wouldn't take long to verify their relationship. "Yeah."

Reese leaned down. Rested the icy barrel of the pistol against her cheek. "I lied."

"You're going to shoot me."

"No. Ammunition costs too much to waste unnecessarily. Besides, I'm not a murderer."

She choked. "You killed Grant and Stanley Jennings."

"No, I didn't. And I'm not going to kill you either."

Zoe knew he was lying about the brothers. But she couldn't help but latch onto a glimmer of hope about her own fate. "You'll tell your dad where I am?"

"I told you I lied about that. He's too soft. Even when he learns you're a cop, he'd come to your rescue. I'm not going to tell him anything. And I'm his beloved only son, so he won't ask."

"But you said you weren't going to kill me."

"I'm not." He straightened and took a step back. "Lack of food and water will do that for me. If you don't freeze to death first."

He walked away taking the thin beam of light and what was left of her hope with him.

She gave up on containing her tears. This was how her life would end. Far from home. Far from the man she loved. Alone in a desolate, frigid, abandoned warehouse. She lifted her face and stared into the blackness, watching for the door to open. Watching for her newly found nephew to walk out of her life.

The now distant footsteps stopped. The *ca-chunk* of the latch bar being depressed echoed. The door opened allowing a glimmer of artificial light to cast his form into a silhouette.

Instead of Reese simply walking out into the night, there was a flash of movement. A thud. And a grunt.

Someone charged in, swinging. Or were there two? Three? Reese staggered. Another thud. A metallic clank of a handgun hitting the floor and skittering away. One of the shadows raised a stick or a club and brought it down with a crack.

And Reese Perkins lay motionless.

A bright beam of light projected from what Zoe had thought was a club and swept the space, landing on and blinding her.

"She's here," Lauren shouted.

"Thank God," the other shadow said.

Zoe squinted. "*Mother?*"

The light swung out of Zoe's eyes and fell on the person standing over a fallen Reese Perkins with a clenched fist, looking like the Angel of Death. A.k.a. Kimberly Chambers Jackson. She glared down at Zoe's fallen captor. "Let that be a lesson to you. Don't ever mess with my daughter."

Pete stormed into the Erie Medical Center's emergency department with Baronick on his heels. The security guard eyed his badge and uniform, checked Baronick's ID, and pointed them to the nurse at the desk.

"Zoe Chambers," Pete said, daring the woman to deny him entrance.

She hit a button to open the automatic doors. "To the left. Room five."

As they breezed into the ER, Baronick tapped him on the shoulder and pointed at a trio of uniformed officers guarding a room to the right. "You go check on our girl. I'm gonna talk to the cops."

Pete found his fiancée sitting on the edge of an ER bed, her right arm in a sling, her face covered in blood. "What the hell?"

She looked up at him, and a smile spread across her face. "Pete."

He crossed to her side, longing to scoop her into his arms, but afraid to hurt her. He touched her face. "What happened?"

"Reese Perkins," she said. "He's my nephew—"

"And he kidnapped you. I know that much."

She looked puzzled. "How?"

"I called him." Lauren entered the cubicle, carrying a paper cup of coffee, which she handed to the patient. Kimberly trailed her with one of those sickly pink hospital wash pans filled with soapy water. She set it on the rolling table at Zoe's bedside and wheeled it closer, elbowing Pete out of her way.

Kimberly sniffed once, twice, and sneezed into the crook of her elbow.

"Bless you," he said, keeping his gaze on Zoe's face. And all that blood. "What did he do to you?"

"The shoulder?" She sipped the coffee. "He duct-taped my hands behind me, and when his truck hit a ditch, I fell off the seat onto the floor. We're waiting for the x-rays, but the doc doesn't think it's dislocated."

"What about your face?"

Kimberly squeezed out a washcloth. "That's not her blood. It's his." She looked at Pete. "I wondered the same thing when I first saw her."

Zoe grinned weakly. "I headbutted him. I'm pretty sure I broke his nose. I didn't even realize I had his blood all over me until Mother saw me and screamed."

Kimberly muttered something Pete couldn't hear and gently began wiping Zoe's face.

Zoe reached for the washcloth. "I can do that, Mom."

But Kimberly pushed her hand away. "I've got this. Just drink your coffee and relax."

Zoe looked as befuddled as Pete. Kimberly? Doting on her daughter?

Kimberly shot a glare at Pete. "It took you long enough to get here. She'd be dead if she waited for you to come to her rescue."

Pete winced. *This* was the Kimberly Jackson he'd come to know and tolerate.

"Mother," Zoe protested. To Pete, she said, "I wouldn't be dead. Only very cold."

"All right. Someone tell me what happened."

Lauren moved to his side. "I was hiding upstairs at Scott's house when I called you. I tried to sneak out one of the windows when I saw Reese leaving with Zoe. That's when Scott came upstairs and caught me."

"The brother," Pete said.

"He questioned me about his son's claim that Zoe was a cop. I convinced him she really was his sister. While he called some of Reese's buddies to figure out where he might have taken her, I called Kimberly."

"Patsy was taking a shower," Kimberly said. "I left her a note telling her to wait at the hotel. I drove back to that man's house as fast as I could."

"'That man' meaning Scott," Lauren said, as if Pete might be confused.

He wasn't. Not about who was whom. But the idea of Florida-resident Kimberly speeding through uncleared Erie streets in a snowstorm painted a picture he couldn't block out.

"By the time Kimberly got there, Scott had a pretty good idea where his son had taken her, so we all piled in the Navigator—"

"Nice vehicle," Kimberly said. "I might have to get one."

Zoe rolled her eyes. "Like you need a monster SUV to get around Florida."

"Don't be insolent." Kimberly rung out the cloth and started on the other side of Zoe's face. "I saved your life, after all."

"Yes, you did."

Lauren cleared her throat and continued. "Scott had us drive to some abandoned warehouse. He worked there years ago and sometimes took Christopher—that's Reese Perkins' real name—to work with him. According to one of Christopher's buddies that Scott called, he still liked to go there to hang out and party with his buddies."

"Party," Kimberly scoffed. "Chains and shackles. I hate to think of what kind of partying they did with those."

"The police have a lot of questions for him," Lauren said.

"So do I," Pete said.

Baronick breezed into the cubicle. "Me too." He paused, taking in the group hovering around Zoe, his gaze settling on the patient. "You okay?"

Before she could answer, Kimberly said, "We're waiting on a doctor to read her x-rays. No one gets in a hurry around these places, do they?"

"Mother," Zoe scolded again. She looked at Baronick. "I'm fine."

"You're not fine," Kimberly snapped. "I warned you about searching for this brother of yours, but did you listen? No."

While the mother-and-daughter bickering rambled on, Baronick tipped his head at the hall. Pete followed and slid the glass door closed behind them.

"Christopher Lewis Nixon, a.k.a. Reese Perkins, has a broken nose and a bad attitude," the detective said. "He's not talking."

Pete imagined putting his hands around the neck of the man who'd terrorized Zoe. "He'll talk to me."

Baronick stopped him before he headed toward the guarded room down the hall. "You'll get your chance. That's what I came to tell you. They're willing to let us have our crack at him first. The

Erie Sheriff's Department will transport him to Monongahela County tomorrow morning." He glanced at his watch. "Make that *this* morning."

"Good." Pete glanced through the glass at the woman he planned to marry. The woman he'd come perilously close to losing.

TWENTY-SEVEN

Zoe watched Pete and Wayne through the glass door of her ER room. Both were in full blown cop mode. Deadly serious. Determined. And in Pete's case, barely concealed rage. The events of the last twenty-four hours flashed through her head. She looked at her mother, rinsing out a white washcloth in a plastic basin of water, now pink with Reese's blood. Her nephew's blood.

Sitting in a hospital bed, surrounded by medical equipment and bright lights, she realized how differently this night could've ended. Had it not been for Kimberly, Lauren, and Scott, she'd be sitting on a concrete floor, alone in the cold and the dark, chained and left to die a slow death.

The adrenalin on which she'd been running drained like water from a bathtub with the stopper pulled. All she wanted was to curl up in Pete's arms and sleep for a week.

The discussion in the hallway ended. Pete opened the sliding glass door and entered. Wayne followed. From Pete's dark frown, she knew something was going on. Before she could ask, her ER doctor appeared in the doorway.

"Excuse me, gentlemen." He edged them aside and took in the growing audience crowded into the cubicle. "I'm afraid there's a two-visitor limit."

Kimberly folded her arms. "I'm not going anywhere. I'm her mother."

Lauren moved toward the door. "I'll go to the waiting room."

Zoe stopped her. "Doctor, why don't you tell us what the tests show. Then I'll run them out. Otherwise, I'll have to repeat everything you said."

He looked at each of them before coming back to Zoe. "Are you sure? There are patient privacy regulations—"

"HIPAA," she interrupted. "I know. It's fine."

He gazed at her, apparently gauging whether she was under duress. Deciding she wasn't, he shrugged. "X-rays show no fractures. No dislocations. However, I can't rule out soft tissue damage, such as a torn rotator cuff. I strongly advise you make an appointment with an orthopedist as soon as possible."

"Does that mean I can get out of here?"

"Absolutely. The nurse will be in shortly with the paperwork and a script for some pain meds. Until then..." He made a point of eyeing each of her visitors. "Cull the herd."

The doctor turned to leave only to be met in the doorway by Scott.

"Cull means less, not more," the doctor called over his shoulder at Zoe before striding away.

No one else moved to leave. Pete and Wayne stood shoulder to shoulder like a human barricade.

Scott stayed in the doorway. "I'm sorry to bother you. Just wanted to see how you're doing."

Zoe stiffened, remembering how he'd let his son take her out of his house at gunpoint. But Scott had also led the rescue effort that saved her. She waved him in. "Doc gave me my marching orders."

Kimberly sidled closer to Zoe and placed a protective arm around her shoulders. "She's fine. No thanks to your son."

"Mother," Zoe protested. Scott looked remorseful enough without the Queen of Guilt piling more onto him. "Don't."

He shook his head. "No. She's right. I claim a large portion of the blame for what happened to you."

Kimberly softened. "You also deserve a large portion of the credit for saving my daughter's life. We'd never have found her without your help. Thank you."

Stunned, Zoe looked at her mother. Kimberly Jackson?

Expressing gratitude?

Pete continued to glare at him, his eyes growing colder by the moment. Scott took in the uniform with a sideways glance at Wayne in his dark suit and coat.

"Scott," Zoe said, hoping to cut through the ice. "This is Pete Adams. My fiancé. Pete, this is Scott Nixon." Her voice snagged in her throat. "My brother."

"Your fiancé?" Scott stiffened. "You're engaged to a cop?"

A memory of another "brother" using a similar tone regarding Pete's profession chilled her to the bone. "Yes. I am."

The two men glared at each other, Pete defensive, Scott distrustful.

Scott broke the staring contest, lowering his gaze. "Look. I know my son has issues. I've known for a long time. But he's not a killer."

"That remains to be seen," Pete said.

Scott's eyes came back up. "I know my boy. I know what he's capable of, and that does not include murder." He glanced at Zoe, the conflict clear on his face. "He's no angel. I know that too. But he wouldn't have let you die there."

She wasn't at all sure of that.

"In case you haven't heard," Pete said, "he'll be transported to Monongahela County later this morning."

Scott nodded. He met and held Zoe's gaze. "I guess I'll see you down there." He turned to Pete. "I won't let you railroad him. Cops have done it to us before. I'm hiring the best attorney I can find." Back to Zoe. "I'm glad you're okay." He lowered his face and left the cubicle.

The room fell silent except for the beeps and whistles of the monitors in neighboring cubbies. Zoe looked at each face surrounding her and settled on her mother. "You and Lauren should go. Patsy's probably climbing the walls over at the hotel."

Kimberly stood taller. "I'm not leaving without you."

Pete moved closer. "I'll stay with her until she's released." He tipped his head toward Wayne. "We'll make sure she gets to the hotel."

Kimberly folded her arms. "I'm her mother."

"I'm her fiancé." His attitude softened. "And I'm not letting her out of my sight."

Kimberly stared him down, her blue eyes narrowed. She inhaled deeply. And sneezed.

Lauren moved toward the door. "Come on, Kimberly. I'll buy you some cold medicine." She patted Wayne's arm. "You too, handsome. These two want to be alone."

The "handsome" remark raised Wayne's eyebrows and brought a smile to his lips. "Right behind you," he said to Lauren. To Pete, he said, "I'm gonna check on our prisoner. I'll meet you out front."

Kimberly, however, didn't trail after them.

"Mom, go."

"Are you sure?"

"I'm positive."

She eyed Pete. "You take care of my daughter. You hear?"

"Yes, ma'am."

Kimberly nodded reluctantly. "I'm going to offer Scott a ride home. He came with us and doesn't have a car."

Her mother's thoughtfulness startled Zoe. Pleasantly. "That'd be nice. Thanks."

She and Pete watched Kimberly leave. Once she was out of earshot, Pete raised an eyebrow at Zoe. "Who was that woman? And what has she done with your mother?"

Zoe snorted. "I've been asking myself the same thing. You should've seen her at the warehouse. She went all ninja on Reese. Kicked the crap out of him."

"I'm going to have to be nicer to her in the future."

"Me too." Zoe grew serious. "What's going on with the case? I saw you and Wayne talking in the hallway."

Pete's grin vanished, replaced with his patented poker face. "I'll tell you about it later. Right now, I want to get you out of here." He bent over, bringing his face close to hers. "By the way, I meant what I said to your mother." His lips slanted suggestively. "I'm not letting you out of my sight. Not tonight anyway."

Zoe's cheeks warmed. She lifted her mouth toward his. "Good."

Pete managed to get two hours of sleep. Maybe. And what little time he spent in bed, he'd been curled up with Zoe, holding on and trying not to think about how badly things could've gone.

At breakfast in the hotel restaurant, Kimberly demanded Zoe ride home with her. Zoe whispered to him she was too tired to argue. Louder, she agreed to travel with the women in the Navigator because she'd seen the backseats of police vehicles.

"They're disgusting," she said.

Pete gave in for three reasons. Four counting the fact that Zoe was right about the backseat of Baronick's car. One, the Erie roads were still a disaster and the Navigator would be a safer ride. Two, Pete intended to go directly to the Monongahela County Jail where Christopher "Reese Perkins" Nixon had been transported overnight. And three, Pete planned to use Baronick's computer on the drive to run a background check on Scott.

Road conditions were only a problem for the first third of the drive south. Below I-80, the snow vanished. By the time they arrived in Brunswick, the sky had brightened to a vivid blue, and Pete had learned Scott Nixon's only run-ins with law enforcement had to do with a handful of drunk and disorderlies several years back—nothing recent—and a handful of parking tickets, which he'd paid.

Inside County HQ, Pete found Seth and Abby, who had a folder tucked under one arm, waiting for them. "What are you two doing here?" Pete asked. "Who's holding down the fort back home?"

"Nate agreed to come in on his day off," Seth said.

"We got a call from the burglary task force about Perkins' arrest," Abby said.

"Christopher Nixon," Baronick corrected.

She made a face at her brother. "You know who I meant."

Pete ignored the sibling bickering. "The task force believes Perkins is part of the ring?"

"Definitely," Seth said. He glanced at his partner with a proud smile. "And Abby nailed the connection. Tell him."

"You can tell him."

"You were the one who put it together."

Pete folded his arms. "*Someone* tell me."

Seth faced Abby, waiting.

She nodded. "You know I've been kinda fixated on the diamond Zoe found at Horace's house and how it matched the pair of earrings stolen from an elderly lady."

The ones Pete suspected had found their way into Belinda Turner's possession. "Yeah?"

Abby opened the folder she'd been holding and pulled out a set of photos. She handed the first one to Pete. It was one of those inexpensive professional portraits of a smiling silver-haired woman wearing a pair of diamond earrings.

"That's the burglary victim I mentioned." Abby tapped the photo. "Those are the earrings she reported stolen." She handed Pete a second photo, a closeup evidence photo of one earring. "And that is what Reese Perkins—" She glared at her brother. "I mean Christopher Nixon—was wearing when taken into custody."

Pete studied the two photos. "I hate to burst your bubble, but don't all diamond earrings look the same?"

"A lot do. But two things stand out to me." Abby moved to Pete's shoulder to view the photos with him. Pointing, she said, "These are both yellow gold, and they both have a three-pronged mount rather than a four-pronged one."

"That doesn't make them a definitive match."

She stood firm. "No. But it doesn't rule out the possibility."

"Plus, Perkins only had one piercing," Seth said. "Convenient when you lose a stone from one of a pair."

"You have a spare," Pete mused.

"Exactly."

"Still not conclusive," Baronick said. When Abby glared at him again, he shrugged. "But a piece to the puzzle as we build our case. Good work, Officer."

The compliment clearly surprised her. "Thank you."

"Shall we go hear what Mr. Nixon has to say about the matter?" Baronick asked. To the eager young officers, he added, "Yes, you too. Although you'll have to watch from the observation room."

TWENTY-EIGHT

Pete led the way into Interview Room A where Nixon, a.k.a. Perkins, waited with his attorney. Anthony Imperatore stood to shake Pete's and Baronick's hands. A sign of mutual respect. And of warriors about to do battle in this small ring.

Pete studied the man who'd held Zoe captive. Prior to that moment, he'd only seen a mugshot—a slightly younger version wearing a bored expression. In the flesh, he appeared older but equally bored. He also looked worse for wear. His nose was taped, and dark circles blackened both eyes courtesy of Zoe's head-butt. Pete restrained a satisfied grin. *That's my girl.*

Baronick caught Pete's arm and directed him to the chair closer to the door. Pete glared at him. They both wanted to sit directly across from the suspect. Baronick probably feared Pete would reach over the table and choke the life out of their prisoner.

The detective knew Pete all too well. With a nod, Pete relinquished the prime position.

Baronick settled into the seat facing Nixon, placing an unopened folder on the table. "My name's Wayne. Do you prefer I call you Chris? Christopher?"

"Perkins," he said. "My name's Reese Perkins."

Pete kept his seat but shifted forward. "Do you think calling yourself by a different name gives you a fresh start? You've loaded your real name and your other aliases with more charges than they can hold, so you take on a new persona and think that's going to give you a free ride?"

Fire gleamed in Perkins' eyes, giving Pete a clue as to why he scared the Jennings brothers so badly.

"Chief Adams," Imperatore growled.

Baronick cut in with a too cheery, "Perkins it is." The detective shot a shut-up look at Pete before turning back to their suspect. "Are they treating you okay? Is it warm enough?" He made an exaggerated attempt at shivering. "I think it's cold in here. Do you think it's cold?"

"I'm fine."

"Good. Glad to hear it." Baronick crossed an ankle over one knee. "I understand you were there last Saturday when Horace Pavelka shot Dennis Culp."

"Yeah."

Pete watched the guy's expression. He wasn't going to be a talker.

"Can you tell me what you saw?" Baronick asked, his tone friendly, conversational.

"Dennis was being an asshole, so the dude in the car shot him."

"How was Dennis being an asshole?"

"He had a baseball bat and was using it. The dude in the car was protecting himself."

Nothing new or surprising. Except for Perkins' willingness to back up Horace's defense.

"Were you and Dennis friends?" Baronick asked.

"Nope."

"Yet you were with him and the Jennings brothers that morning."

Perkins smirked. "Everyone's gotta be somewhere."

"Exactly what was your relationship with Dennis and the Jenningses?"

Imperatore placed a hand on Perkins' forearm. "You don't have to answer that."

He pulled his arm free of the attorney's touch. "I wasn't planning on it."

"You said you weren't friends with Dennis. Were you acquaintances? Coworkers?" Baronick asked. "Total strangers?"

Perkins continued to smirk. In silence.

"Move it along, Detective," Imperatore said.

Baronick held up both hands, the epitome of innocence. "I'm just trying to determine how well your client knew these three men. They're all dead now." He looked at Perkins, feigning concern. "If I were you, I'd be afraid I was next."

Unless you were the one who killed them, Pete thought. Or at least two of them.

"I can take care of myself."

Before Pete could say it, Baronick pointed at Perkins' face. "Obviously. Who gave you that busted nose? Nice shiners, by the way."

Pete covered his mouth to hide his smile.

Perkins narrowed his blackened eyes.

"I understand you got clobbered by a *girl*," Baronick said smugly.

Perkins opened his mouth, but Imperatore cut him off. "Do not respond."

Baronick held up both hands. "Hey, man, I'm sorry. I overstepped." He tapped the file on the table. "Here's the thing. We believe Horace Pavelka got a taste for killing after he blasted Dennis Culp. It must've felt pretty good to finally get back at those who'd bullied him for all those years. I was hoping you could tell me about Grant and Stanley Jennings. About how they picked on poor Horace."

Perkins studied Baronick, trying to determine his level of sincerity perhaps. "They were assholes too."

"Did you know Horace?"

"Nope."

"But you did know Grant and Stanley."

"Didn't say that."

"You knew them enough to label them 'assholes.'"

Perkins shrugged one shoulder. "It doesn't take long to figure that out."

"Let me see if I have this straight. You don't know Horace

Pavelka. And you didn't know Dennis Culp or Grant or Stanley Jennings. Yet you were with all four of them last Saturday when Culp was killed. Is that correct?"

Perkins fixed him with the bored stare. "Yep."

"What were you doing?"

Imperatore tapped the table with a pen. "You've worn out that particular topic, Detective. My client witnessed a shooting. That's all."

"Okay." Baronick made a point of looking at the notes he kept on his phone. "Were you aware that the Jennings brothers had a stash of stolen merchandise in their basement?"

Pete watched for Perkins' impassive mask to crack. Instead, it hardened.

"Nope. Told you. I didn't know them."

"Well, let me enlighten you." Baronick slid the folder closer and withdrew a photo, looking at it but not showing it to Perkins. "In the last few months, there've been a string of burglaries around the county. Mostly electronics. Some firearms. A few pieces of jewelry."

Pete caught a glimpse of the 8x10 as Baronick turned it toward Perkins. An evidence photo taken in the Jennings brothers' basement showing some of their loot.

Perkins never blinked.

Baronick showed several other photos taken at the same time. Different angles. Different merchandise. The stone mask shielding Perkins' expressions softened to his original bored state.

"Ever seen any of this stuff?" the detective asked.

"Nope."

Baronick stacked the photos and tapped the edges on the table to neaten them before setting them aside. He pulled out another photo, angling it toward Pete. The elderly lady wearing the earrings. "How about this woman? Know her?"

For the first time, Pete noticed a chink in Perkins' armor. The twitch of an eyebrow.

"What's this about?" Imperatore asked.

Baronick ignored the attorney, continuing to address Perkins.

"No? You should. She brought her Cadillac into Bud Kramer's Garage for some mechanical issues about a month ago."

It was Pete's turn to blink. When had Baronick found *that* out?

The detective placed the photo on the table in front of Perkins and pulled out another. "This," he said, "is a photo of your personal property, taken when you were arrested last night." Baronick placed it on the table next to the photo of the burglary victim. "Nice earring." He leaned forward, bracing his elbows on the table. "Yellow gold. Three-pronged. Exactly like the pair our burglary victim is wearing."

"Do not say anything," Imperatore ordered.

Pete suspected he needn't have bothered. Perkins was smart. Too smart to incriminate himself.

"We're done here," Imperatore added.

Pete stood, blocking the door. "I don't think so. We haven't even started discussing last night when your client kidnapped my fiancée."

Perkins' eyes widened for a moment. Then the smirk returned. He hadn't known about the relationship between Zoe and Pete.

Imperatore closed his briefcase and rose. "And we aren't going to. Questions relating to the alleged events which may or may not have taken place yesterday will be dealt with in Erie County at a later date. Unless, of course, you want to discuss our intent to file assault charges against Ms. Chambers and her mother."

Baronick moved to throw an arm in front of Pete. "That would make for an interesting day in court, Counselor," the detective said.

Imperatore motioned Perkins to his feet and guided him past Pete to the door. Perkins held Pete's gaze, looking even more smug, until the door opened.

Perkins started out, then paused. He turned toward Baronick. "You're right about one thing." The attorney protested, but Perkins ignored him. "Horace Pavelka is the man you want. A lifetime of being bullied will eventually push a man over the edge."

* * *

Her right arm in a sling zipped inside her Carhartt barn jacket, Zoe leaned against her horse, breathing in his scent and the sweet smells of hay and grain. She'd always found barn aromas to be soothing but never so much as today. She didn't even need the pain meds the Erie doctor had prescribed.

Lauren appeared at the stall door. "Are you okay?"

"Yeah." Zoe stroked the thick winter haircoat on his neck, working the fingers of her left hand deep into the warmth. After the last couple of days, she was back where she felt safe and grounded.

"Patsy and your mom are ready to go."

Despite her head cold, Kimberly had booked a new flight to Florida on the drive home from Erie. Zoe felt sorry for the other passengers, doomed to the recycled air spreading the germs. She was sure she, Patsy, and Lauren would be coming down with it too. Thanks, Mom.

The plan was for Patsy to drop Zoe and Lauren at Pete's and then take Kimberly to the airport. But Pete wouldn't be home, and Zoe needed more equine therapy. "Can you do me a favor?"

"Considering I feel responsible for getting you into this mess, I suppose I owe you one."

"Don't buy into my mother's guilt trip. I don't blame you for any of it."

"What do you need me to do?"

"I want to stay and putter in the barn a while. Would you mind picking up your car at Pete's and coming back to get me?"

Lauren smiled. "No problem. But you should still say goodbye to your mom."

"I'll be right there."

"Don't be long," Lauren said and ducked out of the barn.

Zoe leaned against Windstar, her eyes closed, and breathed deeply. Then she patted the horse on his sorrel rump and left him munching his hay. Outside, the rain had stopped. Apparently, Monongahela County hadn't seen a single flake of the snow that buried Erie and Clarion. Patsy and Lauren waited beside the

Navigator.

Patsy aimed a thumb at the farmhouse. "Kimberly wants to talk to you before we go."

Zoe sighed. Great. Mother probably wanted to demand she never contact Scott again.

Kimberly stood in the kitchen, looking considerably less put together than three days ago, when she'd arrived. She wore the same winter white fur coat, but her hair hung loose around her shoulders. And her red nose matched her reddened eyes.

"I'm sorry you missed your first flight home," Zoe said.

"I'm not."

The response, especially the soft tone, startled Zoe until she realized the meaning behind the words. If Kimberly hadn't been there last night... "No, I guess I'm not either."

She sniffled into a tissue. "I wanted to speak with you in private before I left. About the wedding."

"Oh." Zoe shoved her left hand into her barn jacket's pocket. How could she refuse her mother's generous if misguided offer after what she'd done? "About that." Zoe inhaled, preparing to suck it up and plan a Floridian wedding.

"You should have the wedding *you* want. Not the one I want." Kimberly met her gaze. "I'll help any way you want me to. But you should have the ceremony here."

Zoe stared at her mother, aghast. "What kind of cold meds are you on?"

The acquiescence vanished. "Don't be impudent."

Ah. There she was. Zoe lowered her face, attempting to hide her smile.

"I'm serious. I was wrong to make plans without your input."

Zoe looked at her. Admitting she was wrong didn't come naturally to Kimberly. "Thanks." Zoe almost caved. Pictured a massive wedding in Florida with all of her mother's friends and none of her own. "How about we compromise?"

Kimberly hiked a questioning eyebrow.

"I'll have to talk it over with Pete first, but how about we have our small wedding here and then have a reception in Florida?"

An eager smile spread across Kimberly's face. "At the Vinoy?"

"Wherever you want."

"I like that idea."

Zoe held up a finger. "But let me get Pete on board before you make any reservations."

"Deal." Kimberly closed the distance between them and drew Zoe into an awkward and careful hug. "I better go. I don't want to miss another flight."

Zoe watched her mother head for the door. "Mom?"

Kimberly turned to face her. "Yes?"

"About last night. Thank you."

Kimberly's eyes glistened. Her lips parted, but words didn't come.

"You've never gone all mother bear like that for me before."

Her mother pressed the tissue to her nose and dabbed the corner of each eye before bringing her gaze back to Zoe. "You've never needed me before."

Zoe used the metal spring curry comb lefthanded on Windstar's thick coat. The grooming process was more for her benefit than his. She knew as soon as she turned him out, he'd take great pleasure in rolling in the mud, replacing all the dirt she raked from him.

The silence out here on the farm soothed her soul. No neighborhood kids shouting on the street. No traffic noise. Only the sounds of the other three horses in their stalls, munching hay, and the whisper of the wind rattling a loose board on the barn's siding.

Her mind wandered through a variety of subjects. Her truck—would it be ready? She needed to call Melvin Quinn at the garage to find out. But she didn't have a phone, thanks to Reese Perkins.

She shook her head. The last thing she wanted to think about right now was him.

What day was this? Friday. She counted. Less than four days until the election. She needed to get out and campaign for Franklin. One last push. If Dr. Charles Davis won the coroner's position, she'd have to give up her job there—a job she'd come to love despite the gore and the smell.

A distant rumble grew louder. A car on the road out front. She listened as the vehicle slowed. The sound of tires on rutted blacktop changed to the sound of tires on gravel.

Lauren made good time.

Zoe set down the curry and walked to the barn door. The car coming into her driveway wasn't Lauren's gray Chevy. It was a dark Ford compact that Zoe didn't recognize. The sun breaking through the clouds reflected on the windshield blocking her view of the driver.

The car stopped in front of her. Both the driver's and passenger's doors opened. And Belinda and Horace stepped out.

"Oh my gosh." Zoe strode toward them. "I'm so glad to see you."

TWENTY-NINE

Pete sent Seth and Abby back to Vance Township. He needed to get back there as well, but Perkins' parting words sat on his gut like a sack of lead. "Did your guys follow up on the fellow who helped Belinda Turner escape?"

"You're reading my mind," Baronick said.

A scary thought.

He gestured for Pete to follow him down the hall, into the detectives' division, and to a cubicle in one corner. "Chief Pete Adams, meet Detective Rick Stein." After the handshakes, Baronick said, "Update us on the Turner/Pavelka investigation. I know you talked to the guy Kissell tracked down at the bar."

"Yes, sir, I did. He claims he'd never met Belinda Turner before and had no idea she was evading the cops. She told him she needed a ride to visit a sick friend. He dropped her off at the front door of the hospital and drove away. Didn't see if she went inside or not."

"What about security cameras?" Pete asked.

"Footage shows she stood at the entrance for a few minutes and then walked away without going inside. I also checked with the front desk. Horace Pavelka is not a patient."

"He must not be too far away though," Baronick said. "She was on foot."

"Not for long." Stein thumbed through some papers on his desk and came up with a computer printout from Econo Drive, a local car rental place about six blocks from the hospital. He handed the sheet of paper to Baronick. "She leased a car, a Ford Fiesta.

We've put out a BOLO on it, but that's where her trail ends."

"What about GPS tracking?" Pete asked.

Stein shook his head. "Econo Drive doesn't have tracking equipment installed on their vehicles."

Pete growled. "So we're back at square one."

"Square two," Baronick said. "We know the make, model, and license number of the car she's driving. We'll find her. If we get really lucky, Pavelka will be with her when we do."

Pete's phone rang. His station's number came up on the screen.

"You need to get back here," Nancy said when he answered. "Now."

He didn't like the sound of her voice. "What's going on?"

"Zoe just walked in with Horace Pavelka and Belinda Turner."

Seth and Abby were probably halfway between Brunswick and Vance Township. "Is Nate there?"

"He's dealing with a traffic accident in Elm Grove."

Dammit. That meant Nancy was alone at the station with them. "Do not let them leave." Pete broke into a run toward the door. "I'll be there in fifteen minutes."

Baronick was on his heels. "What's wrong?"

Pete hit the door and kept going, not waiting for the detective but aware he was right behind him. "You can cancel the BOLO. Pavelka and Turner are at my station. With Zoe."

Seth and Abby's cruiser was already parked at the station when Pete screeched into the lot. Baronick in his Challenger wheeled in right behind him.

Pete slammed through the front door, nearly ripping the bells from their tethers. "Where are they?" he asked Nancy, who sat at her desk looking entirely too calm.

"In the conference room."

He covered the distance in three long strides.

Zoe sat at the long table, facing the door. The fugitives sat side by side across from her. Seth and Abby stood next to them. They all turned when Pete and Baronick entered. Unlike the irrational mental picture Pete had battled all the way from Brunswick, Zoe didn't look like a hostage. And Belinda and Horace appeared exhausted and scared instead of hostile.

Zoe must have seen Pete's uncertainty. She stood and nodded toward the couple. "They're turning themselves in. And you need to hear what they have to say."

Pete dismissed his younger officers, who mumbled something about being in the bullpen working on reports if he needed them.

Normally, Pete would have split up the pair of fugitives and interviewed them separately. In this case, they'd already been together on and off for days and had had plenty of time to coordinate their stories. He circled to Zoe's side. "You should leave," he told her.

She grinned. "Not happening."

He'd anticipated the response and moved to her side. "You're too invested in this case," he whispered.

"They turned themselves in to me. It's a homicide case. I'm deputy coroner."

"I don't see a dead body in here. Do you?"

Her grin became a stony glare. "I'm not leaving."

Pete growled a sigh.

She did at least relinquish her chair to him, claiming a seat against the wall. Baronick closed the door behind him and positioned himself at the head of the table.

"Tell them what you told me," Zoe said to the pair.

Belinda and Horace looked at each other. When he didn't speak, she turned her gaze to Baronick, then to Pete. "Horace didn't kill anyone."

Pete held up a silencing hand. "You should know you have the right to remain silent—"

"We know our rights," Belinda said. "We don't want an attorney. We just want you to know the truth."

"All right." Pete opened his notebook and clicked his pen. He looked at Horace. "What happened Monday at your house?"

Horace opened his mouth. Closed it again. And turned to Belinda. She nodded at him. He faced Pete. "I saw Grant and Stanley coming for me and ran. I climbed the path behind my house to the park and waited for them to leave. I thought if they believed no one was home, they'd go away. But then I heard a gunshot. I freaked out. After a while I sneaked back down the path to my house to see if they were still there and saw you. I didn't know what happened, but I knew the Jennings brothers were after me. And whatever happened at my house, *you* would think I was the one who did it. So I went back to the park and called Belinda."

"I picked him up," she said. "At first, we rode around. We didn't know who'd been shot. While I drove, Horace made phone calls and checked social media, but nothing had been posted yet. I wanted him to turn himself in. I mean, he didn't do anything. But he was terrified."

And still was, if Pete was any judge. Horace kept his head lowered, shoulders hunched, as Belinda spoke.

"He said he wanted time to think. I remembered my family's old fishing camp near Confluence. We went there to regroup and try to find out what happened. Except we didn't have any cell service, so we went into town to a diner that has Wi-Fi."

The Turkey Foot Café with the best pie around. Pete recalled what the waitress had told him.

"That's when we learned a man had been killed," Belinda said. "They didn't say if it was Grant or Stanley, but what they did show was our photos. We were named as 'persons of interest.'" She made air quotes.

Horace slouched deeper into the chair.

Belinda reached over and took his hand. "Horace lost it. He was terrified someone might have seen the news and would turn us in, so we left and went to the cabin."

"*They booked it outta here like their hair was on fire,*" the waitress had said.

Belinda brought her eyes back to Pete. "I pleaded with Horace to turn himself in to you. You were so kind to him—to us—when you drove him home from jail that morning. But he was totally freaked out. They were saying he was a murder suspect. And if the victim was either Stanley or Grant, the other one would be even more angry."

"And I'd already killed once." Horace finally lifted his face, his eyes gleaming. "Shooting Dennis was self-defense, but no way would anyone believe I was innocent this time."

Pete glanced at Baronick, who raised an eyebrow at him. Horace had a good point.

Horace must've caught the silent communication. "I refused to come back then. Maybe I shouldn't have come back now either."

"No," Belinda said. "This is the right thing. You did nothing wrong."

"They don't believe me."

Zoe rolled her chair up to the table beside Pete. "I believe you, Horace."

Pete shot a look at her. *Be quiet.* To Horace, he asked, "Why'd you leave the cabin?"

Horace glared at Belinda. "Because she admitted Stanley knew about it. The cops were after us and Stanley Jennings knew exactly where she'd take me. So I smashed my phone." He met Pete's gaze. "I know you guys can track those things. I wanted her to smash hers too, but she wouldn't."

Pete made a note of the tone Horace used when referring to Belinda. The veneer of their Bonnie and Clyde bond was cracking.

"I agreed to take the battery out of mine," Belinda protested. "But I didn't think we should be completely unable to access the real world."

"Where'd you go?" Pete asked.

"A cheap motel near Uniontown," Horace said. "I paid cash. I planned to lay low for a while and see what happened." He glanced at Pete. "See if you guys caught the real killer."

"Any idea who that might be?" Baronick asked.

"None."

The detective came forward, resting his arms on the table, leaning closer to Horace. "Grant Jennings was killed in *your* house.

With *your* gun. And you have no idea who did it?"

Horace's eyes widened. "My gun?"

"You own a .38 revolver, right?"

"Yes." His voice was little more than a childish squeak.

"If you didn't shoot Grant, who else knew about your gun?"

What little color was left in Horace's face drained. Pete could almost hear the thud of pieces falling into place inside the guy's head. Slowly, Horace turned to look at Belinda. "She did."

Zoe waited in the hallway with Wayne while Pete moved Belinda to the interrogation room.

"What are you thinking?" she asked the detective.

"I think the romance is dying a slow death. Now that we've split them up, I expect each to start pointing the finger at the other."

Pete approached them, having closed the door on Belinda. "And somewhere between the two stories lies the truth." Fixing his icy blues on Zoe, he said, "What the hell happened? Why did they surrender to you?"

"I was at the farm when they pulled in. Belinda'd been trying to get Horace to turn himself in, but he didn't trust the cops. She finally convinced him to come to me." Zoe massaged her aching right shoulder. "I know Horace isn't a killer." She couldn't shake her memory of that night all those years ago when he'd come to her rescue.

"I don't think he is either."

Wayne crossed his arms. "What are you talking about? Might I remind you about Dennis Culp? Horace Pavelka freely admits he blasted the guy with a shotgun that he kept conveniently stashed in his car."

Zoe faced Wayne, mirroring his stance. "He's the victim of a lifetime of bullying. Everyone agrees Dennis' homicide was self-defense."

"Not everyone," Wayne muttered.

"I've known Horace most of my life. I've seen Dennis Culp in action. If you look up bully in the dictionary, you'll find a picture of Dennis."

"I don't doubt that. But Pavelka started carrying a shotgun in his car—"

"For protection."

Wayne shook off her interruption. "Or to take the easy way out of his problems. He anticipated Culp's continued heckling—"

"Heckling?" Zoe heard her voice getting louder and didn't care. "Dennis came after him with a baseball bat."

"He anticipated Culp's continued *harassment*," Wayne said, his own volume ratcheting up, "and decided to put an end to it by purchasing and carrying a firearm. *Two* firearms. In my book, that sounds a lot like premeditation."

Zoe turned to Pete for backup, but he was scowling into space. She jabbed him with her good arm, and he flinched. "Help me out here," she said.

He looked at her, then at Wayne. "I don't buy Horace as a murderer."

She shot a triumphant look at the detective.

"He's not smart enough," Pete continued. "But the woman? I can see her as the brains behind the organization."

"What?" Zoe asked.

"The theft ring."

"What theft ring?" She felt like she'd stepped out of the movie to get more popcorn and missed a vital scene.

"You believe Belinda Turner's the leader?" Wayne asked.

Zoe looked at him. Clearly, she was the only confused one around here.

"We've got Horace, Belinda, Reese Perkins a.k.a. Christopher Nixon."

At the mention of her nephew's name, the ache in Zoe's heart threatened to crush her.

Pete shot an apologetic glance at her. "Dennis Culp and the Jennings brothers," he continued. "I'd been thinking Perkins was the brains, but now I think he's the muscle. Belinda's the ringleader and the others were the worker bees. Expendable worker bees."

Wayne gave a devilish grin. "Belinda's the queen bee."

"More like a black widow."

"You're both out of your minds," Zoe said. She didn't know Belinda well but couldn't picture Horace's girlfriend leading a crime ring.

Pete faced her. "Think about it. She knew where Horace kept his handgun. She could've killed Grant and still managed to pick Horace up at the park. She was found with Stanley, covered in his blood."

"And we know whoever killed Stanley was someone he trusted," Wayne said. "Someone he'd allow to get in close physical proximity to him."

"Not to mention, she had a history with him," Pete added.

Wayne nodded, apparently liking the way the puzzle was coming together. "Belinda was smart enough to elude the police officers surveilling her house."

"Have you forgotten?" Zoe said. "Belinda's the one who talked Horace into turning himself in."

"She probably intended to throw Horace to the wolves," Pete said, "and then walk away as the poor innocent, trusting girlfriend."

Wayne stopped nodding. "I don't know. Something still doesn't feel right."

"I know," Pete said. He started toward the conference room where Horace waited. "Let's go get some answers."

Wayne caught Pete's arm. "No. You question Belinda Turner. I'll take Pavelka. You're too soft on him."

Pete glared at the detective. "All right." He looked at Zoe. "Tell Nancy to give you a lift home."

"No way." She eyed Wayne. "I'm going with you. Pete might be too soft on Horace, but I intend to make sure you don't go too hard on him."

THIRTY

Tears streaked Belinda's face when Pete entered the interrogation room. She shot him a fierce, blaming look. Before closing the door, he shouted toward the front of the station. "Nancy. Bring me a box of tissues."

He reminded Belinda of her rights—she still said she didn't need a lawyer—and pointed out the conversation was being recorded. She shrugged.

Nancy knocked at the door and left the requested tissues with Pete, who plunked them on the table in front of his suspect. Belinda stared at them but didn't move.

"It's okay," Pete said. "You've had a rough few days. You're entitled to a few tears."

Her angry glare softened. She plucked a tissue from the box and wiped her eyes.

Pete started with a softball. "How long have you and Horace been seeing each other?"

"Almost three months." She sniffled. "I can't believe he would think I shot Grant."

"I didn't hear him say that." Pete smiled at her. He needed her to trust him. To keep talking. "I think Horace was feeling cornered. Desperate."

"So he throws me under the bus?" She chuffed a laugh. "Nice."

"But you did know where he kept his gun?"

She hunched her shoulders, suddenly very interested in the tissue clenched in her hands.

Rather than risk having her invoke her right to an attorney,

Pete decided to take a different route. "Tell me about Reese Perkins."

This brought her attention back to Pete. "I've already told you. I only know him through Stanley."

"Do you have any idea how long he and Stanley were friends?" Pete used the word loosely.

Belinda pondered the question. "Stanley and I started dating in June. I got the impression he and Reese hadn't known each other all that long before that. Maybe a couple months, more or less."

Pete jotted a note to check on how long Perkins had been employed at Bud Kramer's Garage. "Did Stanley ever mention how they met?"

"No."

"What'd they do together?"

She scowled. "I don't understand."

"Were they drinking buddies? Did they watch sports together?" When Belinda continued to look puzzled, Pete grinned. "Were they gamers?"

"Stanley wasn't into video games. Why are you asking me about Reese?"

"Because we have him in custody for kidnapping and he isn't talking. I was hoping you might shed some light on him."

Her face relaxed. "I didn't get the impression Reese and Stanley—or Grant for that matter—socialized. Reese never talked much. Especially to me. And I sure didn't try to strike up a conversation with him. If they were talking when I walked in, he'd shut up." Her forehead creased. "I only overheard them once. They were discussing work."

"What kind of work?"

"I don't know. Like I said, they shut up as soon as they saw me. But I remember Reese saying something about *the job*. Maybe Stanley and Grant were using him on one of their construction projects."

Pete studied her wide blue eyes. She didn't strike him as a hardened criminal trying to conceal her own involvement in a theft ring. But then again, that innocent act could be a finely-honed skill, one which blended perfectly with her girl-next-door looks.

He thought about the diamond earring Reese had been wearing. The one that matched the pair reported stolen. Maybe those weren't the only ill-gotten gains these guys had decided to keep for themselves.

"Did Stanley ever buy you any expensive gifts?"

The question brought a puzzled scowl. "Heck no."

"No jewelry?"

"You have to be kidding me. Stanley? He borrowed money off me and never repaid it. He sure didn't buy me jewelry."

Pete scribbled a note. "How much money?"

She caught his meaning and stiffened, shaking her head. "Not enough to kill him over, if that's what you mean."

"How much?" he repeated.

"A hundred bucks."

"Did he say what it was for?"

"Stanley owed his bookie. I told you he wasn't a gamer, but he was into sports betting." She made a face. "He just wasn't very good at it."

"You really should have an attorney present," Zoe told Horace.

The white-hot glare Wayne aimed her way was impossible to miss even with Zoe focused on the bullying victim.

"I don't need an attorney." Horace's rounded shoulders, bowed head, and weak voice told her all the fight had drained out of him.

"That's right." Wayne's clipped words may have been in response to Horace but were aimed at Zoe. When she looked at the detective, he mouthed, "be quiet," at her and pointed his pen toward the far end of the long table.

Instead, she plopped into the chair next to Horace. If he wouldn't accept a legal advocate, she'd make darned sure Wayne didn't add to the accumulated history of bullying.

The detective, a notepad in front of him, faced Horace and softened his voice. "Tell me about Belinda. How long have you known her?"

Horace kept his hands in his lap, but Zoe noticed him counting on his fingers. "Two months, three weeks and five days."

Wayne's eyebrows raised. "Wow. That's precise."

"I'm a baker. I deal in measurements."

"How'd you meet her?"

A smile crossed Horace's lips. "She came into the bakery where I work and asked me to have coffee. I couldn't believe this cute girl was interested in me. She said she wanted to apologize for never stepping in when Stanley and Grant harassed me." He looked up at Wayne. "She used to date Stanley."

"So you'd actually met her before that coffee date."

"No. I'd seen her with Stanley. But I'd never *met* her."

"Did she break up with him before or after you two started going out?"

"Before." Horace's eyes narrowed. "I think."

Wayne remained silent, waiting for a more definitive answer.

"I know she wasn't happy with him. And not only because of how he treated me. I always assumed she'd ended things with him before she asked me out."

"You've only known this girl for three months, yet you seem to trust her pretty implicitly."

"Yeah." But Horace added an uptick at the end of the word. A touch of doubt.

If Zoe picked up on it, she knew Wayne did as well.

"You showed her where you kept your .38."

"Those guys...Dennis Culp and Stanley and Grant...were spending more and more time in my neighborhood. I swear they were stalking me. That incident with the baseball bat last weekend wasn't the first. I was afraid."

"For yourself."

"And for Belinda. I mean, she'd left Stanley for me. I feared he'd hurt her. So I showed her where I kept my gun."

"Where was that?"

"In a drawer in my kitchen."

"And you kept it loaded?"

"No. But I kept the bullets in the same drawer."

"Did you tell anyone else where you kept it?"

"No."

Wayne made a note. "Tell me what transpired on Monday after Chief Adams left you at your home."

"Belinda stayed for a few minutes and then took off—"

"You'd only been home from jail for a matter of minutes before she left?"

"She said she had some errands to run. I told her to go. All I wanted was a hot shower and a long nap."

"Understandable," Wayne said. "Go on."

"I was still tidying the kitchen when I heard a noise outside. It was Grant and Stanley's truck pulling up to my house. I started freaking out."

Zoe placed a hand on Horace's forearm. "You shouldn't talk to him without an attorney."

Wayne glowered at her. "Out," he ordered, jerking a thumb toward the door.

"No," Horace said. "I don't want an attorney, but I do want Zoe to stay." He gave her a weak smile.

Wayne's jaw clenched so hard, the muscle in his cheek jumped. "Fine. But I don't want to hear a word from you," he said to Zoe. "Horace, you were saying?"

"I was trying to figure out what to do when my neighbor lady came to my back door."

"What neighbor lady?"

"Jan Gates. She lives next door and has always kept an eye out for me."

"Why didn't you mention her before?"

"I didn't think it was important."

Wayne growled a sigh. "Then what happened?"

"Jan said she knew I wasn't up for another confrontation with those guys and told me to go up to the park and wait. She said she'd call me when the coast was clear."

"And did you?"

"Yeah. Except she never called. When I heard the gunshot, I was afraid it was her that got killed. I waited and waited to hear from her. I even tried calling her but got no answer. Finally, I sneaked down to my house. That's when I saw Chief Adams going in my kitchen door. I panicked. I went back to the park and called Belinda to come get me."

Before Wayne could ask his next question, Zoe had one. "What did your neighbor lady do after she told you to go to the park?"

Instead of ordering Zoe to shut up or leave, Wayne looked at Horace.

Horace gave her a puzzled scowl. "She walked with me to the base of the trail and then continued on to her house. I assume she went home."

Stanley Jennings was into gambling? This made for an interesting wrinkle. "Did he mention who his bookie was?" Pete asked.

"Not to me," Belinda said.

Pete scribbled *check with local sports-betting operations* in his notebook. Then he locked his gaze on hers. Time to get back to his original line of questions. "Why did Horace show you where he kept his gun?"

She looked away. "He was terrified those guys would try something."

"And by 'those guys,' you mean..."

"Stanley. Grant. Dennis. And Reese." She swallowed. "He wanted me to be able to protect myself if something happened while he wasn't around."

"Did you spend much time at his house alone?"

"Not a lot. I have a key. Sometimes I'd arrive before Horace did. Or I'd stay there while he ran out to get something at the store. Stuff like that."

"Anyone else know where he kept the gun?"

"I don't know."

Pete thumbed through his notepad. "Let's talk about Monday.

You were at his house when I brought Horace home from jail."

"Yes. Like I said, I have a key."

"How long did you stay after I left?"

"Not long. I had some shopping to do and planned to come back later in the afternoon, after Horace had a chance to shower and get some rest. He didn't sleep well in jail."

"I left around 11:25. So you left...when? Eleven thirty?"

"Probably closer to 11:35."

Pete checked his notes. Grant was seen entering the house around eleven forty-five. "Sounds like you barely missed the excitement."

She glared at him. Her lower lip trembled as if she wanted to say something but decided against it.

"Tell me what happened after you left."

"I started toward Brunswick. I wasn't quite there yet when my phone rang. It was Horace, and he was hysterical. Said he thought someone got shot at his house and could I come get him."

"He *thought* someone got shot?"

Belinda folded and refolded her tissue. "That's what he said."

"Did he tell you who he thought was the victim?"

She scowled, thinking. "He didn't know. He said Grant and Stanley had come to his house. And he snuck out, because he was sure they were going to get even for him shooting Dennis. He was waiting at the park above his house when he heard the gunshot. He told me he called his neighbor to find out what was going on, but she didn't answer, so he went back down the hill and saw the cops." Belinda met Pete's gaze. "You. He saw you. That's when he called me to come pick him up."

"At the park."

"Yeah."

Pete replayed her words. "Did you say he called his neighbor?"

"Yeah. The woman next door. Her name's Jan. She keeps an eye on him." A hint of a smile played across Belinda's face. "She's like a mother hen where Horace is concerned, so I tolerate her nosiness. At first, he was afraid she was the one who got shot."

A sharp knock on the interrogation room's door stopped Pete

from asking his next question. "Excuse me." He opened the door to find Zoe and stepped out into the hallway.

"Someone else was at Horace's house Monday morning," she said. "His neighbor, Jan Gates."

"She was there? Belinda said Horace called her."

"Later, yeah. But Jan came to his door when she saw the Jennings brothers outside. She's the one who told him to hide at the park. She walked him to the footpath, then went back to her house."

"Interesting." Jan had neglected to mention that part when Pete had questioned her.

Zoe's baby blues sparkled. "I have a feeling she might know what happened that morning."

THIRTY-ONE

"What do you want?" Jan asked when she opened her door to Pete. "No one's been shot around here today."

"Glad to hear it. Mind if I come in?"

"Actually, I do. I have an appointment, and I'm already late."

Pete noticed she was better dressed—dark jeans, a clean sweater, and a cardigan without holes—than during his two recent visits, and her hair had been gathered in a neat ponytail. "It'll only take a minute. I have a few follow-up questions regarding Grant Jennings' death."

She mulled over the request before stepping to the side.

The interior of the house looked no different than it had days ago with the exception of a leather purse big enough to hold one of Zoe's cats slouched on the table next to the door.

As in his previous visits, Jan didn't offer him a seat. He followed her into the dingy living room where she wrapped her cardigan more snuggly around her and turned to face him. "Ask your questions."

"You said you heard the Jennings brothers' truck outside around eleven forty-five, correct?"

"Sounds about right."

"Then what happened?"

"I heard a gunshot and a few minutes later, the truck took off."

"What about before the gunshot?"

Her eyes shifted to the side and quickly came back to his. "I don't know. I was watching my show on TV."

"Really? Horace said you knocked on his door and warned

him."

"Did I? My memory's not so good."

"Jan, there's nothing wrong with your memory." Pete fixed her with a don't-bullshit-me look. "Why'd you go next door?"

She glared at him. "Because I like the guy. He's a little stupid but sweet. I know what it's like to get beat up. I didn't wanna see him get hurt again."

"Then tell me what happened. All of it."

Jan huffed. "Fine. I knocked on Horace's door. Turns out, he'd already seen the truck out front and was in a panic. I told him to leave. Go up the path to the park and stay there until they left."

"Did you tell him you'd call him when that happened?"

"Maybe. I guess so."

"And did you?"

"I tried. The call didn't go through. Damned unreliable cell service."

"What'd you do then? After you told Horace to leave."

"I went back to my house to keep an eye on the truck. Heard the gunshot. Then the truck left."

"That's all?"

"Yep."

"Do you see my problem with your story?"

Her flinty eyes narrowed. "What?"

"Who fired the gun?"

She didn't offer a response.

"You told Horace to leave. You said you saw one of the brothers go inside while the other stayed in the truck."

"Yeah," she said, making it sound like a question.

"Who else was inside that house?"

"Don't know."

"You sure you didn't see anyone else?"

She thought about it. "The girlfriend had been there earlier. I didn't see her leave."

"You said her car was gone."

Jan met Pete's gaze, her eyes brighter than he'd ever seen

them. "It was. But who's to say she didn't park it down the road and sneak back?"

Exactly what Pete had been thinking. "But you didn't notice it?"

"No. Wasn't looking." Somewhere in the room, a phone rang. Jan grunted. "Excuse me." She crossed to the handbag next to the door and rummaged through it.

Pete kept coming back to Belinda Turner. All girl-next door, fresh-faced innocence. And yet, she'd been present and covered in blood when Stanley'd been shot. She may have said she was trying to save him, but her car was also buried in the mud. Otherwise, she'd have been long gone.

"I have to take this." Jan pointed at the phone in her hand, interrupting Pete's rumination.

He acknowledged her with a wave. She shuffled into the other room.

Belinda was savvy enough to evade the police officers watching her house. Smart enough to con a bar patron to give her a lift to visit her "friend" at the hospital. Pete could easily picture her batting those dark lashes framing those blue eyes.

Girl-next-door innocence.

She had the means to kill Grant. She knew where Horace kept his gun. Opportunity? What if she'd seen the Jennings brothers' truck as she was leaving? She could've turned around or merely pulled over and parked, depending on where she encountered them. A regular presence in the neighborhood, she wouldn't have drawn attention as she walked to Horace's house.

Motive? The theft ring. Maybe the brothers were demanding more of the cut. Or maybe Belinda no longer wanted to split the take five ways. Or six. Was Horace also part of it?

Dennis was the first victim. Maybe his bullying was a convenient excuse for Horace to eliminate one of the partners. After that, Belinda did the math and determined a three-way split amounted to a lot more income than a six-way one.

Reese Perkins could confirm Pete's suspicions. If they could get him to talk. But if Pete could definitively place Belinda in the vicinity when Grant was killed, he'd have enough pieces of the puzzle to satisfy the DA and press charges.

Jan hadn't seen her. But what about other neighbors? Someone in Langstown must've seen Belinda and didn't realize they held a vital piece of information.

Pete looked toward the doorway where Jan had disappeared. He could hear her muffled voice as she talked on her phone. "I'm going to question your neighbors," he called to her. "Thanks for your help."

He headed for the front door. As he closed his fingers around the knob, he glanced at the purse, gaping open, its contents jumbled from Jan's digging for her phone. A large plastic baggie caught his eye. More precisely, the sparkle of its contents.

He paused. Glanced toward the other room. No sign of Jan. He gingerly opened the purse further. The baggie contained a tangle of gold and silver chains. Jewelry. A few items with gems. He withdrew a handkerchief from his pocket and used it to pinch a corner of the baggie and heft it out for a better look. Assorted necklaces, earrings, bracelets, and broaches—good quality if he was any judge—filled the gallon-sized bag. A chill started at the base of his spine.

What was Jan Gates doing with that much expensive jewelry?

Perhaps she was simply taking some old family pieces to one of those stores that buy gold.

Pete shifted the bag in his hand, rolling the contents around inside the plastic. And spotted the earring. A gold post with empty prongs where a diamond might have once been. The chill froze his infamous—and unreliable—gut.

"It's a damned shame you're so nosy," came Jan's flat voice from behind him.

He turned. Slowly.

Jan Gates stood in the doorway to the other room, her phone in one hand.

And a small semi-automatic in the other.

Zoe stalked the police station's hallway, from Pete's office door to the front vestibule and back. Something about Horace's story troubled her. Not his claim of innocence. She'd never doubted that. But she couldn't quite grasp what nagged at her.

With Pete gone to speak to the neighbor lady, Wayne had moved to the interrogation room to further question Belinda and had left orders for Zoe to stay out of the conference room, away from Horace.

So she paced. After the sixth or seventh lap, the troublesome issue that was stuck in her brain slammed to the forefront. Despite Wayne's directive, she stormed into the conference room.

Horace looked up and swiped a hand across his face. Had he been crying?

"You said something that's been bothering me." Zoe claimed the chair across from him and leaned forward. "You said at first you were afraid it was your neighbor lady who'd been killed."

Horace folded his hands on the table and studied them. "I mean, who else would it have been? I never dreamed Belinda would've…"

"What if she didn't?"

He looked up. "But—"

"What if Belinda had nothing to do with any of it? Who else might have shot Grant?"

Horace stuttered. "I—I don't know."

"Who else was there?" Zoe held up one finger. "Stanley. But your neighbors say he never got out of his truck."

Horace scowled.

Zoe held up a second finger. "Your neighbor."

Horace met her gaze. "Jan?"

"You said she walked with you to the trail leading to the park, right?"

He nodded. "And then went home."

"Did you see her go inside?"

He thought about it. "No. I was too busy trying not to fall on that muddy path."

"Could she have gone back to *your* house instead?"

"I suppose..." Horace rubbed his neck. "But why?"

"I don't know. Yet." Zoe hauled her phone from her hip pocket and keyed in Pete's number.

As it rang for the third and fourth times, a pool of heat simmered behind her eyes. The call went to voicemail. At the tone, she said, "I need to talk to you. Now. Call me."

"What's going on?" Horace asked.

She was on her feet, headed for the hallway. "Pete's at your neighbor's place, and he's not answering his phone."

Dammit. This was the second time in a year Pete had allowed someone to get the drop on him. Maybe he was getting too old for this shit.

"Give me your gun," Jan said, her cigarette-abraded voice even more gravely than usual. "With your left hand."

"Not happening." Last time, he'd ended up with a bullet in his leg.

Jan gave her small pistol a shake as if he hadn't noticed it before. "You don't have a choice."

"Neither do you. You heard my phone." She hadn't allowed him to answer it. "Someone's going to wonder where I am and send backup."

"Or leave you a voicemail about Little Johnny skipping school." But Jan's eyes darted toward the door behind him. A nervous, desperate woman with her finger on the trigger. Not a good scenario. "Give me your gun." She enunciated each word as if he hadn't heard her the first time.

"No." Pete had been in this house enough times to know the layout without looking. An old stuffed chair and sofa, neither of which would stop a bullet. Neither would the flimsy side tables provide any cover. He measured his odds. He was wearing his Kevlar vest under his uniform. At this distance, she'd have to have a hell of an aim to make a head shot. Or be lucky. What was that saying? *I'd rather be lucky than good any day?* He hoped the luck was with him today instead of her. He lifted his arms away from his body, palms open, showing he had no intention of reaching for his Glock. Yet. "You don't want to shoot me, Jan."

"You're right. I don't. But if you don't give me your damn gun, I will."

She would either way, he figured. "What do you think you're going to do?" he asked, keeping his voice calm. Friendly. "If you shoot me and take off, they will catch you. You can't outrun the radio." As if illustrating his point, he reached up and tapped the mic on his shoulder.

Jan jerked the gun at him. "Keep your hands away from that. I know your tricks. Don't go trying to open the line so your cop friends can overhear everything I say."

He lowered his arms. Slowly. "I wouldn't dream of it."

Jan's eyes narrowed and shifted. She was thinking. Weighing her options.

"You don't want to kill me," he said, gently. "You aren't a killer." A lie.

She scoffed. "Sure I am."

An obnoxious, piercing tone—one Zoe'd never heard before—pulsed from the front office as she arrived at the doorway. Nancy, wide-eyed and pale, perched on the edge of her seat.

"What's going on?" Zoe already feared the answer.

Nancy glanced up. "Pete just triggered a signal one." She wheeled back to her desk.

"What's a signal one?"

Nancy silenced her with a raised finger. She clicked the mic. "Vance Thirty, this is Vance Base. Come in please."

Nothing but static.

Footsteps thudded from the rear of the station. Seth and Abby charged down the hall toward the office. The interrogation room door opened, and Wayne stepped out.

"Vance Thirty, this is Vance Base. We've received a signal one from your location. Are you okay?"

Nothing but static.

Nancy swore. Something else Zoe'd never heard before.

"What's going on? What's a signal one?" she demanded.

"Officer needs assistance." Wayne strode up behind her, joining Seth and Abby. To the young officers, he ordered, "Gear up." As they vanished down the hall, Wayne turned to Nancy. "What's Pete's last known location?"

Before Nancy could respond, Zoe said, "Jan Gates' house." Zoe reached out and clutched Wayne's wrist. "What if Jan didn't go home like Horace thought? What if she went to his house to confront Grant?"

Wayne's jaw clenched. He again looked at Nancy who frantically worked the computer connecting Vance Township to County Emergency Ops. "Response?"

"Every law enforcement officer within fifty miles is on their way to Langstown. Including SERT."

"Good. If it comes down to it, I'll drive their friggin' tank right through Jan Gates' front door."

Seth and Abby rejoined them, armed with what must have been the armory's entire inventory.

Wayne slapped his sister on the back. "Let's do it." He trailed the pair out the door.

Zoe started to follow.

He turned and placed a hand on the front door, blocking her. "You. Stay here."

"Ain't happening."

"I don't have time to argue."

"You're right. Let's go." When he didn't budge, she said, "I'm a paramedic. If Pete's hurt, we need an immediate medical response." She couldn't allow herself to think about her other job.

Wayne studied her a moment before nodding. "Let's go."

THIRTY-TWO

"That idiot Grant Jennings never saw it coming," Jan said. "And Stanley was so convinced Horace did it, he let me walk right up to him and pop him."

Pete knew help was coming. He hadn't keyed the mic on his shoulder to allow their conversation to go out over the air. But he had managed to hit the red signal-one button. Jan didn't react to the two calls from Nancy, oblivious to Monongahela County police protocol. As he'd hoped, Jan wrote them off as just more radio chatter. All he needed to do was keep her calm and talking.

He gestured to the .22 in her hand. "That the gun you used?"

"On Stanley? Yep."

"Why'd you kill him and Grant?"

"Because they were idiots. Both of them. The vital component of our team was keeping a low profile. Fly under the radar. Reese worked at Kramer's Garage. When a nice car came in, he'd get names and addresses from the insurance cards people leave in their glove boxes. He never had to risk getting caught by looking at paperwork in the office. We'd case the house. Dennis and the brothers would break in when no one was home. We were supposed to sit on the stuff. Collect enough to make it worthwhile, then stop and wait until the heat was off."

"It's a good plan." Pete managed what he hoped looked like a casual glance around the room, mentally logging every piece of furniture that might provide cover, every throw rug that might trip him up.

"It was. But it depended on all of us keeping our noses clean."

"Keeping a low profile," he echoed.

"Exactly. I told those morons to leave Horace alone. He's a nice guy. Good neighbor. Quiet." She smiled wistfully. "He even baked me a cake on my birthday. He's sweet."

"Was Horace part of your team?"

She blew a raspberry. "Hell no. He had nothing to do with any of it. Except for blasting Dennis, who totally had it coming to him. God, I hate bullies. Then I realized Horace had done me a favor. Not only did he get rid of a troublemaker within our ranks, he gave the rest of us a bigger percentage of the cut."

"What about Grant?"

Jan shook her head again. "After Dennis, I told those idiot brothers to drop it. Nothing good could come from their insistence that Horace pay. It only put them on the front page, which is precisely where we did not want to be. When they showed up out front on Monday, I went over to Horace's and got him out of the house. After he was gone, I slipped inside his place. I'd seen his gun in the kitchen drawer once. I loaded it and waited. When Grant came storming in, he was royally pissed to find me instead of Horace." She chuckled a laugh that sounded like rocks inside a can. "He threw a temper tantrum. Turned his back on me. Big mistake."

"But why leave the gun behind? You say you liked Horace, yet you framed him by leaving the murder weapon—his gun—at the scene. Why not take it with you?"

"And be caught with it? I don't think so. Besides, I knew you'd never be able to convict him. He's one of the good guys. Any halfway decent lawyer could get him off."

"You were supposed to call him when the coast was clear. Why didn't you?"

"Don't be stupid, Chief. I didn't call him because the coast *wasn't* clear. There was a dead body in his house."

Pete thought he heard sirens. Faint. Distant. Or was he conjuring up the sound he wanted to hear? "Tell me something, Jan." He aimed a thumb over his shoulder toward the plastic bag of jewelry. "If you were so insistent on laying low—not selling any of the stuff you stole—why did you wear the diamond earrings?"

Her mouth pressed into a deep inverted "U," but she didn't reply.

"You were wearing them, right? On Monday? When you were in Horace's kitchen, gunning down Grant Jennings?" When she still didn't respond, Pete went on. "That's when you lost the stone. The rightful owner had reported the setting was loose."

Jan spit out a string of epithets that would have embarrassed even a longshoreman. "I wondered where it went." She shook her head. "That was a mistake on my part. I broke my own rule. I saw those earrings and fell in love. I'd always wanted a pair. Always. That deadbeat husband of mine drank all our money, so I never had anything nice." She huffed. "I guess Dennis and the brothers weren't the only idiots on our team."

Her gaze shifted. Had she heard something outside? Pete took a step closer to the sofa. It wouldn't stop a bullet, but she'd have a harder time hitting a target she couldn't see.

His movement brought her attention and the gun's muzzle fully back to him. "Don't move."

He raised both hands higher. "Okay." He tipped his head toward the purse. "What about the rest of the jewelry in the bag?"

She shot another glance toward the window. "You cops found the stash in Grant and Stanley's basement. Then you busted Reese." She sounded almost...heartbroken. "My team's gone. All I had was the jewelry I'd kept here. I thought I'd take it to a friend of mine who'd dispose of it for me. I wouldn't get rich but at least I'd get something for my trouble."

"Then what?"

"Start over somewhere else." Her eyes lowered. Slightly. So did the barrel of the gun. "That was the plan all along. Except I was supposed to make the move with Reese."

"You and Reese?"

She didn't reply. Didn't need to. Pete had seen that look too often before from women in love with some jerk being hauled off to prison.

This time, Pete definitely wasn't imagining the sirens. Jan

heard them too. The faraway look in her eyes snapped into laser-focus on the window. Seizing the opportunity, he moved. Pulled his Glock. As he dived behind the sofa, stuffing and wood splinters exploded around him, and the *pop, pop, pop* of Jan's .22 rang in his ears.

All of the emergency runs Zoe had made over the years in an ambulance didn't prepare her for the adrenalin overload of careening up Langstown Hill in the passenger seat of Wayne's Challenger. In front of them, Seth and Abby, lights and sirens in the township's cruiser. Behind them, a trio of State Police SUVs. According to the terse voices on the radio, SERT and a dozen more county, state, and local units were only a minute or two out.

Wayne took charge even before they reached Horace's street, barking orders for some responders to approach from the opposite direction, deploying others to the park on the hill behind the houses.

Zoe fought to maintain her seat as they screeched around the final turn. When they roared up to Pete's SUV, she reached for the door handle, but Wayne's hand clamped on her arm at the same time he stood on the brakes.

"Stay in the car."

"But—"

Seth and Abby tumbled out of their car, armed with assault rifles. State troopers raced toward them from the other direction and skidded to a halt.

Wayne tightened his grip. Forced her to look at him. "Pete would kill me if I let anything happen to you."

The detective's worried expression did nothing to soothe her. "*I'm* going to kill you if you let anything happen to *him*."

Officers in black body armor, slinging vicious-looking weapons, swarmed past the Challenger.

Wayne's smile didn't reach his eyes. "I guess I'm pretty much screwed, huh?"

"Damned if you do, damned if you don't," she said, returning his humorless grin. "Let me go in there. I'm not armed. I'm not a threat. Jan won't shoot me." Even as Zoe said the words, she knew it was a stupid idea.

"Not. Gonna. Happen."

Before she could make another attempt to sway him, three quick pops of what could've been fireworks, but everyone knew were gunshots, rose above the sounds of boots on pavement, above the whoop of sirens. Above the thud of Zoe's heart.

Pete led with his Glock, peeking over the sofa's back to locate Jan. She, like Pete, wasn't about to provide an easy target. She stumbled backward, heading toward the other room.

He pressed the trigger. Recovered from the recoil. Fired again.

She cried out, hit, but not down. Her small, but deadly, pistol stayed leveled at him. He squeezed off a third round before dropping and scrambling, not wanting to be in the same spot she'd last seen him.

Pop, pop.

A sliver of wood blew at his face. Instinctively, he closed his eyes. The splinter, the size of a nail file, sliced across his cheek.

At least, he hoped it was only a splinter.

He stole another glimpse over the sofa. Jan had retreated through a doorway into what he knew was the kitchen. Had she continued out the side door? Injured, armed, and very dangerous, loose in the neighborhood?

He climbed to his knees. Then to his feet. Kept his Glock raised, aimed at the doorway. He forced his breathing to slow, forced his peripheral vision to broaden. While he *thought* she'd taken cover in the kitchen, he hadn't *seen* her.

One step brought him in front of the sofa. Virtually naked without cover. A second stealthy step moved him closer to the other room. Balanced on the balls of his feet, ready to dive or drop. He spotted the blood. Tear-shaped, glistening drops marring the dull flooring, pointed not toward the kitchen. But toward the darkened hallway.

A blur. A flash. Another *pop*.

This time it wasn't a wooden splinter that struck him, knocked his breath out as if he'd been kicked by a mule.

He staggered but focused the Glock on his memory of the muzzle flash. The recoil lifted the gun in his hands. On the downswing, he fired again.

And crumpled to the ground.

The first trio of shots froze Zoe's brain. Wayne was out of the car, merging with the herd of officers in shades of black and gray stampeding toward Jan Gates' house. Zoe wanted to join them, but her legs, like her brain, had turned to ice.

Two loud cracks followed, thawing her, lifting the weight. She flung open the Challenger's door and sprinted after the wave of cops, mindless of the simplest of facts. She wasn't wearing Kevlar. Wasn't carrying a shield.

Where was Pete?

More fireworks burst from inside the innocuous-looking house. All contained. No shattering windows. She thought she heard a scream.

The officers in front of her funneled up the steps. Across the porch. Shouts of "Police! Drop your weapon!" The crash as they slammed through the door. More shouts.

At the base of the stairs, a hand seized Zoe from behind, wheeling her away from what she needed to see. She stared at a helmet, unable to make out the face behind it.

"Ma'am, you can't be here," said the muffled voice behind the protective gear.

She choked. "I'm a paramedic."

"You still need to move away from the area until it's cleared."

Zoe wished she could see the guy's eyes. It was like talking to an alien in black. Like standing in the middle of a bad movie set. Except this was really happening.

Pete was inside.

Again. Not again.

The gunfire stopped and the silence roared inside her skull. Ignoring the gloved hand clutching her shoulder, Zoe frantically searched the tense faces of the cops above her, those who knew what was going on.

Voices, some comprehensible, most not, punched through the deafening silence.

"Ma'am." The hand on her left shoulder tightened.

Through the chatter, she made out the words, "We need an ambulance!"

She pivoted. Tried to break the alien SERT member's hold. Pete needed an ambulance. A paramedic.

He needed *her.*

"Ma'am..."

"Let me go."

Wayne appeared in the doorway above them. He scanned the scene until his gaze landed on her. He pointed. "Zoe. In here."

She was only marginally aware of him telling the others that the scene was secure. Her security didn't matter. Not then. Not when it was Wayne—not Pete—at the door beckoning her.

Zoe thudded up the steps, her lungs constricting. She wished she had her jump kit.

The sea of cops between her and the door parted. Wayne held the shattered storm door open for her. "EMS is on its way," he said. "ETA two minutes."

She expected to see Pete on the floor, curled in a pool of his own blood. That was the scene she remembered from the last time. A scream of anguish perched at the back of her throat. Choking her. Ready to burst forth.

This time, she didn't see him at all.

Maybe he wasn't there. Maybe she'd been mistaken. Maybe he'd never been here at all.

A sofa faced away from her, stuffing poking out from a series of holes in its back.

Not a cop's house. The thought rushed through her mind

unbidden. *A cop would never place furniture requiring them to sit with their back to the door.*

Seth and Abby knelt in front of the sofa. Four more officers gathered in the shadows at the rear of the room.

Seth caught Zoe's gaze, his face tight. He gestured to her.

Her feet carried her forward. She struggled to swallow the scream still stuck in her throat.

Pete sprawled on the floor in front of the bullet-riddled sofa, motionless, his eyes closed. Blood streaked his face.

Oh, God. Her legs weakened. She was too late.

Abby touched his arm. "Zoe's here."

Pete groaned. Bent one knee, placing his tactical boot flat on the floor. And opened his eyes. "Hey," he said, his voice devoid of breath.

But he was alive. Zoe dropped to her knees beside him. "Hey, yourself." She took a quick head-to-toe survey. The only blood she could see was that on his face. "Are you...okay?"

Another groan. He moved one hand to a spot at his lower ribcage. "I'm hit."

"What?" she squeaked, reaching for the spot, expecting blood. Finding none.

Wayne loomed over them. "His vest stopped it. Maybe cracked a rib. But he's not the one who needs you." Careful of her injured shoulder, he tucked a hand under her left arm, lifting her to her feet. "Back there." He gestured with his chin. "Jan Gates needs medical help. It's bad."

"But—" Zoe wanted to stay with Pete. To examine every inch of him. To make sure he was perfectly fine.

He groaned again as he pulled himself to sitting, with help from Seth.

"You—don't—shouldn't—" Zoe stuttered.

Pete waved her away. "I'm good." He didn't sound good.

But he was alive.

As Wayne guided her toward the patient who needed her, Zoe became aware of the hot tears wetting her cheeks. She brushed her arm across her face. "If he has a cracked rib, he might have a punctured lung."

"And EMS will be here to treat him." Wayne looked at his watch. "In two minutes. Jan Gates may not have that much time."

"Dammit." Pete's ribs hurt like hell. The EMS crew jostling the cot they forced him to ride on didn't help.

Zoe stood at the rear of the ambulance as they hoisted him in. The worry in her baby blues made him feel guilty for complaining.

Once her colleagues anchored the gurney in place, she climbed in beside him. The paramedic she'd called Ken grinned at them. "I'll give you two some privacy and ride up front with Randy."

"Thanks," she said, her voice thin.

Ken slammed the rear doors. The driver slid the door separating the patient compartment from the cab shut.

"Alone at last," Pete said through clenched teeth.

Zoe fingered the Kevlar vest draped across his thighs. He'd insisted on keeping it with him, claiming he wasn't signing over the evidence. In truth, the thing had saved his life and he wasn't willing to part with it yet. He wondered what was going on in Zoe's mind as she traced the small hole.

He reached down to cover her hand with his. "I'm going to be fine."

"I know."

"How's Jan?" She'd caught two of his slugs. The first one slowed her down. The second one stopped her.

"She lost a lot of blood. And, if I was to guess, has a collapsed lung. But she's one tough cookie. I think she'll make it. She's in good hands."

He squeezed Zoe's. "Not as good as the ones I'm in."

She forced a grin.

Pete caught the shimmer of tears rimming her eyes. "I'm going to be fine," he said, more forcefully this time.

"I know." She removed her hand from the vest and leaned in, one eyebrow hiked. "You got lucky."

No lie.

"You might have a cracked rib."

He'd bet on that.

"You'll have to take it easy for a while."

"Yes, ma'am."

She glared at him. Mock anger for the "ma'am."

He chuckled but dammit, it hurt.

Once he stopped clenching his jaw, she leaned back, gazing at the ceiling. "*I* got lucky."

"You?"

She lowered her eyes to his, the shimmer still there. "I almost lost you."

Even the movement of reaching out to her hurt like hell, but he ignored the pain, focusing instead on the pain on Zoe's face. "I'm not going anywhere."

"You can't promise that."

For one very long moment, he feared she was about to end their engagement. Tell him she couldn't live like this. Waiting for the phone call. Or anticipating the knock at the door. His first wife hadn't been able to handle it. Suddenly the cracked rib couldn't compare the crushing weight on his heart at the thought of losing her.

She took his hand before he could withdraw it. "Life's too short. None of us knows how long we have. I'm aware of it more than most. I've seen the traffic fatalities. The first heart attack that's also the last." She inhaled a ragged breath. "The gunshot victims."

"The crazy family members coming out of the woodwork," he added with a grin.

She eyed him, her face blank. Then he got what he wanted—that smile. She lowered her face, shaking her head. "Those too."

Pete fingered the diamond on her third finger. "Marry me."

She snorted a teary laugh. "I already said yes, you dope."

"I mean now. Today. Or this weekend." The words poured out, unedited. A result of the near tragedies of the last few days? Or the emotional vacuum left once the adrenaline drained? "You're right.

Life's too short. I don't want to waste another minute of it. My buddy Chuck has been after us to come to Vegas. We could elope. Might be cool to get married by Elvis."

Zoe choked. "You're on drugs."

The pain meds starting to kick in could be another reason. "I don't care."

She slid to the edge of the jump seat and leaned over him, planting a kiss on his lips. "Yes, I will marry you. No, not today or this weekend. And definitely not in Vegas by Elvis." She tipped her head and grinned that sexy grin of hers. "I want you fully mended and functional for our wedding night."

Even the pain killers couldn't dull the rush of heat surging through him. "Yes, ma'am."

THIRTY-THREE

Tuesday night had been long and inconclusive. The polls pronouncing the coroner's race too close to call hadn't been kidding. Zoe stayed up until she couldn't keep awake any longer.

When the phone rang Wednesday morning, she opened one eye. The clock on the nightstand glowed six a.m. Pete's side of the bed was empty, and the phone only rang once. He must've picked up in the kitchen. Probably a work-related call for him. He was on desk duty following the shooting and his injury—only bruised ribs, no breaks. Seth once again served as acting chief of police and kept phoning with questions. She suspected he knew the answers but wanted to keep Pete from feeling useless.

She closed her eye.

She'd started to drift back into blessed slumber when Pete's soft voice at the bedroom door brought her fully awake. "That call was from Franklin Marshall."

She sat up. "And?"

"He wants you to meet him at Walden's in an hour."

"Did he win?"

"He wouldn't tell me. Said he wants to give you the news in person."

That didn't sound good.

An hour later, Zoe nursed a cup of coffee at a table in the café on Phillipsburg's Main Street, remembering her encounter with Dr. Davis on her way back to the ambulance after picking up lunch. Was that really only a week and a half ago?

The restaurant's front door opened. She looked up,

anticipating Franklin. Instead, Pete and Wayne strolled in. "What are you guys doing?" she asked.

Wayne claimed a seat at her table. "Same as you. Franklin ordered me to meet him here."

She looked at Pete, who sat next to her and across from Wayne. "I'm just curious. Besides, I don't have to be at the station until eight."

The waitress approached them with plastic-laminated menus and a pair of steaming stoneware cups of coffee, which she set in front of the men.

"Do you know who won?" Zoe asked Wayne as he stirred cream into his mug.

"Nope. Last I heard, it was—"

"Too close to call," she finished for him.

"Uh-huh." He sipped his coffee. "By the way, how are the wedding plans coming along?"

She shot a look at Pete who made a point of being absorbed in the menu even though he knew it by heart. "We're thinking of a Valentine's Day wedding."

"Wow. That's soon."

Not soon enough, but Kimberly had approved. "We'll have a small ceremony and reception here, then fly to St. Petersburg for the reception Mother's planning."

"St. Pete?" Wayne said. "Not a bad spot for a honeymoon."

Pete grunted.

Wayne glanced toward the window and the snow flurries falling through a gray Pennsylvania sky. "Especially in February."

"Except for my mother's presence."

"Well, there is that."

"And I have to find someone else to bake my cake."

"Why?" Wayne set his cup down. "Horace completely exonerated."

"Yes, but Belinda broke up with him. He's taken off on an extended sabbatical to get over the events of the last couple weeks."

Pete leaned back in his chair. "He mentioned putting his house up for sale and moving."

It was Wayne's turn to grunt. "Can't say I blame him. Bad enough he blasted a guy in front of the place, but having another guy killed in your kitchen by your next-door neighbor? That's a lot to overlook."

"Speaking of the next-door neighbor," Zoe said, "is there anything new on Jan and the case?"

"Jan Gates is well on her way to a full recovery from her confrontation with Pete. And she and Reese Perkins, a.k.a. Christopher Lewis Nixon, are tripping all over themselves to implicate each other." Wayne raised an eyebrow at Pete. "Good thing for you since you royally muffed up."

Pete kept his eyes lowered.

"By getting shot?" Zoe said.

"Actually, that helped his case. No. His mistake was the illegal search and seizure of the stolen jewelry in Jan's possession."

Pete shrugged. "I would've gotten a warrant, but there was the little matter of a gun in my face." His phone chirped. He slipped it from his pocket, read the message, and tapped a reply.

"Perkins is facing a number of grand theft auto charges, including the red Dodge he torched and the one he had in Erie," Wayne told Zoe. "But we can't find any outstanding homicide charges against him or any of his aliases."

She thought of the night in Erie. Her nephew wasn't a known murderer. She wasn't relieved. Instead, she suspected he was very good at hiding the bodies.

Wayne sipped his coffee. "On the subject of pickup trucks, did you ever get your backup lights fixed?"

Pete chuckled. "Zoe's favorite topic."

She kicked him—gently—under the table. "Not yet. They're still working on locating the short. But at least they've replaced my leaky gas lines." She sighed. "I'm getting tired of borrowing Sylvia's car."

"Sylvia's getting tired of loaning it to you." Pete's phone chirped again. He glanced at it. Picked it up.

Wayne gave Zoe a mischievous grin. "You could trade your old truck in for something new."

Pete typed a reply to whatever text he'd received. "That's what I keep telling her."

Zoe glared at Wayne, then Pete, and back again.

The restaurant door opened and Franklin, haggard and pale, walked in. Zoe swallowed. He definitely didn't look like he was celebrating a win.

He spotted them and shuffled to their table, claiming the fourth seat.

"You look like hell," Wayne told him.

Franklin huffed. "Thanks."

Pete set his phone down. "Well?"

Franklin met Zoe's gaze. "I'm afraid you're going to have to give up your position as deputy coroner."

She exhaled. Two years ago, when she'd accepted the job, she'd had expectations fueled by TV shows. Back then, the reality of autopsy sent her fleeing to the restroom. But over time, she developed a tolerance for the smells and a passion for the work. "I'm so sorry, Franklin."

He nodded grimly. "Thanks. My kidneys are getting worse by the day, and I've been moved up on the transplant list."

She'd almost forgotten about Franklin's kidney failure. "Maybe it's a good thing you lost the election then."

He blew a raspberry. "What do you mean, 'lost'? I won."

Zoe stared at him, trying to process his words. "But…"

"It wasn't a landslide by any means; however, Davis phoned me, conceding the election around four this morning."

"But…"

Franklin managed an exhausted smile. "I'm promoting you. Chief Deputy Coroner. If you'll accept the job. For the sake of my health, I need to lighten my workload. It'll mean more training for you. And once I have the transplant, you'll be in charge while I recover." The smile faded. "It also means I'll need you full-time. You'll have to leave the ambulance service."

The job offer set Zoe's mind spinning. The idea of no longer working for EMS sent it crashing to earth. She looked at Pete.

He raised both hands in a don't-ask-me gesture. "It's your decision." His phone chirped a third time. He read the message and looked at her. "Excuse me a minute." He rose and strode to the restaurant's back door.

Zoe turned to Wayne.

He raised both hands as well. "Like Pete said. Your decision."

She looked at Franklin. "Can I think about it?"

"Sure, but don't take long. This campaign has taken a toll on me."

That much was obvious. His coloring was horrible, and dark circles framed his sunken eyes. She nodded. "I'll let you know in a day or two."

The back door opened, and Pete, looking smug, strode in with a man following him. Zoe did a double take as the pair approached the table.

"Scott?" She hadn't seen or heard from her brother since he'd walked out of her cubicle in the Erie ER.

"Mind if we talk for a minute?" He glanced at Pete and the two men seated at the table with her. "In private?"

She stood and motioned to an empty table across the room. "I didn't expect to see you again," she said once they were seated.

"I wasn't sure myself." He gestured at her shoulder. "Are you all right?"

She reached up and massaged the aching joint. "I'm sore. The doctor has me in physical therapy for now."

"Good." Scott placed his palms down on the tabletop and studied the backs of his hands. "Pete called me the other night. We talked. About Chris. And you."

Pete called Scott?

Zoe waited for her brother to continue, unsure of which of her thousand questions she wanted to ask first.

"I'm sorry about what Chris did to you. Like I said that night at the hospital, I've always known he..." Scott's voice trailed off. He swallowed. "I guess every parent with a troubled kid says the same thing. 'My son wouldn't do that.' We need to believe there really is good in them. For our own sakes, we need to trust they'll do the right thing in the end. Otherwise..." Scott lifted his eyes to hers. "Otherwise we question everything we as a parent have done. Everything."

She nodded, still not sure what to say.

"That night at my house, I didn't want him to take you with him. Whether you were a cop like he said or not."

"Why didn't you stop him?" The words were out of her lips before she could think.

Scott opened his mouth. Closed it again. "I didn't believe he'd harm you. I know, I know. I was an idiot. But I wanted—*needed* to believe my son wouldn't do that."

They sat in silence. Zoe tried to put herself in his shoes. She had no children. Would never have children of her own. But what if she had? What if a child of hers turned out bad? Did bad things? Wouldn't she—any parent—come to her child's defense?

Maybe. Maybe not.

"Look," Scott said. "I don't expect you to forgive me. I was wrong. And I'm really glad you're okay. I just wanted to tell you I'm sorry. About everything. And if you ever decide you want a brother in your life, I'm available." He patted the table like a bongo drum and stood. "Oh. Pete mentioned your wedding. And not having anyone to walk you down the aisle."

She glanced over at her fiancé who was watching her. He'd talked to her brother about their wedding?

"I'm available for that too," Scott said. "But I totally understand if you have other plans or don't want me there." He started for the door.

"Wait."

He turned, facing her.

"The wedding's still a few months away...and I'm not sure about a lot of the details...but if...and I do mean *if*...I decided to have you give me away...well, I'd want to get to know you better...a lot better, before I could make that decision."

Scott smiled, a tight, uncertain smile. "I'm good with that. I cancelled my trip to Arizona, so I'll be around for a while."

She pointed at the table where Pete, Wayne, and Franklin waited to order breakfast. "Have you eaten yet? Would you like to join us?"

He looked toward the men. Pete gave him a nod. "I'd like that."

Side by side, Zoe and her brother approached the others. Pete dragged a vacant chair from a neighboring table. She raised a questioning eyebrow at him.

He leaned closer and whispered in her ear. "Life's too short."

An impending wedding. A new brother. Zoe swore the earth shifted beneath her. Life was about to take a major turn.

Aw, what the hell. She rested her hands on the back of her chair and looked at Franklin. "Yes."

The coroner blinked. "What?"

"Yes. I'll take the job."

ANNETTE DASHOFY

USA Today bestselling author Annette Dashofy has spent her entire life in rural Pennsylvania surrounded by cattle and horses. When she wasn't roaming the family's farm or playing in the barn, she could be found reading or writing. After high school, she spent five years as an EMT on the local ambulance service, dealing with everything from drunks passing out on the sidewalk to mangled bodies in car accidents. These days, she, her husband, and their spoiled cat, Kensi, live on property that was once part of her grandfather's dairy.

**Books in the Zoe Chambers Mystery Series
by Annette Dashofy**

Printed in Great Britain
by Amazon

36007197R10165